THE THINGS THAT
ARE DIFFERENT

THE THINGS THAT ARE DIFFERENT

A Vic Lenoski Mystery

Peter W.J. Hayes

LEVEL
BEST BOOKS

The Things That Are Different

A Vic Lenoski Mystery

First Edition | July 2019

Level Best Books
www.levelbestbooks.com

Trade Paperback ISBN: 978-1-947915-17-6
Also Available in e-book

Cover and Interior design: Shawn Reilly Simmons

Printed in the United States of America

To Charles Hertrick, my eighth grade English teacher, Maggie McMillin, my eleventh and twelfth grade English teacher, and Monty Culver, creative writing professor at the University of Pittsburgh, who all urged me—repeatedly and with startling patience —to write more, to trust my writing instincts, and to stick with it.

You're fighting, not playing the piano, you know.

Always work the ref's blind side.

— FRITZIE (THE CROAT COMET) ZIVIC
World Welterweight Champion, 1940 - 1941
A Pittsburgh guy.

CHAPTER 1

Vic Lenoski slid from behind the steering wheel, stepped into the road and straightened into the warmth of a May dusk. Liz Timmons, his partner, emerged from the passenger side of the car and squared her shoulders. The crows feet at the corners of her eyes tightened as she squinted at the collection of fire engines, ambulances and police cars scattered along the block, as if an angry five year old had abandoned his toys. The air stank of smoke. Here and there firemen, police and EMTs clustered on the water-sodden grass, leaning toward one another to talk over the thrumming of a water pump, their shoulders slumped, hands pocketed. The yellow tape blocking access to the scene sagged across the road, as if it had hung there for a hundred years.

"Makes me tired just lookin' at it," Liz said. She turned to him, her dark skin somehow sallow in the fading light, a frown creasing her forehead, her eyes distracted and blank. Vic didn't like it. She'd had that look a lot lately, as if she couldn't take or wasn't interested in work any more.

"Not easy when you're thinking you should have got here faster." As he talked he automatically scanned the spectators clustered on a nearby front lawn for a blond-haired teenage girl. No one. Annoyed at himself for doing it, he locked the car and headed toward a young cop waiting behind the crime scene tape. Vic raised his badge and watched the cop try to focus watering, red eyes. He repeatedly blinked as if his eyelids were filled with grit. The sleeves and thighs of his township uniform were smudged black with soot.

Vic dropped his arm and raised his voice to be heard over the thundering pump on one of the fire engines. "Vic Lenoski. Pittsburgh Bureau of Police. This is my partner, Liz Timmons. I know we're outside our jurisdiction but the DA's office asked us to take a look. Because of the victim."

The cop nodded so hard Vic thought he might hurt his neck. "Yes sir. Chief said you guys were coming." He lifted the tape.

Once they were underneath Vic gestured at the cop's uniform. "You were the first on the scene?"

"Yes sir."

"Tell me about it. Looks like you went inside."

He nodded again, the movement gentle and careful this time, as if he didn't want to shake that memory loose and relive it. "Yes sir. Um, got the call about 3. Security service and a neighbor called it in. I got here at 3:06. Flames were coming out of the upstairs windows. I confirmed the fire on the radio and then tried the front door." His voice shriveled to a hoarse whisper and he stopped to suck in a breath. "I didn't know if anyone was inside. After the front door I tried the garage doors then ran around the back. Got in that way. Place was full of smoke, I shouted, went through the kitchen and into the living room." He paused to find a breath. "It was bad, I couldn't breathe or see. I shouted some more. I could hear someone upstairs screaming." He rubbed his cheeks, the tears from his eyes smudging the soot.

"No problem, Pokorny," Liz said softly. "Being inside a burning house is bad. People don't get what the smoke does to you."

Vic glanced at the young cop's name badge, wondering why he hadn't checked it earlier.

"Yes, ma'am," Pokorny said. "Anyway." He lifted his head and stared at a distant place just over their shoulders, his eyes as red as stoplights. "I got to the stairs but they were burning.

There wasn't a way up."

"I hope you got out then," Vic said.

"I gave it one shot. Got maybe two steps up. The scream-ing was…" His breath caught and he fell silent.

As Vic waited he noticed how the skin on Pokorny's face was red under the soot. But he saw something else in Pokorny's brown eyes; it was as if a new space had opened behind them. Vic guessed that was where the sound of those screams would live for the rest of his life.

"You did well, son," Vic said softly.

Pokorny's eyes shifted and locked onto Vic. "I should have tried again. Just run up."

"You crazy?" Liz said. "You'd be dead too."

"Look," Vic added. "I know you want to do the right thing, but half the cops I know would have stayed outside. The fire was too far gone."

Pokorny didn't say anything, just turned his head and looked down the suburban street. Vic followed his eyes and saw the boxy look-alike two-story houses and identical lawns that ran to the edge of the asphalt road. The pump engine shut off, throwing silence over the area like a bomb blast. The vol-ume of voices from the fire trucks and emergency vehicles fell as people adjusted to the silence. Vic didn't know what else to say. He hoped the young officer would take some time to think about the day, to work through it.

Liz tapped him on the arm and nodded toward the fire-fighters.

"Thanks," Vic said, watching Pokorny's profile.

Vic turned and spotted a white helmet on one of the fire-men. Guessing it was the chief he aimed toward him, stepping over fire hoses that crisscrossed the ground like a giant's forgot-ten shoelaces. Liz fell in beside him. Vic took two more steps, stopped and turned around.

"Hey, Pokorny," he called.

Pokorny stiffened but turned to him.

"You said you tried the front door, and then the garage

doors, but you went in through the back door, right?"

"Yeah."

"How'd you get in through the back door?"

Pokorny frowned. "Just tried it. The screen door was open, so was the back door."

"You mean not locked, right?" Liz asked, drawing next to Vic.

Pokorny's frown deepened. "Yeah. No. Screen door was closed and not locked, but the back door was open."

"It was ajar?" Vic asked.

Pokorny's forehead cleared. "Yeah." He paused for a moment, his red eyes inward and working back and forth. A tear slid down his cheek. "Absolutely. It was ajar. It surprised me. Middle of the day, people are usually out. I remember because it was different than what you'd expect."

"It *is* different," Vic said. "Good memory. When you write up your report be real specific about that. I want it documented."

"Yes sir." Pokorny's mouth eased. It wasn't a smile, but as Vic turned toward the man in the white helmet he hoped that maybe Pokorny would realize that by remembering that detail, today he'd done something right.

CHAPTER 2

The township fire chief was tall and meaty, with a round, red face and thick white mustache. When Vic and Liz joined the group he was telling a story about a wild fire he'd chased as a rookie, describing the way the flames moved over the dry grass in front of the wind and hopped from blueberry bush to blueberry bush. As he talked Vic caught his eye, just before the chief delivered the punch line about how that wild fire was exactly where they were standing, before the housing plan was built.

Vic knew the story was the chief's way of lightening the mood after a bad day. As a murmur and soft laughter travelled around the firemen and EMTs the chief's eyes strayed back to Vic, so he held up his badge. "You got a moment, chief?"

He nodded and turned to a sergeant standing beside him. "Wrap it up. Leave one truck here hooked up, in case we get a flare up. Let's keep four guys here, I'll need 'em. You know the drill."

The sergeant called out the order and the group disbanded, leaving Vic and Liz alone with the fire chief.

"Thanks for taking the time," Vic said. The chief nodded at Liz and waited for Vic to keep talking. "I'm Vic Lenoski, this is my partner, Liz Timmons, we're Pittsburgh Bureau of Police."

"I'm Dave Mendeloski. Rich told me you were coming." They shook hands all around.

"Rich?" Liz asked.

"Richard Landry. Township police chief. Insists everyone call him Richard, so I call him Rich just to jag him. He's around back of the house. You know the victim?"

"Not really," Vic said. "But she might be one of the public defenders for Allegheny County. Worked out of the downtown courthouse. DA asked us to take a look."

Mendeloski stared at the house. "We found her body in bed. Middle of the day."

"She was on vacation today," Vic said.

"Maybe she likes those power naps." Mendeloski used his chin to point at something behind them. "Here's Rich."

Vic turned to see a short police officer with a belly overhanging his utility belt huffing across the yard, his face red from the exertion. Vic guessed he was in his late fifties. They waited in silence until Rich joined them.

Ignoring Liz, Richard asked, "you the guy from Pittsburgh?"

"Yeah, both of us," Liz said, her tone tart.

Richard kept his eyes on Vic. "We're running the scene. I don't get why the DA wants you here."

"The victim worked for him?" Liz cut in again, before Vic could speak. "One of your boys died in Pittsburgh we'd offer you the same courtesy."

Richard pulled himself erect and glared up at Liz. "Why the hell would one of my boys end up dead in Pittsburgh?"

Before Liz could say something like 'so he could avoid working for you,' Vic spoke quickly. "Chief Landry, I'm Detective Vic Lenoski, this is my partner, Liz Timmons. I appreciate you opening up your scene to us. We're just here to observe and keep out of the way. But the victim worked for the DA's office, who, as you know, oversees the entire county, including your township. Assuming the victim is who we think it is, he'd like to know what happened."

Richard shifted on his feet. "You're talking about Frank Marioni? That DA?"

Vic nodded. "Yeah."

Richard spit on the ground. "ID'ing the victim? You kidding me? That's gonna take a couple of weeks, given how burned the body is. You tell your Marioni that."

Vic glanced at Mendeloski and saw a twinkle in his blue eyes. He understood why the fire chief called him 'Rich.' He turned back to Landry. "ME check the body?"

"Not yet. He's on his way."

"If he's sobered up," Mendeloski said. Richard shot him a hard look. "Just kidding," he added, looking innocently at the sky. Vic guessed he wasn't kidding much at all.

"Mind if we look in the house?" Vic asked, and looked at Mendeloski. "Assuming you're okay with us going in."

He shrugged. "I'll go in with you. Part of the second floor collapsed into the living room, avoid that and we'll be fine. I've got a fire inspector coming later to review the scene, so I don't want it stirred up."

"We'll be careful. Let's go," Vic said quickly, before Richard could intervene.

They all tromped up the driveway and around the side of the house, picking their way through the mud and puddles remaining from the fire hoses. The skin of water covering the back yard reminded Vic of a blister. Waiting beside the door was a tall, thin cop with a pale face and scraggly blond mustache. The screen door hung open on one hinge and the back door was jammed open with a piece of charred wood. Before they entered the house Vic stopped and studied the door jamb and stop around the lock. Apart from a layer of soot everything was unmarked.

"You think someone broke in?" Richard asked.

"Well, first on the scene said the screen door was closed but the back door was ajar."

Liz pointed at the screen door. "Cylinder on it, automatic closing. Everything works right it would be closed. Fits what Pokorny said."

"Pokorny told you that?" Richard asked.

"He was first on the scene, right?" Vic found himself struggling to keep his voice even.

The Chief spat on the ground. "His report isn't written and I have to approve it. Until I do nothing happened."

Vic looked down at the chief. "And why the hell is he working the perimeter? He's got smoke inhalation. The EMTs need to help him."

"He's a rook. Rooks work the perimeter. Little taste of smoke won't hurt him."

Vic's face heated. He glanced at Liz. In the fading light her skin looked much darker, her eyes whiter, and their message was *have at him*.

"Did you even talk to him?" Vic shifted close to the Chief and leaned over him. "His eyes look like they're bleeding. He's having trouble breathing. His face is burned and he blames himself for not running through a wall of fire to save the victim. He heard her screaming. And you put him on the perimeter?"

Richard's doughy face reddened even more. "I'm the chief, he's a rook. I make the rules. End of story." A speckle of spit followed the last word out of his mouth.

"Yeah, but rule two is always take care of your guys. Always. No goddamned wonder you make everyone call you Richard. If you didn't they'd call you Dick."

The chief bumped him with his chest, so close Vic knew he was a smoker. "Get out of my crime scene."

"You want the DA hearing you got a thin skin and don't want to help him? Listen to me, Richard." Vic stretched out the name. "We are not going to take your glory and we're not gonna say you suck at investigating. But we're gonna find out what happened to our public defender. That makes her an ADA: your assistant district attorney and mine. You understand me? And you're missing the bigger picture here. For once you got a couple of real detectives to help you investigate. You got resources. This is your chance to look like a hero, but you gotta cut the crap and work with us. You understand me?"

In the silence Richard took a light breath through his mouth. His brown, angry eyes searched Vic's face.

"So how about we start over?" Vic said carefully.

Rich blinked and stepped back. "My rules." He glanced at the thin officer standing by the door. Vic followed his gaze and saw anger in the cop's pale blue eyes. Richard turned back to him. "One. I give you information when it's been approved by me. Only then. Two. I preapprove all reports to the DA. You read me?"

Vic could think of about six ways to work around those rules, so he nodded. "Sure thing. You got it."

"Damn right I do." Richard turned and started for the front of the house, the tall cop following him. "You guys are on your own," he shouted over his shoulder.

"That's a much better idea," Mendeloski said, as Richard disappeared around the house. "From now on I call him Dick."

CHAPTER 3

As they stepped inside the house Vic fought down a gag at the stench of soot and the corrosive chemical smell that underlay it like electricity. Liz coughed hard. Water squelched under their shoes with each step.

"I'm thinking it started upstairs," Mendeloski said after a moment. "Most likely master bedroom. That's where most of the damage is and that's what dropped into the living room. We saved most of the downstairs, if you can call it that." He spat into a corner, clearing his mouth.

Mendeloski led them down a narrow hallway to the front of the house and after a few steps Vic saw the sky through a hole in the roof to his left. They stepped over some fallen timbers and reached the foot of the stairs. The living room was a mound of wooden debris and roof shingles. About halfway down the pile something barely recognizable as a foot stuck out from the pile of debris on what looked like the charred remains of a bed. The foot was black, blistered, the toes tiny stubs.

"Is that a foot?" Liz asked. She held a handkerchief over her mouth and nose.

"Yeah," Mendeloski said softly. "That's why I kept some guys on the scene. I'll need 'em to dig out the body."

"Any idea how it started?" Vic asked.

"Fire inspector needs to tell us."

Vic looked at him. "Chief, you've been around fires before. Just between us three. If you had to guess?"

"In the old days I would have said smoking in bed, but it doesn't hold. She had a home security system with smoke alarms so we got the call fast. But apart from her bedroom there's another place that's well burned." He pointed at the top of the staircase. "See how the top steps are burned out and the way the next steps down are scorched? Makes me think point of origin was the bedroom and a secondary started at the top of the stairs. Two origin points. Not what usually happens."

"Arson," Liz said, through the muffle of her handkerchief.

"Inspector needs to say it, I can't," Mendeloski answered. "But between us three I'd bet on it."

Vic stared up the stairs at the charred hole where the treads should have met the second story landing. He thought about what would have happened if Pokorny ran upstairs.

"Okay," Vic said, "not sure we can do more here."

They squelched outside and around to the front of the house, all three gulping a few deep breaths once they were outside. All that remained of the emergency vehicles were a fire truck, an ambulance and, near the crime scene tape, Pokorny's cruiser. In the fading light Vic made out Pokorny's back as he stood by the tape staring down the road. The other end of the scene was also blocked by tape. It was manned by the tall officer they had seen at the back door, but he stood facing into the crime scene, watching them. Police Chief Richard Landry, or Rich, or Dick, was nowhere to be seen.

"Christ," Mendeloski said. He put two finger to his lips and whistled so loud everyone within a hundred yards stopped and looked at him. He motioned to an EMT standing near the ambulance. As the EMT crossed to them Vic stared at the burned out house and the hole in the roof above the living room. In the fading light it looked as black and hollow as a tooth socket.

"Chief?" asked the EMT, when he reached them.

Mendeloski pointed at Pokorny. "See the guy on the perimeter? Sounds like he ate smoke. Check him out and clean him up, will ya?"

"Sure thing, Chief."

11

They all watched the EMT head back toward the ambulance before Liz said quietly, "Well, DA is gonna say something about this."

Mendeloski shoved his hands deep into his pockets. "Glad I'm just the fire chief. Soon as the ME gets done I can go home. Sounds like it's just starting for you guys."

Vic looked at him. "Thanks, Chief. We appreciate the help."

"Sounds like she was one of ours, in her own way."

"She was," Vic said, watching Pokorny lift the scene tape so a white Ford Explorer could enter the scene.

"That's the ME who coveres this region," Mendeloski said. "Bars musta closed early."

"How do we get his report when we're done?"

Mendeloski shook his head slowly. "Hate to tell you, but that's Dick's department. You gotta go through him."

"We're just born lucky," Liz said.

Vic watched the ME clamber out of this car. His shoulders were slumped, his face haggard, but what bothered Vic was how he seemed lost in his own world. He wanted someone on top of his game. He thought of Freddy, their pathologist, and his broad Berlin accent. "Body is going to end up with Freddy, let's get him to take a look as well," he said to Liz.

"I'm with you."

From Liz's tone he knew she didn't like the look of the ME either. Vic felt a chill at the same time a thought come to him. "Chief," he asked, "you know something about smoke inhalation. What happens if you're sleeping and a fire starts. Do you wake up?"

The chief shook his head slowly, watching the EMT lug an equipment bag toward Pokorny. "Depends, but usually if you eat enough smoke you're confused and out of it within a few minutes. Fire eats up the oxygen in the room and you're done. That's if the chemicals in the air from furniture and building materials haven't killed you."

"Pokorny said he heard her screaming."

"If she was, that's bad."

Liz drew closer to them. "But wouldn't she try to escape? We saw inside she was still in bed."

The blue eyes in Mendeloski's meaty face hardened. "You'd think, but like I said, sounds bad. If she knew what was happening to her it's a real bad way to go."

Liz turned away. "God."

"Yeah," the Chief echoed.

Vic didn't say anything. He didn't like how the details stacked up. Too many things were different than what he would normally expect. A tremor ran through him.

"Exactly," Mendeloski said.

Vic glanced at him and realized he had seen the shiver.

Mendeloski pointed his chin at the land around them. "I know how you feel. This place gives me the goddamned creeps. You heard that story I told earlier, about the wild fire I fought out here before the housing plan went in? I didn't tell them the other thing that happened. That fire moved so fast it flanked us, me and another guy got caught in it. I thought I was done. All those blueberry bushes burning like goddamn steel furnaces. First time in my life I was spew-shit scared. And then one of our trucks just drives right through the flames, back wheels spinning and the whole thing bouncing around like a whale on the beach. Chief's at the wheel. We hop on and out we go. Took two months to grow back my eyebrows. So I don't like this place, although it was a damn good lesson in what it takes to be chief. You know sometimes you get the feeling someplace is haunted or sacred? It's this place for me. It's like we shouldn't be on this land, like it's sacred somehow. Like the fire is a warning."

"I know what you're talking about," Liz said, and Vic wondered if she was thinking about New Orleans and hurricane Katrina.

"Any others die in this plan?" Vic said.

"No, but we got time yet. Plan's only fifteen years old."

They all stood in silence for a moment, the light fading around them. Vic stuck his hand out. "I missed your first name,

Chief."

He smiled. "Dave. Parents gave me David, but I was always fine with Dave. Maybe because people get hung up on Mendeloski. Too long and complicated. I always figured that's why my guys call me chief. It's easier to spell."

As they shook hands all around Vic said quietly, "I think they call you chief because they like it that way."

Mendeloski grinned at them. "You wouldn't say that if you knew most of them spell it c-h-e-e-f. Anyway, good to meet you guys. Listen, give me a business card and I'll send you a copy of the fire inspector's report. I get a copy of that."

On their way back to the car Vic and Liz shook hands with Pokorny. With ointment on his face and newly washed out eyes, his voice was more upbeat.

As they drove back toward Pittsburgh Liz said quietly, "I don't like any of this, Vic."

Vic thought about the public defender. "Gretchen Stoll," he said slowly. "Hard way to go. Did she have a husband and family?"

"Husband only, another lawyer who works downtown. E-mail I got said he's just been notified."

Vic stared at the road ahead. "Yeah. I don't like it either, and the DA's going to like it even less."

"And why did the DA ask us to take a look? He's got his own investigators."

Vic eased the car through a curve. "Well isn't that an interesting question?"

CHAPTER 4

That night, alone in his house, Vic exercised in his basement while carrots and cauliflower roasted in the oven. Still hot from working out, his knuckles stiff and arms heavy from the punching bags, he removed the vegetables from the oven and started a pan of scrambled eggs. The heat made him sweat and he wiped his forehead and face with a work-out towel draped over one shoulder. After plating the vegetables and eggs he settled in front of the television and ate from his lap, watching the local news and sipping from a large cup of ice water.

This was his routine now. He didn't miss the take-out food and whiskey. He felt better for the difference, as if he'd climbed clear of a mine after a cave-in. Finishing his food he washed the dish and pans and settled them into the drain rack. Coffee mug in hand he stepped into the dining room and stood in the dark, staring at the ghostly white images of the documents and photographs taped across the entire facing wall. He turned on the standing light in the corner and colored post-it notes jumped to light, marking clusters of documents and specific passages in the paper stacks at the base of the wall.

He ignored it all and crossed to the long windowsill and a series of small framed photographs. Each was of Dannie, his daughter, at various ages from two to her fifteenth birthday. He studied each one in order, lingering over the last two. In the photo of her at twelve her blond hair was pulled back in a pig-tail and she was laughing. Vic could tell that the photographer had made a joke to draw out her laugh and that she had fallen for it, but people liked to do that with Dannie, they enjoyed making her laugh. But sometime before she turned fifteen, her jawline had strengthened and a new look entered her blue eyes. She looked more confident, but tempered by determination. The change in the two photos caught in his chest and he put the last photograph back down. He wiped his lips with the back of his hand.

"Okay, it's time," he said out loud. He folded his arms over his chest, closed his eyes and rocked slowly. For two months he had spent each evening studying the documents related to Dannie's disappearance, using a color coding system he'd developed himself. They were categorized now, green for Dannie's movements before the abduction, yellow for the interviews after she disappeared, orange for possible leads, blue in the places where he spotted a discrepancy or thought that more questions could be asked. Only a few blue post-its stared back at him, but he had expected that. Dannie had left for her friend's house late one afternoon and never arrived. The task force had investigated her movements minutely and ruthlessly. What was left to him now was only to memorize the documents, to understand the rhythm of the investigation that conflict-of-interest rules had barred him from joining. He wanted to be sure of the documents when he started his own search.

And it was time.

Immediately after her disappearance, as the task force rushed through their interviews and chased leads, he had followed every development. Liz, who had talked her way onto the task force, slipped him the reports. Every evening he reviewed the findings, but as the inescapable truth that Dannie was lost slowly dawned, he found he needed several whiskeys to review the reports. Then five. That morphed into eight until the discipline of individual drinks dissolved and his days swam together. He wasn't completely sure when Anne, his wife, left to live with her mother and sister, or when the task force investigating Dannie's disappearance was disbanded. He just knew that one day he woke up next to the wrong woman with the conviction that finding Dannie was up to him and no one else, that no matter how much the search for her might scare him, he had to do it.

He crossed to the card table in the center of the room. The table was empty except for some discarded file folders and a single, large brown envelope. He picked up the envelope and lifted the flap. Inside were three thin bundles, each held together by a paper clip. He sat down, separated the papers and carefully read the documents.

Except for the dining room the house felt empty, the basement and upstairs dark. Half an hour later, when Vic finished reading, the moment still felt right. Starting anything, he knew, meant starting with yourself. He didn't yet know what to do with the histories of the three young women who had disappeared within a few months of Dannie, but after reviewing the documents related to Dannie's disappearance, he knew it was all he had.

CHAPTER 5

"**Y**ou guys have fifteen minutes, do it in five and you get jelly beans." Allegheny County's District Attorney, Frank Marioni, rose from behind his desk and pointed at a squat jar of jelly beans. His smile was as wide as an ambulance and his teeth just as white. Liz and Vic crossed the long expanse of electric blue carpet and shook hands with him over his desk. Marioni's brown eyes were sharp in the olive glow of his skin.

Vic plunged ahead. "We went to Gretchen Stoll's house yesterday afternoon. There's a body, but it isn't ID'd yet. But so we're clear, it was her house, her bed and she hasn't shown up at work or used her phone or credit cards since about an hour before the fire call."

"Sounds like it's her." Marioni deflated and sagged into his chair.

"We talked to the fire chief and the local police chief," Liz added.

"Reports?" Marioni's head bobbed up.

Vic glanced around and realized there were no other chairs in the room, just some built-in wooden bookshelves holding rows of legal texts. The logo of Allegheny County on the wall behind the desk was the size of a garbage can lid.. "Probably another week or so. But we picked up some preliminaries, if you want to hear them." He waited, half hoping Marioni would say no.

"Yeah, go."

"Preliminary," Vic said. "Just us and the local fire chief shooting the shit. We need to confirm all this."

"Right." Annoyance crept into the DA's voice. His eyes darted from Vic to Liz and back again.

"Not an accident," Vic said. "First cop on the scene said the back door was ajar. Not unlocked, ajar. He got inside and says he heard the victim screaming." He waited, but the DA just stared at him, his face frozen. "The fire chief says that's unusual for burn victims, they tend to pass out as the fire sucks the oxygen out of the room or they get overwhelmed by fumes. Then the same chief says that in his book—and again, this is before the fire inspector's report—but he thinks the fire had two sources. One in the victim's bedroom, the other at the top of the stairs, as if someone wanted to make sure no one could get downstairs, or up to save the victim."

"That last part is us speculating," Liz added. "But it's logical if this is murder."

The DA closed his eyes for a few seconds. When he opened them he looked stricken, but something seemed off about it to Vic, as if he was practicing the look for later.

"Exactly," Vic said, trying to pin down what bothered him about the DA's expression. "But we need to see the reports to confirm everything. Also, I'd like Freddy, our pathologist, to look at the body and confirm anything his ME might come up with."

"Sure."

"I may need your signature on some paperwork to make that happen."

Marioni grinned at him. "Did you just hear me say 'sure'?" He spoke lightly, but Vic heard annoyance underneath it.

"Just so you know what's going on when the paperwork hits your desk."

"Don't get me wrong, Vic, I appreciate the heads up."

Oddly, despite the easy tone, Vic felt like they were having an argument. He shifted his feet. "If this is what it seems, we'll need to look at Gretchen's case files and talk to her colleagues in the public defender's office. See if she said anything to them."

"Absolutely. When do you see the reports?"

"Should be in a few days. The only one that has me worried is the local police chief. He didn't like us butting in."

"Who's that?" The DA spoke so quickly that Vic knew he was reacting to a problem he thought he could solve.

"Richard Landry," Liz said.

The DA stared at them both for a moment and then leaned back in his chair. "No shit. That dick."

"As the local fire chief now calls him." Vic relaxed, sure he and the DA had found common ground. "How do you know him?"

The DA raised his arms and clasped his hands behind his head. "Three or four years ago. One of his squad got nabbed on the South Side for drunk and disorderly. Guy was standing in the middle of the street trying to expose himself to the cars going by, but lucky for him he was too drunk to get his pants down. Kept falling over, otherwise we'd have nailed him for more. We jail him, the next morning the chief shows up where you're standing, asks if we can work out some professional courtesy and tries to hand me a bottle of single malt. My brand. He'd asked around, the asshole."

"How'd that go?" Liz asked.

The DA kept a straight face but his eyes twinkled. "I called in my secretary, told her Landry had put the bottle accidentally on my desk, and she needed to hold it until he left, but to make sure he took it. Then I told him the only professional courtesy he'd get was me not pressing charges for bribery. Pretty sure I lost his vote with that one."

"What happened to his officer?" Vic tried to keep his own grin under control.

"Wouldn't cut a deal, took it to court. Tall skinny guy. Blond. His lawyer said the guy's military service had left him with PTSD and the poor guy was just letting off steam. Jury gave him a walk. Felt sorry for him, war hero and all."

Liz cut in, "Explains why Chief Dick didn't want us asking around for you."

Vic said, "Maybe I'll take him a bottle of single malt."

Marioni shook his head. "He wouldn't get the joke. I couldn't believe it when he held out the bottle. I guess he thought we were in some hick town in Alabama and that's how things work."

They fell silent for a moment, and afterwards Vic said, "So that's what we've got. Sorry it isn't better news."

The DA waved a hand. "Look, you're right. If the official reports confirm it you'll have full access here for your investigation." He glanced at Vic. "Just like you asked for."

The feeling they were having an argument came back. Out of the corner of his eye he saw Liz nod and knew it was meant for him after their conversation in the car.

"That's fine by us," Vic said. "But we do have a question. Why are you asking us to do the investigation? I mean we don't mind going to the scene, but why wouldn't your county detectives handle this? They report to you."

Marioni removed his hands from behind his head and leaned forward. "Fair question, so I'll be straight with you guys. Transparency. You two are independent of my office. I use my own guys, next thing I know the news people are screaming, saying I'm using them to cover something up."

Marioni watched Vic as he spoke, and Vic was careful not to look at Liz. Marioni's statement didn't pass the sniff test and he guessed Liz didn't buy it either. He also knew it wasn't something he could solve right away. "Well, we should talk to our Commander. Crush has us working other cases."

Marioni shook his head. "I talked to him this morning. He's good with you guys handling it."

Vic sensed Liz glance at him. They were boxed in; she knew it and he knew it. He studied Marioni and said slowly, "Then we'll get started. Anything you can tell us about

Gretchen?"

Marioni brushed off the top of his desk with his right hand. "Big picture? She was twelve years in the public defenders office. From what I hear she was good. I thought sometimes she went a bit hard after people, some of them she'd refuse to plea deal, take them to court. Every once in a while she would have some problem with evidence or something and someone walked, but that happens to all of us one time or another. So, I guess the way to say it is that she pushed hard when she thought she needed to, and assuming no technical slip-ups, she did her job. Can't complain. Their office is going to miss her."

"Thanks, that's helpful. I'll forward the reports as they come in."

"Great." He stood up suddenly, the movement surprisingly fast. "Listen, I'd like you guys to talk to me on a regular basis. Case updates, crap like that. Let's do that in person, just us. Document the meetings and don't hide anything, but I don't want a huge e-mail tail. Just like you guys, in our job we make enemies. And I've got an election in six months. That means everything is in play. You guys good with that?" He glanced from Liz to Vic, nodded and checked his watch. "Shit. Twenty minutes. I have to run." He pointed at the jelly bean jar. "Help yourselves, guys. I'll tell my secretary to give you access to me whenever you need it. And I'll get everything set up for you to start interviews tomorrow."

Marioni came around the desk and stopped in front of Vic. "Vic, I was real sorry to hear about what happened to your daughter. And then no one found out what happened. I have two daughters. Can't imagine it." He reached out his hand and squeezed his arm just above the elbow.

"Something will turn up," Vic said carefully.

"I'm sure it will. In the meantime, find out what happened to Gretchen, will you?" He turned to Liz. "You too, Liz. I feel good with you guys running this." He stepped back so he was talking to both of them. "Gretchen is family. We need people to know we take care of our own." He looked at Vic. "We haven't been doing that very well lately." He shook both of their hands again and headed for the door.

Liz dug into the jelly bean jar, pulled out a closed fist and worked a jelly bean free. She popped it into her mouth.

"Man," Vic said softly as they both turned for the door. "That last part sounded like he was talking to a TV interviewer. He's already campaigning."

"Here." Liz held out her fist. Vic opened his palm and she dropped two black jelly beans into it. Vic looked at them.

"I don't eat the black ones. You want other colors get them yourself."

"Kinda particular, aren't you?"

"You see any white ones in the jar?"

Vic glanced back and didn't, although he knew white ones were made. They exited into the main office and crossed to the doorway. In the outside hallway their footsteps echoed off the polished floor.

As the elevator ground toward the first floor Liz stared straight ahead, then said slowly, "Transparency? Really?"

"Yeah. Only thing I can think of is this has something to do with City Council wanting an independent review board for police crimes. Maybe he figures if he uses us he can say he's used independent investigators before. His political opponents can't paint him into a corner."

"And we know how politicians hate being painted into corners. But why is he even that interested? The public defenders office doesn't report to him, it reports up to the County Commissioner."

Vic considered a long scratch on the brass of the elevator door. "Maybe that's it. He's looking for dirt on the County Commissioner and wants us to find it, not the detectives who report to him. That way he's blameless."

Liz huffed in disgust. "At least with Crush, when he does stupid stuff we know he's just looking for a promotion. This shit is way worse."

They both fell silent as the elevator ground toward the

first floor. Vic's mind shifted. For several days he had planned to ask Liz to walk him through Dannie's case file, but now the words stuck in his throat. It was too real. Finally he managed to squeeze out, "You know Dannie's case file?"

"Yeah." Liz popped another jelly bean into her mouth.

Vic saw flecks of grey in her closely cropped hair. He shook the loose fist he had made around the two black jelly beans and felt them bounce against his palm. "I read through it. I'd like to hear your take on it. You were on the task force. They'll be things you know that aren't clear in the report."

Liz swallowed as the elevator jerked to a stop. The doors creaked open. "About goddamn time you asked." She stepped ahead of him into the hallway.

CHAPTER 6

T hat afternoon, Vic slid the car into a parking spot outside a four story rectangle of a motel. It loomed over them, it's pale cream lines carved from a hammered tin sky. A light rain spat on their windshield. Ten yards away cars rolled along a four lane road bisecting sprawling strip malls and discount box stores. The air felt muffled and empty.

"I didn't know there were this many chain stores in the world," Vic said, cutting the ignition.

Liz looked up from her phone, her cheeks drawn and eyes bloodshot. She studied the motel. "Your house burns down this is what you get. Long term rental suites. If you even got the money for insurance. You think any insurance company is putting you up at the Ritz?"

"Yeah, I get it. What do we have?"

"Eric Stoll, Gretchen Stoll's husband. Lawyer, same as her, but he works at one of those hoity toity Grant Street law firms. Specializes in real estate and trusts." She flicked her finger across her phone's screen. "Huh. Went to law school in Chicago, got recruited out of there, I guess. He passed our bar exam like ten years ago."

"Gretchen was already at the DAs office by then."

"Yeah. Looks like they married seven years ago." She fell silent and Vic let her read, watching the cars shushing by on the access road, their tires trailing misty rooster tails of rainwater.

"He's clean," Liz said, after a few more seconds. "I mean

nothing even on his driving record from the last five years."

"Come on, he's a lawyer." Vic checked the cars in the parking lot and spotted a BMW 7 series. "He drive a BMW?"

Liz's finger flicked across her screen again. "Good call, detective."

"Superior observation skills. It was either that or a Nissan pick-up."

"Aren't you the funny one. I told him we'd be here at ten."

"And it's ten." Together they exited the car and crossed to the entrance, the drizzle cold on Vic's face. The door to Eric's suite was halfway down a carpeted corridor with a repeating design that tried to tip Vic off balance. He knocked on the door, more to steady himself than anything else.

The door swung open almost immediately, as if Eric was waiting for them. He was tall, just over six feet, and Vic was overwhelmed how everything about him seemed thin. His waist, his hair, the diluted quality of his blue eyes, the fabric of his hiking pants and sleek polyester shirt. They shook hands all around, Eric overshooting Vic's hand so his fingers fluttered on Vic's wrist like a bird's wing.

"Coffee?" Eric asked. "I just made some in case you wanted any." Even his voice sounded reedy.

"Not for me, thanks." Vic glanced at Liz.

"Sure," she said. "I'll get it," and stepped into the tiny kitchen. Vic saw that Eric had laid out everything for the coffee in a neat row on the kitchen counter. When Liz joined them, balancing a mug, they arranged themselves on the couch and armchair. The single black eye of a large flat-screen TV watched them from its perch on a nearby chest of drawers.

Eric broke the silence as if he had been rehearsing for their arrival. "I assume this is pro forma?"

"I'm not sure what to call it," Vic said. "But given the circumstances we need to talk to you, obviously. We appreciate you taking the time. We realize this can't be easy for you."

"It's horrible. This is a tragedy. I can't imagine a world without Gretchen." His voice trailed off, as if saying that much was painful. He dragged long fingers through his thinning hair. Oddly, Vic didn't sense any sadness.

"We still don't have a final ID, but we're very sure it's Gretchen," Liz said. "But perhaps you could just walk us through what happened over the last couple of days? When you last saw Gretchen or were in contact with her. Why she might have been home yesterday?"

Eric nodded quickly, tendons flexing in his skinny neck. "She'd taken a personal day. They have a heavy schedule at the DA's office and she just wanted a break. She was so *committed*." He looked about. "I told her she'd put in enough time, that she should take a job with one of the law firms. Better money and hours. That's what most of the ADAs do. But she *loved* it. Taking care of people who don't have the means. She said it was *service*." He wiped his mouth suddenly, as if he knew he was off topic. "Sorry. I just worry about some of the people she met through her job. Who she defended. But she was so committed to it. She believed it was the right thing to do." He fell silent, his eyes shifting from Liz to Vic and back, a note of pleading in them.

"We understand," Liz said. "I worked with Gretchen a couple of times. Not recently, but a couple of years ago. I agree about her commitment."

"Exactly!" Eric sat back, as if Liz had picked the perfect word.

"Perhaps we could get back to yesterday?" Vic asked softly.

"Right!" Eric shifted in his chair. "Um, anyway, she took a personal day. She didn't have any plans. She texted me about ten and said she was going to check on the house we're buying. It's in Sewickley. We bought it already, actually, but we have a contractor working on it, we have to redo the kitchen and stuff." His voice trailed off again, as if he had just realized that the project was now up to him.

Vic nodded, thinking that Sewickley made more sense for a lawyer than the inexpensive suburb where the Stoll's house had burned. "And that was the last communication from her?"

27

He nodded. "Yes. Do they know how the fire started?"

Liz shook her head. "Not yet."

Vic noticed that Liz hadn't taken a drink of coffee. He leaned forward. "Mr. Stoll, you mentioned you worried about Gretchen's clients. Did she ever make any comments about them? Anyone in particular? Do you know if anyone ever threatened her?"

Eric stared at Vic, then glanced at Liz. "What are you saying? I thought this was an accident. Are you saying it wasn't?" His eyes widened.

"We don't know. Liz placed the untouched mug on the coffee table. "We're just trying to cover all the options. Until we have the medical examiner's report we need to keep as many leads active as we can."

Eric rocked slowly. "I don't think so. Everyone *respected* her. She had great job reviews at the DAs office. She never complained about anyone. She just wanted to *help* people."

Vic looked at the window. He had the feeling that Eric was trying to convince himself of something. He hated asking the next questions, but he had to do it. "Mr. Stoll, I'm sorry to ask, but was everything fine between you and Gretchen? Marriage was on solid ground, that kind of thing?"

Eric started to say something but stopped.

"I'm sorry, Mr. Stoll," Liz added. "It's a question we have to ask."

He nodded as if he wanted to agree but didn't believe her. His nose rose a bit in the air. "Yes. We had a good marriage." He glanced from Vic to Liz and back and Vic sensed something change in him. He gazed directly at Liz. "Is this how it's going to be?" His voice rose. "You just asking any questions you want, no matter how personal they are? But so you understand. We were rock strong. She was a *saint!*"

"We just need a clear picture, Mr. Stoll." Vic changed his posture on the couch, wondering about Eric's use of past tense when he talked about Gretchen "We also understand that you were at work all day yesterday."

"Yes." His answer came quickly and Vic heard an edge to it. "And there's about twenty people who can confirm it."

"Thank you, Mr. Stoll." Vic placed his business card on the coffee table. "My e-mail is on the card. I'd appreciate it if you could e-mail me the name of the contractor your wife went to see yesterday. And I would really like you to think about her past clients, whether anyone might have a grudge or ever threatened her. Unfortunately, in her line of business, it would be natural."

"And when do I know what actually happened? When do I find out? I'm just supposed to wait? What do I do about her estate?"

Vic nodded. "Unfortunately that's out of our hands. We need to wait for the reports from the medical examiner and fire inspector. But you should know that we did find some irregularities. Perhaps there's nothing to them, but we need to be sure."

Liz cut in quickly. "Just out of interest, did your wife use the back door of your house much?"

Eric stared at her as if he had forgotten she was there. "Hardly ever. Unless we were using the patio. She went in and out through the garage."

Vic stood up. "Thank you, Mr. Stoll. As I said, we'll get back to you as soon as we know something. Again, I apologize we can't give you anything definitive yet, we need tine for the specialists to do their work."

Vic glanced at Liz in time to see her take a long swig from the coffee mug. She rose but there was a tiredness to her movements. Eric stood up, his eyes glazed.

Vic nodded at him. "We can let ourselves out.

Eric didn't react so Vic crossed to the door, Liz behind him. They let themselves into the hall and stayed silent all the way to the car. As Vic pulled onto the highway headed into Pittsburgh Liz finally spoke up.

"No ID on our vic and he's talking about her like she's been dead for years and we need to turn her into a saint. And close out her estate?"

"Yeah, not what I was expecting. I thought he'd be worried about if she really died in the fire."

"Makes you wonder."

Vic eased the car around a slow-moving pickup. "Yes it does."

CHAPTER 7

By 9:30 the next morning Liz still hadn't arrived at work and was unresponsive to Vic's texts. Vic stared at the e-mail from his commander's new administrative assistant, Eva, trying to decide what to do. The e-mail was simple. Crush, as their commander was nicknamed, wanted to see Vic and Liz immediately. Vic swilled down the last of his coffee and headed for Crush's office.

Instead of knocking on Crush's door, Vic made a beeline for Eva. She was new to the job and fresh out of college, and looked it, from her unlined face and wide eyes to the guarded way she watched everyone as if the world of adults mystified her.

"Any chance we can delay this?" Vic asked, half whispering so Crush wouldn't hear him.

Eva froze, but before she could answer Crush shouted to him from the depths of his office. As relief flooded Eva's face, Vic winked at her and stepped through the office doorway.

Crush rose from his chair, his skin-tight uniform shirt straining the buttons on his chest. "I hear you got a positive ID on Gretchen," he said, his dark eyes darting over Vic's shoulder, searching for Liz.

Several months earlier Crush had tried to suspend Vic but it hadn't stuck. Since then Liz had served as the intermediary between them, usually handling the conversation when the three of them were together. It was an accommodation they all preferred.

"Yeah," Vic said. "Um, Liz is out running something down. But about Gretchen, we got the e-mail last night. Gretchen's not been seen, used any of her financials or appeared at work. Husband and relatives haven't heard from her. The body was in her house and was the same height, the husband said she had the day off. That was enough for the ME to call it, at least until DNA samples come in. Body was delivered to Freddy last night, he told us to call him tomorrow and he'd give us top line on the autopsy results."

"Why is Freddy doing the autopsy? ME can't handle it?" Crush shifted his hands onto his hips, hesitated and dropped them to his sides, before finally placing the flat of his knuckles on his desk and leaning forward. Vic sensed Crush didn't like being alone with Vic any more than he liked being alone with Crush.

"My suggestion," Vic said, not about to let Liz get in trouble for his decision. "We checked it with the DA after we knew it was a suspicious death. Figured it made more sense to have our best guy on it."

"You talked to the DA?" The muscle ridges along Crush's shoulders flexed and Vic was reminded of his eighth grade anatomy lessons.

"Yeah. He wanted an update."

Crush rocked his body on his knuckles, his eyes like unsheathed knives. "From now on you let me know when you're going to talk to the DA, you understand?" He head butted in Vic's direction for emphasis. "Clear it through me first, dammit."

"I'm supposed to ignore the DA if he wants me to do something?"

"Just clear it through me!" Crush slammed his fist on his desk. "He's an elected official. You're out of your depth again. He's got an election coming up. He needs clear driving and smooth shit. We're gonna give him that. So you go through me!"

"Sure." Vic shrugged the word out, wondering how many

more people he had to bring into the loop before he could send a report to the DA.

"Now get out of here! Go detect."

Vic stepped out of the office, his hands clenched in fists. As he did Eva pointed at Crush's office and rolled her eyes. Somehow the tension inside him evaporated. He fought down a grin, leaned close to her and said, "You're gonna fit right in."

CHAPTER 8

Liz arrived at work at ten without explanation, and at one o'clock Vic and Liz let themselves into a conference room in the DA's office to begin their interviews. Someone had paneled the room in wood about eighty years before and no one had done anything to the room since. Near the door, the grey carpet squares were stained and worn. A narrow window ran down beside the door, but apart from that the room was windowless. As Vic settled into a lumpy and mismatched office chair Frank Marioni bounced in. He walked around the table and they both stood up to shake hands. Marioni shook hands with them as if his life depended on it. Or at least their next vote, Vic thought to himself.

"You guys ready to go?" Marioni asked, his dark eyes darting from one to the other.

"I think so," Liz said. "We have everyone lined up. We're starting with the people who interacted with Gretchen the least and then we'll work in to the people who know her best."

"You guys sound like a special counsel."

"Just gives us a clearer picture," Vic said. "First we get the rumors and scuttlebutt, then we can compare all that to the information from the people who knew her best."

"Good. Anyone gives you a hard time or won't talk, you let me know. We owe this to Gretchen. I don't want screwing around." His head turned from one to the other as if it was on a swivel. "You guys got any updates?"

Liz looked at Vic, giving him the go ahead.

Vic shifted on his feet, sorting what he wanted to say. Somewhere in the room a hot water radiator creaked. "Not so far, still getting stuff lined up. Our pathologist is ready to examine the body, and we'll have phone records soon."

Marioni's eyes bounced from Vic to Liz and back. "Keep me updated."

"Also," Vic said carefully, "we were wondering if we could see Gretchen's entire personnel file. We just got part of it."

Marioni spread his hands. Somehow it made him seem bigger in the room. Vic guessed it was something he'd learned to do at fundraisers. "Sure. Why not? You looking for something in particular?"

"Not really, just wanted to confirm all her old addresses. Gets us to people who might have known her in the past."

Marioni nodded his head as if he thought he was on TV and wanted to look decisive. "Good idea. Anything else?"

"Nothing we think is relevant," Vic said.

The conference room door opened and Crush walked in, the light gleaning off his shaved head. His white uniform shirt was starched into concrete. Vic had the sudden through that it was a different shirt than the one he had seen that morning.

"Commander Davis." In a split second Marioni was across the room pumping Crush's hand.

"District Attorney." Crush dipped his head slightly. "Dave."

Marioni swept his arm toward Vic and Liz. "Your team is doing great work. Outstanding. I'm sure we'll get to the bottom of this quickly."

Crush smiled. "Exactly, but I thought I'd come over and sit in on the first few interviews, make sure everything is moving in the right direction. We all want to get this right."

Vic found himself up on the balls of his feet and made a conscious effort to tamp down his anger. He glanced at Liz. She was staring at the wall as if she could open a hole to the outside with her eyes. Vic was sure that Crush had shown up to impress the DA and show he was in control of the investigation. He realized he should have anticipated the move.

"Great!" Marioni shook hands with Crush again and circled back to shake hands with Liz and Vic. Liz forced a smile. As he shot out the door he called, "Let's get this done."

Once the door banged shut Liz and Vic turned to Crush and waited. He glanced from one to the other.

"Figured I'd sit in on a couple of interviews," Crush said with a tone of 'what's wrong with you guys?'

"We heard," Liz said.

Crush clapped his hands together. "Glad you could make it, Liz. So, who's first?" Vic guessed Crush didn't want to have a discussion about why he showed up, or why he was wearing a freshly starched dress uniform.

Liz opened her portfolio and slid a piece of paper across the table to him. "That's the list."

Crush picked up the sheet and circled around the table to sit at the head. Once he was settled he stared at the paper. Liz pulled out a pen and clicked the button on top over and over. After a few moments of it she shifted to tapping the shaft on the edge of the table.

"Good," Crush said. "So the first interviews are the people who know her best? That'd be the most efficient. More information faster."

Liz stopped tapping her pen. When she didn't say anything Vic started talking. "We thought we'd try it the other way around. People who know her the least are first. That way we find out the rumors about her before we get to the people who know her best and have the most accurate information. The problem isn't getting the most information the fastest, it's having a way to evaluate the information we get. And the people who know her best can explain why a rumor about her might be out there."

"Right." Crush slapped the palm of his hand on the tabletop. He leaned forward to speak but the conference room door opened and a young man stepped inside. Despite the fact he was over six feet with a thick head of hair he came across as so young that Vic wondered if he could buy a drink.

"You guys here for the interview about Gretchen?" he asked, glancing around the room. Vic could had sworn he squinted at the brightness of Crush's white shirt.

For a moment Crush didn't say anything, then leaned back and pointed at Vic and Liz. "You have the right place. Detectives Lenoski and Timmons will handle it."

The young ADA turned to Vic and Liz, then pointed at a chair directly across the table from them. "Is that good?"

"Looks good to us," Liz said, and everyone waited until he sat down, the radiator hissing like an exhausted cat.

Crush sat through the first two interviews, but after the second interviewee left the room he made a show of checking his smartphone. "Something came up," he said. "You guys take it from here." He was out of the room so quickly Vic wondered vaguely if he had been there at all.

"What the hell?" Liz asked.

"Politics. He wanted to show off to the DA."

"Well yeah, but what I mean was he doesn't know how to interview a group of people?"

"Is knowing how to do the work a job requirement for a boss? Never seemed that way."

As Vic talked Liz was distracted by her cell phone, picked it up and started to thumb out a message.

Vic watched her for a moment. "How's it going with Levon?"

Liz finished typing and pressed the send button. She looked at him, her lips tight. "And why would I ever tell you? You guys are friends. I tell you one thing and you're on the phone to him blabbing."

"Wow, because that's what guys do. Just like high school."

"Vic, I spend most of my days with you. I don't need to be telling you what I do in my time off."

"I kind of meant the question in a friendly way, I wasn't digging up details."

"Good."

The door opened and another ADA stepped into the room. "This the place?" she asked.

"Yes it is," Liz said quickly. "You're Hanna Richards?"

"Yep." She sat down in the chair across from them. Vic guessed she couldn't be thirty years old. Her hair was long, brushed and carried a sheen, her pants suit expensive and her brown eyes brimmed with intelligence, even if the skin underneath them was marred by deep shadows. As they worked through the questions she seemed bored, but two-thirds of the way through the interview her lips tightened in response to one of Liz's questions. Vic saw it and cleared his throat. Liz looked up from her notes.

"Sorry," Vic said. "I didn't follow. We were asking about Gretchen's caseload and wanted to know if she worked the same number of cases as everyone else. You said the *caseload* was the same. You emphasized the word. I got the feeling you meant something there."

Hanna shrugged. "I did. Her caseload was the same. I answered your question."

"Nobody's on trial here," Liz said. "We're trying to figure out who might want to take her life. Maybe think of the question as more open ended."

Hanna nodded, but a hardness invaded her face. "Like I said, her workload was the same. We all have thirty or forty cases going at the same time. But somehow she was never as busy. We plea deal most of our cases, but they still take work. But she never worked late like the rest of us and she came in like an hour later than everyone else. I don't know how she did it. I'd figure her caseload was about to crush her, and then, bam, a bunch of her cases would plea out or get dismissed and she'd be fine. It was weird."

"Or lucky?" Liz asked.

"We aren't in the luck business. You skip the work and some judge eats you for lunch. But she always landed on her feet. Some of the guys called her Magic Mary."

Liz arched her eyebrows. "I don't get that."

"Her middle name was Mary. Gretchen Mary?"

"They called her that because of the workload?" Vic asked.

Hanna drummed her fingertips on the table, her nails clicking, and cocked her head at Vic. "Yeah, I wondered about that as well, I mean when guys come up with a nickname like that for a woman you know what they're talking about." She glanced over Vic's shoulder as if she needed a window. "She flirted sometimes, but not in a big way. I never really got that feeling. I think the nickname was actually for the way she handled her workload. For once."

Vic took his time answering. "Thanks. That's helpful." He nodded to Liz, so she would know to go back to their list of questions. Instead she leaned forward.

"Tell me, Hanna, what was her reputation as a lawyer? Good or bad? You must have had an opinion other than 'magical'."

"Look. Our job ninety percent of the time is to plea deal our cases." Her voice rose. "Do you understand? It's not about representing our client. Usually if we go to trial it's because the DA is after our client or our client is so dumb they've convinced themselves they're innocent. It's nuts. We're not doing law. Gretchen was the same. When she did take a case to trial she usually lost big. But that might not be about her as a lawyer. It happens. So I don't know. I can't say." She blew out a breath in disgust.

"Right, but in the balance?" Liz's voice was hard.

Hanna waved her hand over the table top. "Don't you get it? Our job is to move through as many cases as we can. Feed the machine. She was great at that, so I guess for an ADA she was everything you want. In the balance."

Liz shuffled her papers and dug her pen point into her notebook. Vic watched the color on Hanna's cheeks gradually disappear. He hated it, how someone so young could be so disgusted by what they did. Liz asked another question and Hanna answered, but the animation was gone. When they shook hands a few minutes later she didn't meet Vic's eye, as if she was disgusted with herself for revealing her feelings.

"You hear that?" Liz asked, before the conference room door was fully shut.

"Which part?"

"What the damn public defenders do. Work out a plea deal, move the cases through? Don't worry about your client actually getting a fair trial? You get that most of the people represented by public defenders are black?"

"Yeah, I know that," Vic said.

"Jesus."

Vic stayed quiet. It was one of those things everyone in law enforcement knew but didn't talk about. He forced himself to think about how to summarize what Hanna had said so he could trial balloon it when they interviewed others.

Liz was faster. "So we're supposed to think Gretchen was some happy-go-lucky who did the minimum work and came up like roses. Too damn bad for her clients."

"We don't know that yet. We got six people to interview tomorrow. We keep going."

Liz flipped her notebook closed. "Can't wait."

Vic stood and stretched. Through the narrow window beside the door he saw Hanna talking to the bean pole of an ADA they had first interviewed. He had a pretty good idea what they were talking about. He let his eyes roam and saw someone at the far end of the room, leaning against a file cabinet and watching him. Something jangled in the back of his mind. He knew the man, but couldn't place him. He stared at him a few moments longer, memorizing his face, then collected his things.

CHAPTER 9

That evening was the night Liz had agreed to review Dannie's case file with him, but when Vic opened his front door to the sound of the doorbell, it was Anne, his wife, he locked eyes with. She waited beside Liz, the top of her head even with Liz's shoulder, her eyes sharp and searching Vic's face for a reaction to seeing her.

"Hey," he said quickly to Anne. He opened the door wide so they could enter. As Liz brushed by she said, "I asked Anne to come." It sounded more like a command than a statement.

Vic saw Anne glance at the stairs, her face hard, and knew the reason. The last time Anne visited, another woman had come down the stairs from the second floor, naked under Anne's robe. Liz shed her windbreaker but Anne turned to him, her face stiff.

"Are you okay with me being here?"

Her hair was different, he thought. It reached just below her ears and was shaped to the roundness of her face somehow. Even with the hard set of her eyes it softened her features. He liked it. "Of course I am." Then he understood what she was really asking him. "I would have called, I just didn't know how much of this you wanted to know."

Her blue eyes searched his face before she slid out of her windbreaker. It was a brand that he hadn't seen her wear before, one preferred by teenagers and people in their twenties. He wondered if she had started working out.

"How's your mother?" he asked, for something to say.

"She's well. You aren't going to ask about my sister?"

"Not a chance." Vic grinned, slipping into the humorous banter they used to frame how much Vic and Anne's sister disliked one another.

A twinkle slid through her eyes and she glanced at what was once their living room. Vic warmed inside in a way he hadn't felt in months. "Good," he said. He looked at Liz. "We still doing this?"

She held up a large cup of take-out coffee. "Ready to go."

"Great." Vic led them into the dining room and stood to one side. Liz immediately scanned the wall, her eyes darting from the clusters of documents to the piles on the floor and back again, as if using a dining room this way was a natural thing. Anne shrank back, as if seeing the dining room this way scarred her memory.

"What's the coding system?" Liz asked, pointing at one of the colored post-it notes.

"Green for Dannie's movmements. Yellow for interviews. Orange for leads. Blue for stuff that doesn't feel right."

"There's so few blue ones," Anne breathed.

"That's why they're called the blues," Liz said softly, but her attempt to lighten the moment fell flat. "I ain't seen you work this way before, Vic."

"Just trying to organize it in my head. You guys did a ton of work and it's a lot to track. I didn't appreciate it at the time."

"Only thing you were appreciating then was whiskey." Liz approached the wall.

"Especially after you chased me away," Anne added. The air in the room thickened. Liz stared at a document on the wall as if it contained the nuclear codes. Vic searched for something to say but Anne added, "we need to get started. Liz, you have coffee, Vic, can I get you something?" She spoke in her *time to get to work* voice, and Vic guessed she used it to cover a sentence she hadn't meant to say out loud.

Vic nodded toward the kitchen. "I made coffee." He

avoided Anne's eyes, but he was suddenly attuned to her presence, as if he'd found something he lost a long time ago.

"Right," Anne said quickly. "Still just sugar, Vic?"

"It is." He glanced at her with a smile that she returned as she headed for the kitchen. He was glad. He wanted her to know that he wasn't anywhere close to disagreeing with what she had said.

◆ ◆ ◆

It was almost eleven when Liz finished her summary of the case. Vic watched her face as she finished speaking and sipped the last of her coffee. The grimace she made at the coffee cup told Vic her coffee was cold.

Vic guessed that her description of the investigation re-enacted the spirit of the original one. She'd been energetic and animated at the start, describing in sharp detail the timeline of Dannie's disappearance: how that particular Sunday was grey and cold, the tracking of Dannie's walk from Anne and Vic's house in the direction of her friend's home, the people interviewed in every single house along her route, the brief glimpses of her mined from window watchers and the clerk at a small convenience store where she'd bought gummy bears.

From Dannie's phone records the task force had confirmed the time she was expected at her friend's house. She hadn't used her friend as cover to do something else, they had the texts to prove it. And then, two thirds of the way to her friend's house, her phone had stopped pinging the cell towers. It had gone black, never to reappear. Dannie or someone else had turned it off, or the battery had run out. With the help of the cell phone provider they had marked a three block area where that happened.

And so the second round of interviews began, moving

outward from Dannie's walking route like ripples from a stone tossed in a pond. As Liz described the first ring her voice slowed and dropped, describing Dannie's school friends and teachers. By the time she got to the outermost ring, the registered sex offenders and places where Dannie only had a tenuous link—the library and a local coffee shop—her voice settled into sadness. Vic understood. The larger the ring the less chance of finding a lead.

Vic was familiar with how it felt that deep into an investigation. The sense of something slipping away. The frustration. The anger and the fear of failure. He didn't mention it to Anne but he knew it was in this period that Liz stuck the barrel of her Glock in someone's mouth in anger at the way they talked to her, and suffered a two week suspension.

In the end they had come away empty. All the task force knew for sure was the fifteen minute time frame when Dannie actually disappeared, and the place, a block from her friend's house within the three block perimeter outlined by the cell company.

It was as if someone had reached down and snatched her from the face of the earth.

They sat in silence in the half dark of the dining room for what seemed like a minute. Vic ached inside. Anne stared at the line of Dannie's photographs along the windowsill, her eyes watery. Liz looked as if someone had emptied her out.

Vic spoke first. "You did well, Liz. You guys were thorough."

"Not thorough enough." She swallowed a sob. "It was like the harder we worked the less we got. I don't get how someone completely disappears in the blink of an eye. There's always something. I don't get how we couldn't find it."

"Because it happens. The stuff marked with the blue post-it notes, it's all stupid stuff. Like someone forgot to check the spelling of Dannie's friend's names, so we might have missed an interview. That kind of thing. There's nothing substantive."

Vic stood up, separated a large brown envelope on the

card table and pulled out three photographs. "So here's what we know. From the task force we have no open leads, no real discrepancies in all the interviews and reports. What do you think about this?" He taped three photographs to the wall in a blank space close to the center of the wall. The faces of three young women stared back at them.

"I don't get it." Liz squinted at the photographs.

"These three women went missing about the same time as Dannie's disappearance."

"How old are they?" Anne asked.

"All of them are eighteen."

"We didn't investigate missing persons eighteen or older," Liz said quickly.

"Right, you guys followed procedure and searched on missing persons Dannie's age plus two years older and two years younger. Which is right. That's what we always do. But these women, they were strippers, and all three of them did shows where they pretended to be under age. Catholic girl uniforms, little princess dress and big lollipop. Pigtails. That kind of thing."

Anne crossed to the photographs and stared at them. "They look young for their ages."

Liz joined her for a moment before turning to him. "What are you saying, Vic?"

"I don't know. Maybe someone likes girls who are fifteen or sixteen, or at least pretend to be."

Liz stepped sideways, her head cocked. "Where did you get these photographs?"

"Someone I know."

She watched him, immobile. He almost heard her brain working.

"A someone who owns strip clubs?" she asked finally.

"Something like that."

Liz widened her stance. "You're getting too friendly with the wrong folk, Vic."

Anne turned from the photographs. "What are you talking about?"

Liz stayed quiet and Vic knew she wanted him to answer Anne's question. He guessed Liz felt he owed Anne a lot of answers and this was a good place to start. "Bandini," he said finally. "His daughter was involved in our last murder case and we got her out of a tough spot. He knew about Dannie disappearing and I think this was his way of saying thank you. I'm not sure it takes us anywhere, but it's a new way to think about the problem."

Anne shifted on her feet. "Bandini the gangster?"

Liz turned back to the photographs, leaving him, once again, to answer Anne's question.

"Yeah, although it seems like he's gone straight, or he's really good at hiding the bad stuff."

"Did we investigate these women when they disappeared?" Liz stared at the photos as if she was committing the faces to memory.

"Yeah. But the same way we normally search for strippers. Basic view was that they ran off with their boyfriends, even though two of them didn't have boyfriends."

"So what do we have on them?" Liz turned to face him.

Vic held up the envelope. "Everything we have. I pulled our original reports. There's not much there, except the names of family members who filed the reports."

Anne frowned. "Why didn't those girls get more of an investigation?"

This time Vic didn't bother waiting to see if Liz would reply. "There's no bodies, and they're strippers. You have to understand the search for Dannie was different. The department committed much more manpower and time to it." He waved at all the documents hanging on the wall and stacked on the floor. "That's how you get all that."

Anne sat down again on her folding chair, her face tight. He guessed that she understood the greater effort to find a policeman's daughter, but he could tell she didn't like it.

Liz crossed to the desk, picked up the brown envelope

and slid out the reports on the three women. Her eyes roved the pages but she was interrupted by a ding from her cell phone. She put down the reports and swiped through a couple of screens on her phone.

"Okay," she said. "That's Freddy. He'll do the autopsy on our burn victim first thing tomorrow morning. His ME agrees. He's calling it as Gretchen Stoll." She picked up the reports. "Mind if I hold onto these?"

Vic shrugged. "Pretty much have them memorized, but there is one thing." He took them back and wrote down the names and social security numbers of the three women, along with the names and contact information of the people who reported the women missing. He handed the reports to Liz.

"How you gonna handle it?" she asked. "These are cold cases. Crush finds out you're looking into cold cases he'll rip you one. He thinks Gretchen's case is his ticket to police chief, or whatever he wants to do. Plus you'll have to explain how you found out about these women. You know how he feels about Bandini. He'd probably suspend you again."

"Does he need to know?"

She stared at him for a long moment and her eyes brightened. "Now that sounds like the Vic I used to know. Freddy says we should call him tomorrow at ten. He'll give us a verbal on Gretchen's autopsy." She glanced at Anne and Vic knew Liz was asking her a silent question about whether she needed a ride home.

"Time to go," Anne said, rising from her chair. She gave a last lingering look at the line of Dannie's photos along the windowsill and followed Liz into the living room. They both slid into their windbreakers.

"Thanks," Vic said to Liz. She nodded, clutching the reports on the three missing women.

Vic was aware of Anne watching him. "You're really going to investigate what happened to our Dannie?" She said. "You can do it finally?"

After a moment Vic nodded. "I think I can, yeah."

She smiled and touched him lightly on the arm before following Liz through the front door. Vic watched her go. He wanted to say something to her, but he didn't know how to start. There was too much to say. It was like they were on opposite sides of a rain-swollen river, watching each other, each waiting for the other to make the swim.

CHAPTER 10

The next morning Vic was at his desk by 7:30. It was almost two hours before Liz arrived. As she shrugged off her waist-length leather jacket Vic called over to her. "I sent you a couple of texts this morning."

Liz ignored him and launched her computer. Annoyed, Vic leaned toward her. "By the way, I forgot to mention it yesterday. Before we did the interviews Crush called me in. He wanted both of us but I was the only one here. And guess what? He wants to see all our reports on Gretchen's case before they go to Marioni."

Liz sat back. The bags under her eyes were as rounded as the slump in her shoulders. "So let me get this straight, we gotta run our reports past Chief Dick in the North Hills and Crush. Anyone else?"

"Still early in the day."

"No one thinks we can do our job?"

Vic was surprised at the bitterness of her comment. He softened his tone. "More like people want to look good in front of the DA. When do we call Freddy?"

Liz rose from her desk. "Now. We can use the conference room."

A head popped out from a cube farther down the aisle. "Can I sit in?"

Liz sat down so she was hidden in her cube, leaving Vic to deal with the problem of Keith. Vic wondered if Keith had figured out how Crush used him to track Vic and Liz's movements during their last homicide investigation. Crush's decision to spy on them hadn't surprised Vic at the time, but Keith's enthusiasm at doing it had.

"We got a lot of people on this already," Vic said, trying to let him down easy.

Keith's head disappeared into his cube and a moment later he walked down to him. He glanced at Liz, who kept her eyes glued to her computer screen. Vic couldn't tell if her computer had actually booted up yet.

"I'm sorry," Keith whispered. He held out his phone so Vic could see an e-mail. "Crush wants me to work with you guys. I just got this. I know you don't need me, but I have to do what he says."

Vic skimmed the e-mail. "Sure," he said, hearing how clipped and angry his voice sounded. "Sit in on the phone call."

Liz stood up abruptly. "And I bet you want to read our reports before they go to Crush as well?"

Keith chewed his lip for a second. "No, but I could write them, if it would help you guys."

Vic stared at him and saw Liz blink hard twice. Everyone hated writing reports, offering to write them was unheard of. It was as if your dog had made a mess in your neighbor's yard, just to have the neighbor come out grinning and offer to clean it up.

"Can you write?" Liz asked. Vic could see her brain whirring. Not only was it a pain to write the reports, it was time consuming.

Keith seemed off-put by the question. "Yeah. I can write."

"I mean, you don't think you're Walter Mosley or Octavia Spencer, do you?"

"Who?" Keith shifted back down the aisle a step, as if he needed more distance between Liz and himself..

"Perfect answer," Liz said, shaking her head.

Vic cut in. "What she means is that we'll have to read them after you're done and we may edit them. When we do you can't bitch and get mad about us changing what you wrote. We know more about how to pitch the reports so our DAs can use them properly."

Keith recovered the step he had lost. "I get that. I want to learn how to do that."

Vic glanced at Liz and after a moment she shrugged. She turned to Keith. "And once the reports are done you deal with getting them past Chief Dick and Crush. But we need to know what they change. We have the last say before they go to the DA, and if we change things after they see them, you live with it."

"No problem." A big grin broke out on Keith's face.

"Sounds good," Vic said, surprised at the development. "Let's hear what Freddy has to say."

The conference room was actually Vic's cube, a long-standing joke between Liz and Vic, with the call on speaker. Liz and Keith pulled over chairs. They all waited silently through the sequence of clicks and dings until Freddy's voice made them all jump. Vic could never get over how someone barely 5' 7" could have such a deep and penetrating voice.

"Vic, I tell you," Freddy boomed into the phone. "The last body you give me was cooked. This one is crispy."

Vic squeezed his eyes shut for a moment, hoping the joke would go away. "Thanks, Freddy. You get this is probably one of our public defenders? That's why we wanted you to look at her."

"Yeah, sure. You hate jokes, Vic? But I am serious. I spent more time than my ME. So, female, early forties, fire death. Burns in her mouth nostrils and lungs. And soot. In the lining of her lungs."

"Freddy," Vic said, working his forefinger and thumb along the bridge of his nose and digging into the corners of his eyes. "First cop on the scene said he heard her screaming. Does that make any sense if she died of smoke inhalation?"

"Detective Lenoski, did I say she died of smoke inhalation? Sure, soot in her lungs, but not much. Lots of internal burns. Nose, mouth, lungs."

"So she burned to death?"

"Sure. If you say so. I say she was very close to source of

the fire. Perhaps she goes into shock."

"But how is it she was screaming? The first cop on the scene said he heard her screaming."

Freddy was silent for a moment and Vic learned that Freddy even breathed in a deep and penetrating way. Everyone listened to him draw three long breaths before he said, "Is this polizei sure?"

Vic thought of Pokorny, the local cop who was first on the scene, his stoplight eyes and the new space behind them where the screams would live. "He didn't make it up."

"Smoke inhalation then she would not scream. Burning to death, yes. For a time. Then she would pass out from carbon dioxide."

No one had anything to say for a few seconds and Vic knew everyone was thinking about what that would be like. He turned to Liz. "Why wouldn't she move? Get out of there?"

Liz watched him. "Maybe she was bound?"

"I check tox screens," Freddy said.

"What?" Asked Vic, aware that all of them were staring at the telephone.

"When tox screens come back. I check for drugs. Perhaps she is drugged. Wakes up to fire. I need to check for carbon dioxide too."

Liz and Keith sat back at the same time.

"I guess we should have thought of that," Vic said. "But that'll be a few weeks, right?"

"I put rush on it, I will let you know."

"Thanks, Freddy," Liz and Vic said in unison. Vic leaned forward again. "Liz asked if she was bound. Any evidence she was tied to the bed?"

"I check ankles and wrists again, but I did not see anything the first time. Too much fire. Any bindings burn or melts."

"Thanks, Freddy." Vic hit the disconnect button and sat back. "So someone drugged her and she woke up to the place burning down?"

No one spoke, and Vic was again sure everyone was thinking of Gretchen waking on her bed, her limbs on fire. They all jumped when Liz's iPhone rang. Liz breathed out sharply and pushed her chair across the aisle to her cube. Keith stood up, grabbed the back of his chair and dragged it toward his cube. Vic thought he looked pale, but it might just have been the fluorescent lights. On the other side of the aisle Liz stood with her phone pressed to her ear. She was hunched and Vic could tell from the tightness of her shoulders that the call was a problem. She turned her back to him and spoke a few words before hanging up. She turned back to him.

"I gotta go out for a few hours. I'll be back." She shrugged into her leather jacket.

"What's up?" Asked Vic.

"I gotta go. It's important."

There was something in Liz's face. The muscles said she was angry, but there was a sliver of something in her eyes. Desperation, almost. "Anything I can do to help?"

"Not likely," she said, spearing the strap of her shoulder bag and tugging the bag against her side. Without another word she disappeared down the aisle.

CHAPTER 11

By ten o'clock the next morning Vic and Liz were again seated in the courthouse conference room with the hissing radiator and the empty, hand carved wooden shelves. Two more lawyers sat through their questioning, neither one able to add any information about Gretchen or her workload. The second seemed to make a point of talking more as a way to tell them very little. Vic was relieved to watch him leave along the rutted carpet to the door.

When the door thumped Liz tossed her pen on the table. "I hate jerks like that."

Vic liked that Liz was engaged enough to be angry. "Just because he thinks it's funny to confuse whoever is asking him questions?"

"I get why you want to do that in a courtroom. But here? We're trying to figure out who murdered one of his colleagues."

Vic didn't reply. When the lawyer sat down in front of them he'd guessed he wouldn't be much use. His shirt was stained around the collar and his tie frayed at the knot from frequent rubbing against his beard stubble. The dark half circles under his eyes could have attracted a female raccoon. When he started talking in circles and asking rhetorical questions, Vic knew he'd turned lazy, or drifted to a place where it was easier to confuse people than accurately answer questions and help someone.

The door opened and a squat, broad shouldered man with

salt and pepper hair entered.

"My turn?" he asked. He checked both Vic and Liz with sharp brown eyes.

"Only if you're John Laren."

"I am." He sat in the chair opposite them. He had a strong chin that he stuck toward Vic before swinging it toward Liz. "Have at it, guys."

"Sure." Liz started him through the regular series of questions. He answered each one quickly and to the point. For most of the interview he had little to offer, until Liz asked him how well Gretchen handled her workload. When she did, Vic caught the smallest tell, a movement in the corner of his mouth and half a heartbeat's hesitation. It was the first time he had paused before answering a question.

Vic cut in. "Just to make the point, we don't care about anything but finding out how Gretchen died. We're not sitting on judgment, we're trying to understand as much as we can about her. Good or bad."

John let his eyes linger on Vic for a moment before he turned to Liz. "You may have already heard about this. Some of us called her Magic Mary?"

"We've heard," Liz said. "Tell us about it."

John spread his hands on the tabletop, his palms up. "I came up with the name. Yeah, so I guess I'm the jerk."

"We're not going to be footnoting sources," Vic said. "What made you come up with that name?"

John slid his palm together and interlocked his finger. "It was about three years ago. She and I tag teamed a case. Manslaughter DUI. Some guy in his twenties drank too much malt liquor, passed out driving and ran head on into a car driven by some father on his way home after working a late shift. Father died, drunk kid walked away from it. You ever notice how that happens?"

"Yeah." Liz didn't even try to keep the disgust out of her voice.

"Anyway, the kid came from a good family in the suburbs,

but his Dad decided enough was enough and refused to pay for a lawyer so the kid ended up with us. I guess the Dad wanted to teach the kid a lesson. Probably should have done it fifteen years earlier, but that's how it went."

"Gretchen handled the kid's case?"

"Yeah. Pretty open and shut. Anyway, DA asked me to stay on top of the case, Gretchen hadn't handled that kind of case before and I'd done a few of them. It was only a few years after the new law came in that ramped up the penalties. It was high profile, the guy who died was a veteran working his ass off to keep a roof over his wife and two young daughters, keep them fed, that kind of thing. A lot of sympathy. DA was a Marine platoon leader, you know that, right? He felt for the family. Wanted this to go right."

Liz drummed her fingernails on the table. "And a guilty verdict on the kid would open the way for the widow to sue a rich kid's family?"

"There's that.

"So how did that turn into Magic Mary?" Liz asked.

"While the case was running, I'd meet with Gretchen once a week kind of thing, reviewing her progress, steps she's taking, you get the idea. And the first few weeks she's all over it. Has the evidence locked down, she's all over the court schedule. She was cranking out depositions, witness statements, all good. And then she wasn't."

Vic leaned over the table. "What do you mean?"

"We'd meet and every question I asked she had to check her notes. Then stupid stuff started coming up. Witness statement got misplaced, like the one from the arresting officer. Then she missed a court deadline on something. Wasn't a big deal, it was one of the things you can make up, but I called her on it. You know what she said?"

Liz and Vic waited as John glanced from one to the other.

"She said the kid's mother had come in. They'd talked, she was pretty sure we wouldn't be handling the case."

Liz tapped her pen on the table. "She stopped working on

the case without being officially taken off it?"

John nodded. "I figured that the mother told Gretchen she was getting different legal counsel. The family had the money and I could see her thinking differently than the kid's dad. I mean it's her kid. But yeah, just because someone tells you that, so what, you keep working the case until it's official."

Something stirred in Vic. "So what happened?"

"Well, it went on for another couple of weeks. Same thing. I could tell in our meetings that she wasn't working the case, but we had no notification from another law firm that they were taking over the kid's defense. And then one week I sit down with her and she's got this look on her face. I ask her what's up and she passes me the revised statement from the arresting officer. Remember I said the first one was lost? In his new statement the cop said they did a field sobriety test, but in thinking about it now the kid's performance was a judgment call. Could have gone either way."

"Breathalyzer?" Liz asked.

"Turns out the certification was out of date. So you got a 'maybe drunk' from the cop on the scene and the breathalyzer evidence gets thrown out on a technicality. They hadn't done a blood test. So suddenly the case is maybe the kid drank a couple of beers, it was late at night, he just fell asleep at the wheel. Not a crime, just a tragedy."

"You didn't have statements from where the kid was drinking?"

"He was coming from a buddy's house in Shadyside after a Penguins game. No way to check drinking at a game like that, and his friend said they hung out for a couple of hours after the game and just had a beer or two. No way to prove or disprove any of it."

"The kid walked?"

John unlocked his fingers and showed his palms.

The feeling inside Vic shifted to anger. "What about the family who lost the father?"

"Yeah. I figured the widow would go after the kid in a civil case, but she had no money. A friend of hers did some crowd funding and got her a lawyer, but all she could afford was some lawyer on his way to disbarment. They brought a case but it was settled before it went to court."

"The kid's family gave them money?" Liz couldn't keep the disgust out of her voice.

"Sounds like it. The kid and his parents had a team of lawyers from one of the big firms, and you know how that goes. They probably low-balled a settlement offer, it was more money than the widow's ever known, or her lawyer, so she took it. Done and done."

The only sound was the hissing of the radiator. Vic stared through the narrow window beside the door, into the DAs office and the people moving back and forth. He refocused on John, who was watching them. "And that's when you gave Gretchen the nickname?"

He smiled, but there was no humor in it. "That came later. After that case I just noticed more about what she was doing. I didn't plan to, it just happened that way. I knew what she was working on from our weekly staff meeting. It was like I knew the signs, after that, and I'd see the same thing happening sometimes. Like maybe for a few weeks her updates on a case would be basically the same, and then the case would go away somehow. So a bunch of us are out after work one night and I just say 'Magic Mary.' People picked up on it."

Liz tapped her pen again. "When you say *go away*, what do you mean?"

John shrugged. "Any of lots of ways. Like the drunk kid, sometimes there's a problem with evidence or witness statements. Sometimes a plea deal is worked out, sometimes an internal review decides the case isn't strong enough. It happens to all of us. I can't complain. It's just she had a nose for which cases would collapse. I mean part of calling her Magic Mary was because she was so good at spotting the crap cases and not wasting time on them. You almost had to give her credit."

"And it meant she didn't have to work as hard?" Liz asked.

"It does have that benefit. We waste a lot of time on cases that don't go anywhere. She avoided that. Magic Mary."

Vic shifted his feet underneath him, feeling the stiffness in his knees from working out the night before. "How about the cases that did go to court?"

"Probably about .300, winning and losing. Although I will say, the ones she lost, her defendant got the book thrown at them. They got crushed."

"Maybe she didn't do the work on those cases, either," Liz said quietly.

John shrugged. "I don't know that. Her percentage is about what most of us do. There's nothing really different there. Remember we try to avoid court. Rarely goes well."

The radiator clanked and Vic was aware of the emptiness of the bookshelves behind him. His anger had drifted away and he was tired. He turned to Liz. "Anything else?"

She pursed her lips. "Not right now."

He could tell she didn't like it any better than he did. He turned back to John. "Listen, I appreciate you taking the time. We'll call if we need anything else."

"No problem." John rose and stepped into the rut in the carpet. He had the door halfway open when a question skated into Vic's mind.

"John," he said quickly. John stopped, his hand on the door knob. "One other thing. You said the drunk kid was from the suburbs. Which one?"

John's eyes glittered for a moment as he thought about it. "North Hills," he said finally. "Wreck was on McKnight Road."

"Who was the police chief?"

John grinned. "I remember that. Guy had the same name as that old Dallas football coach, Tom Landry. Name was Richard Landry."

Vic glanced at Liz. "We've met him."

John shrugged. "I never did, I just remember the name."

"Thanks, John." Liz said.

"Yeah. Good to meet you guys."

As the door thumped shut Liz huffed a short laugh. "What do you know. Chief Dick."

"Yeah." But Vic was distracted. Through the narrow window by the door, at the far end of the aisle, the same man as the day before leaned against a filing cabinet. "Give me a second," he said, rising.

Vic let himself out of the conference room and walked down the aisle to the man, still trying to remember how he knew him.

"Vic Lenoski," the man said, as Vic drew close. His voice was confident and smug.

"Yeah," Vic said. "I remember you somehow."

"Shit. I remember when you first made detective. Had that deer in the headlights stare."

Vic waited, the man watching him, "Yeah," he said after a few seconds. "Wouldn't expect you to remember me. I left the force five or six years ago. But we need to talk about Gretchen. You'll get around to interviewing everyone she worked with so I'll save you some trouble. I'm one of the county detectives now, work for the DA, when they actually give enough of a shit to investigate something, or have enough time to actually read the files and see the mistakes. I knew Gretchen. There's some shit you need to know."

"If you got something to tell us we'll listen. I still don't remember your name."

"Dave Norbert."

The name shot through him. "Dave Norbert. You used to be a detective with us."

"One and only."

"Yeah. Good to see you again." Vic wondered if he'd ever told a larger lie.

"Vic, don't even go there. Just give me a time to meet and we'll sit down. All that went on doesn't mean I'm a total asshole. You got a murder on your hands and I got shit you need to know."

"And it'll come out anyway?"

"Wow. You never change. Same hardass. Yeah, it'll come out anyway, but I'm saving you a boatload of time. And it's the right thing to do."

"Okay, Dave." They settled on meeting for lunch the next day.

"Who was that?" asked Liz, when he was back in the conference room.

"Dave Norbert."

Liz cocked her head. "I heard that name. Before my time, though."

"Be glad you don't know him. He's off the force, but the DA's office hired him, which makes no sense. But he says he has information about Gretchen." Vic took a deep breath. He felt dirty.

"And Chief Dick keeps showing up."

"Yes he does," Vic said, slowly. But that wasn't quite it, either. It was the kid who avoided the DUI who wouldn't leave his mind.

CHAPTER 12

Vic stood in his dining room that night staring at the documents taped to the wall. He wore sweats from his basement workout and a small white towel hung around his neck. As he skimmed each document he sometimes wiped the sweat from his face.

His eyes kept drifting back to the photos of the three young women from Bare Essentials, all reported missing close to the time of Dannie's disappearance. He stepped in front of the photos and considered each one, working his fingers to ease the stiffness that lingered from the punching bags.

The house was silent around him. Outside, traffic churned by, as muted as a heartbeat. And in that instant he knew how different everything was.

When Dannie was home, when Anne still lived with them, the house had deadened the outside noises, cocooning them, and at the time he thought it a good and trustworthy thing. But it was a lie. Anger rose in him and he fought it down, glancing at the photographs of Dannie arranged along the windowsill. He had failed her, he knew suddenly. He had believed the lie, that somehow the house could stop whatever was outside from reaching them, from hurting them. Despite everything he'd seen on his job, of all the ways people damaged themselves and others, he'd stopped paying attention and gone soft.

He breathed hard through his nose, anger making up his mind. It was time to investigate the three missing women. Liz had the reports, but he had the names and social security numbers. Turning to the table he found the paper where he'd written them down and tore off the top half, so they were separate from the contact information of the people who reported the missing women. He placed both pieces of paper on the kitchen counter near the garage door.

On his way upstairs his movements were thick somehow, as if the air around him had stiffened, as if the skin of the cocoon was trying one last time to pacify him. Outside a bus humphed along the street, the sound of it leeching through the walls. He heard it clearly and knew that now he would listen for it, and kicked each riser on his way to the top of the steps.

◆ ◆ ◆

At work the next morning Vic hung up his sport coat and slid the folded paper with the names and social security numbers from his inside pocket. He walked to Kevin's cube.

He expected Kevin to be reading sports news on his computer or playing a computer game, but he was only half right. The Penguin's website was open on his computer, but he was reading a three ringed police procedure binder. Kevin glanced up quickly.

Vic nodded at the binder. "Light reading?"

"Evidence chain of custody and stuff." He pushed the binder away as if he was embarrassed to be caught reading it.

"Yeah, I saw there were a couple of updates last week."

"You read that stuff?" His eyes widened.

"Best way not to look like an ass in front of the DAs."

"Um," Kevin glanced into the corner of his cube and a flush spread across the back of his neck. When he spoke he stared at Vic's belt buckle. "I read that if you make a mistake with the chain of custody there's a couple of remedies. It's not a great thing to have happen but you can work around it. Not poison the case."

Vic knew what Kevin meant. During his last murder investigation, Vic broke the chain of custody on a suspect's laptop. Kevin reported it to Crush, and it became part of the case for Vic's suspension.

"Yeah," Vic said carefully, wondering why Kevin brought it up now. "But it's always better to get it right."

"I guess I hadn't realized there were remedies. That even if chain of custody is broken there's ways to make the findings admissible."

Vic decided that, in his own way, Kevin was apologizing. He nodded. "See, reading that thing taught you something already. Now, can you help me do some research?"

Kevin's eyes snapped up. "Sure, what do you need?"

Vic held out the top of the torn piece of paper. "I was researching some cold cases. This is a list of missing women and their social security numbers. They all disappeared like a year or a year and a half ago. I don't know if they ever started working again, or if they pop up in our systems anywhere since then. They were strippers, maybe working girls. But if they are working again now we can close their jackets."

Kevin stared at him. "You're working cold cases?"

"These, yeah. At the time everyone figured they ran off with boyfriends. If they're working again then they're not missing, right? Should be easy."

Kevin's gaze turned inward, and Vic knew he doubted the story. He grew interested in what Kevin would do and decided to push a bit. "You used to work cold cases, right?"

Kevin glanced at his computer, saw the Penguins website and clicked it closed. He tapped his fingers on his mouse. "Sure, no problem. Won't take long. Simple search." He emphasized the last sentence as if he wanted to know why Vic didn't do the search himself.

"Great." Vic wasn't about to tell him that he didn't want the search history for the three women on his computer. He started to turn away but faced him again. "Kevin," he said. "We all get chain of custody wrong one time or another. The point is to stay up to date and try not to, and when you do screw it up, admit it. If you try to cover up a mistake any half decent defense lawyer will nail you on it. Fact of life."

"Sure. Thanks Vic."

Vic walked back to his cube. As he sat down he glanced across the aisle and saw Liz staring at him. He hadn't seen her come in. She frowned and tilted her head as if to say, 'what was that all about?'

He shrugged and turned to his computer. He spent most of the morning reviewing notes from the interviews over the last two days and answering e-mails, until wrinkled chinos appeared next to him. He looked up into a crooked grin and an unruly mop of hair.

"Craig. All good down in Tech?"

"Detective Lenoski," Craig said formally. Vic had noticed that Craig was uncomfortable addressing him by his first name. Craig's father was Vic's first commander, and Vic guessed that Craig saw him as part of his father's generation.

Craig shuffled from one foot to the other. "You sent down the request for the data from a Gretchen Stoll's phone?"

"Yeah. But we don't have the phone itself. I was hoping you could get your ducks in a row in case it arrived. It probably got burned in the fire."

"Sure, but you sent the number. I got a warrant out to the cell company and they sent me back a bunch of stuff. Locations, texts, browser history."

Vic leaned back. "That fast? That usually takes weeks."

"Oh yeah. But I know a guy who works over there. Fraternity brother. He helped me out. They also told me the type of phone, so I got a warrant out to the company that carries her cloud account. That should get me photographs and files."

"Thanks, Craig. You could have e-mailed this, you didn't need to bring it up here."

He shifted back a step and Vic saw Liz tilt her head as if she was listening. Craig grinned his lopsided smile. "Gets me out of

Tech. Good change. I don't mind. Anyway, I thought hard copy might be easier."

The tech department was a single, long windowless room in the basement. Vic believed him. He chose not to ask why Craig thought he might prefer hard copy over digital. "Okay, always good to see you. How's your Dad?"

"Still fishing on the weekends. He's been helping out with new officer training. Seems good with it."

Kevin appeared beside Craig, his face serious. He moved so close that Craig had to shift to his right. He might as well have blocked him out of the way, and Vic knew he did it on purpose.

"Kevin," he said shortly.

Kevin held out a piece of paper. "What I found on the cold cases you asked me to investigate."

"Thanks." He took the paper, surprised that Kevin was already finished. Holding it, he turned back to Craig and raised the thick file. "Thanks again. This'll be helpful."

"No problem." With a glance at Kevin he disappeared down the aisle. Kevin seemed unsure what to do so Vic told him he would review the paper later and turned back to his computer. When he was gone Vic glanced at Liz. She was staring at her computer, shaking her head slowly.

Vic unfolded the paper. By each name Kevin had appended a short note that said: 'No further SS usage.' He wasn't surprised. He refolded the paper and stuck it in the inside pocket of his sport coat, certain that his only leads on the three women would be the people who reported them missing. He opened Craig's file, his eyes scanning the lists of text messages and e-mails. He turned to the back of the file, where the location data was listed. It was the hardest data to work with. About a month of data was listed, the last entry showing 3:01 the day of the fire. Sure enough, when he plugged the location data into Google it came back showing the phone located near the Stoll's house. He worked backwards from that time stamp, checking locations. It didn't take long until he leaned back and called across the aisle to Liz.

"You remember Gretchen's husband said she was going to Sewickley the morning of the fire to meet their contractor?"

Liz nodded.

"Funny, she was there, but that was right before she went to the South Side flats."

Liz sat back. "She told her husband she's going north but she actually went south?"

"And pretty far south."

"What's there?"

Vic shook his head slowly. "Beats me, but maybe after we finish lunch with Norbert we take a drive over there, see what we got. Work for you?"

"First you gotta tell me about this Norbert guy."

Vic glanced at his computer clock. "I'll tell you on the way. It's in half an hour."

CHAPTER 13

Vic and Norbert had agreed to meet for lunch at a small restaurant in Lawrenceville that specialized in empanadas and fried chicken. Norbert had suggested the restaurant. Vic wasn't sure what an empanada was and it added to his dislike of the hot-spot restaurants and art galleries new to the neighborhood. To him, Lawrenceville meant the Zivic brothers and other boxers born and bred in Lawrenceville in the early 1900s. From his own Golden Gloves days he knew what the brothers had meant to Pittsburgh in the early 1900s, well before the success of the Steelers and Penguins.

"What the hell was that with Kevin?" Liz asked, as Vic pulled the car out of the parking lot.

"Asked him to track down the social security numbers of those three women Bandini gave me."

"You think that's smart? He tried to screw you when he was spying for Crush."

"He kind of apologized for that."

"Guys don't change, Vic. I guarantee you this is just a new tactic. This time he was just open about the fact he was working for Crush. He's still feeding Crush information. I guarantee it."

"Bit cynical, aren't you?"

"I dated for a while when I first got here. Guys play nice when they're after something. Problem is most girls give it to them before they find out what the guy is really like."

"Speaking of which, how's it going with Levon?" Vic

asked, referring to a friend Liz had started dating several months earlier.

Liz was quiet for the time it took Vic to cross two traffic lanes to the off ramp that led to Lawrenceville.

"You won't give up, will you?" she said finally. "There is a lot going on with him."

Vic tried to pin down Liz's tone of voice to understand what she was really saying, but failed. "Two tours in Iraq, never met his dad, he's going to be complicated. I see him as the kind of guy who's worth it, though. You saw what happened on our last case. And that was your first date."

"Yeah, I know from that he can handle himself. And he's a good shot. But there's something underneath those tours he won't talk about. I met his mother last week. Real nice lady. Runs her own web business. Levon says she can write code good enough to hack the NSA."

"Good. We might need her some day. So you're meeting relatives? Uh-huh."

"Shut up, Vic."

He stopped at a red light. "Wow. Touchy. So this lunch place, what's an empanada?"

Liz stared at him, her full lips tight. After a few seconds she said, "Time for you to start acting like a cop. What about this guy we're meeting? Norbert. What's up with him? I asked around and people aren't talking. In a 'he's bad news' way of not talking."

Vic found himself starting to get annoyed at how long the light was red. "Rumor at the time was that he faked evidence. He knew they had the right guy, but the evidence wasn't quite there. Rumor was he embellished it and suddenly the arrest stuck. At least that's what I heard."

"Suspect went to jail?"

"Yep. And the crimes stopped as soon as he was locked up. Media ate it up and everyone shook hands and pretended nothing had happened."

"Wow,"

"Yeah.

"Doesn't make me like him any better."

Finally the light flicked to green and Vic goosed the accelerator. "You and me both. Now tell me, anything in Gretchen's financial records we need to worry about?"

"Nothing in a something kind of way. Everything is just a little different than what you normally see, but nothing you can point your finger at. Very few withdrawals, but they're there. Some cash deposits, but nothing too big. No structure or regularity to any of it.

"Maybe Norbert has some ideas." Vic spotted an open parking space ahead, just after a traffic light. Together, he and Liz crossed the street and Vic held the door into the narrow restaurant. Vic recognized Norbert right away. He was sitting a few tables down from the door, watching them come in, a drumstick in his fingers. He waved it at them and Vic nodded back.

They shook hands all around, Norbert still chewing. His black hair was thick and swept back from his forehead and he had a large lower jaw that with the right lighting, makeup and script could have made him a movie star. But Vic thought the lines around his dark eyes and the tips of his mouth had hardened. He was aware of Norbert studying him closely as well.

"Order at the cash register," Norbert instructed, so Vic and Liz trudged to the cash register by the front door, studied the menu and ordered. By the time they returned Norbert's small metal tray was littered with chicken bones. He wiped his fingers carefully with a paper napkin.

"Your show," Vic said as he settled into his seat. "You asked us to come."

"Sure. Where are you so far?"

"Just getting started," Liz said.

Norbert glanced back and forth between them. "Man, you two act like you been married for twenty years."

"Look," Vic said. "You asked for this meet, we did the courtesy of coming here. You got something for us? Otherwise we can just wait until the official interview."

"I only know what I know."

"Which right now doesn't seem like much," Liz said.

"Okay, okay." Norbert sat back. "I knew Gretchen pretty well."

"How so?" Vic leaned toward him.

"Part of my job is helping the assistant district attorneys with investigations. With her it was more than that." He glanced past them at the large front window and the street outside. Vic was surprised to see emotion well up in his eyes. "Gretchen and I were kind of an item."

"She's married." Liz didn't try to hide the disgust in her voice.

Norbert shifted his gazed to her. "Yeah. Like no one else ever screwed around. In the history of the world. Grow up."

"How long?" Vic asked.

"Year. Year and a half. I knew you guys would figure it out so I wanted to save you the trouble. Maybe you can see a way not to tell the husband. Might go easier for him if he doesn't know."

"Really?" Liz sat back. "You're worried about hurting the husband's feelings? Now?"

"You need to back down," Norbert said to Liz. "Keep your damn moralizing to yourself."

Vic cut in. "All right, all right. Both of you. So you were sleeping with Gretchen. That's not the main point. Any idea why someone would kill her?"

Liz folded her arms on her chest. Vic knew she'd heard him, but she was more interested in treating Norbert as a suspect.

Norbert showed the palms of his hands. "No. See, that's what I don't get. I investigated some cases for her, that's how we met. But as far as I know she never got any threats. She never said anything to me about being scared of someone."

"Did her husband know you were sleeping together?" Liz asked.

Vic scratched his cheek. Liz was a step ahead of him. He should have seen right away that if Norbert was sleeping with

Gretchen and her husband knew, that Mark Stoll was a suspect.

"No. I'm pretty sure about that. She was careful. No e-mails or texts. And we always went to her place on the South Side, so no hotel receipts or that kind of crap."

"What place on the South Side?" Vic stared at him, barely aware that the cook had just called his name. He thought of the location data on Gretchen's phone. "I didn't see any South Side property listed among her assets."

"She put it in her Mom's name. She mentioned that to me once. But her Mom's in some nursing home up north. Gretchen has power of attorney over her affairs, so she just bought it and put it in her mother's name. Used her mother's money, for all I know. She kind of bragged about that. No question she paid the taxes out of her mother's money. So, yeah, it wouldn't show up."

Distracted, Vic stood up and collected his lunch from the counter. Liz did the same. When they sat down he asked, "Does her husband know about the house?"

"Doubt it. The guy's pretty clueless. One time I was talking about maybe her husband walking in on us and she said I didn't need to worry, that he didn't know about the house. Then she got into this thing about maybe she'd tell him, that it would make things more exciting. She had a freaky side that way."

"What else?" Liz asked, and Vic could tell that she didn't believe him.

"Just those two things." He nodded at Vic's tray of food. "After you take your first bite of the empanada, pour a little of that Chimichuri sauce into it. It's freaking ridiculously good. Anyway, figured I'd save you guys the trouble. She has an office in that house as well, you'll want to go through it. Pretty sure her will is in there. Different than the one she has with her husband."

"Yeah," Vic said, thinking. "Street address?"

Norbert gave it to them and Liz wrote it down. Vic was surprised to hear a note of sadness in Norbert's voice.

"You doing alright?" Vic asked him.

"Kind of. I only heard about it yesterday. She didn't show

up at work and I just figured she'd taken a day off. Then the DA called everyone together and announced it. Sucks hearing it in public like that."

"And where were you two days ago about three o'clock." Liz asked.

Norbert pushed his tray away, his movement angry. "Just like that? I try and help you guys out and that's what I get. Prove I didn't do it?"

Vic leaned toward him. "C'mon, you know how this works. If you were sitting on our side of the table you'd be asking the same question."

He looked away. "I was working."

"Meaning?" Liz bit her empanada but didn't seem to taste it.

"Stakeout. It was for one of the other lawyers. That new ADA, Crane. He still uses me a lot, it'll take him another six months before he caves and starts mailing it in. Anyway, police arrested a guy for beating up someone, the suspect says the guys charging him are lying and they owed him money, so I'm watching those guys. See if the defendant is lying or not."

Vic didn't follow how staking out the men could prove the suspect's innocence. He let it go. "Anyone see you?"

"No," Norbert said quietly. "I would be pretty shitty at staking out if they did."

No one said anything and Vic picked up his empanada and gingerly took a bite. He liked the taste. Norbert pointed at the plastic sauce container. Vic poured some into the empanada, careful not to soak the pastry crust. "We'll need to take a formal statement," he said, and took another bite. The sauce made a magnificent difference and he found himself lining up another bite.

Norbert grinned. "Good, huh?"

"Tell me," Liz said, tossing her empanada on her tray as if it was radioactive. "Did Gretchen take any other guys down to that house, or were you the only one? Or maybe you don't have a clue."

Norbert shifted his gaze to Liz. "Man, you got a tight ass, don't you?" He leaned forward. "What if she did? Is that any of my business? Maybe she liked a bit of fun on the side. Maybe she liked a bit more than I know about. Not my damn business, is it? We had fun together. That's it."

"And you didn't care that she was stealing her mother's money? Guy like you, I guess we should expect it. It's all about having fun."

Norbert sat back, staring at her. Liz was absolutely still. Vic sipped his water. He knew Liz was trying to make Norbert angry, to shake something out of him he didn't mean to say. But after a moment Norbert leaned forward again, his eyes calm.

"Yeah, so I guess you heard the rumors about me. Why I left the force. I bet it bothers you, right? Doesn't fit with your perfect way of looking at what's right or wrong? You just think I'm crooked. You tell me. We had our guy, we just didn't have good physical evidence. All circumstantial. A guy who got his kicks beating up gay men. Some of 'em will never walk straight again. One's in a wheel chair. Another one can't make a fist any more, his fingers were crushed, he was a painter and he's done now. You know what, I don't even care the victims were gay. You do that shit to someone, anyone, again and again, you belong in jail. So guess what, we found some physical evidence. *I* found some physical evidence. Right in the suspect's house. Nice clean packet of it, even after we'd already searched the place. The guy went to jail and the beatings stopped. And you're gonna say I did something wrong? That it carries over into everything else I do? Screw you, Detective Timmons. I don't lose sleep at night. I guarantee if it was you, if you let him go and more guys got beat up, you'd be the one losing sleep over it. Don't give me any bull-shit. I made my bed and I'm lying in it."

Liz didn't flinch. "Seems like you think about lying in bed a lot."

"Okay," Vic said quickly. "Norbert, listen, we appreciate you telling us this. Means we have some more angles on Gretchen."

"For what good it does now." Norbert was still locked eye-to-eye with Liz.

Vic softened his tone. "We'll figure out what happened."

Norbert broke eye contact with Liz and turned his gaze to Vic. "You I believe." He drummed his fingers on the table top and then stood up. "Let me know when you need a statement." Without another word or glance at either of them he left the restaurant.

Liz picked up her empanada and took a bite, but Vic could tell that she didn't taste it.

"Kinda hard on him, weren't you?" Vic asked as she chewed. "He was pretty helpful."

She swallowed. "Give me one reason to believe anything he says."

"Well, let's see what we find in Gretchen's South Side house. And I gotta tell you, he ever makes a restaurant recommendation again I'm gonna believe him." He chewed for a few moments longer and swallowed, then stared at Liz.

"Seriously. What's up with you lately?"

"Leave it, Vic." She dropped her half eaten empanada on her tray, watching him, anger in her eyes. "Just leave it."

"Fine." He picked up what was left of his empanada and dribbled more sauce on the filling. He had absolutely no intention of leaving it alone. But Liz's phone rang before he could follow up.

Liz fished her phone out of her purse and left the table to talk. Vic finished his second empanada, wondering if he had room for another. Suddenly Liz was standing in front of him.

"I have to go," she said quickly, her voice tight but controlled.

"Thought we were going to the South Side, check out the house? You got that it fits with her phone's location data from right before the fire?"

"No shit. Hard to believe I got that, right? We can do that tomorrow. We need a warrant to get inside anyway. And I have to go. I called a Lyft." She spun on her heel and was through the door so quickly that Vic didn't have time to respond. Instead he sipped his water and watched the people passing on the sidewalk. She was right about the warrant, which annoyed him. As he chewed the last of his second empanada, an idea came to him.

CHAPTER 14

I nside his car, Vic did a quick web search on the family members who filed reports for each of the three missing women. One name was linked to Pittsburgh's university area, the second to someone in the McKees Rocks neighborhood, not far from their station house on the North Side. The third was well north of Pittsburgh in Portersville. Vic knew it would be easier to find time to visit the McKees Rocks and university areas of the city, so he wrote the Portersville address on a piece of paper and did a quick map search to find the address.

He followed Route 79, the interstate linking Charleston, West Virginia to Erie, Pennsylvania. The exit to Portersville was about forty minutes north of Pittsburgh, but when he reached the stop sign at the end of the exit ramp all he saw were tree-covered rolling hills. They stretched away into a haze that left the sky rinsed out. With each shift of the wind, wide swaths of trees turned up the pale undersides of their leaves as if they were surrendering. He frowned and followed the sign pointing toward Portersville.

A few miles later the town appeared, clinging to the edges of the two lane road. On one side was a low-roofed industrial building that stretched for a hundred yards and stopped at the gravel lot of a takeout pizza restaurant. Facing that long building was a row of small Victorian houses converted into an insurance office, a tanning salon and other businesses. The paint on the buildings was faded from years of sun, snow, rain and neglect. Like the few other vehicles on the road, Vic didn't slow down.

About half a mile outside town he spotted the road he needed, turned left and fifteen minutes later read the name Stutz in reflective letters on a mailbox. He turned onto a rutted, gravel driveway that led to a two story clapboard farmhouse. A barn sat to its left. A rusty swing set was to the right of the house, flanked by a homemade sandbox of rotting wood and a thick-trunked oak. He parked in the driveway's small pull-off area near the front door. He had considered calling ahead, but he knew it was always better to talk to people before they had time to prepare.

The woman who answered his knock was in her forties, her brown hair pulled back in a ponytail from a face with high cheekbones and a tall forehead. She wore baggy and stained sweats and held a pink-cheeked baby no older than two. She considered Vic with the look of someone wary of men, the crows feet at the corners of her eyes etched into her skin as if they were metalwork.

"Sorry to bother you ma'am. Are you Barbara Stutz? I'm from the Pittsburgh Police." He held up his ID. "I understand Barbara filed a missing person's report about 18 months ago?"

The woman placed her free hand on the screen door knob as if she was debating whether to slam it in his face. She searched the area behind him with sharp, green eyes.

"I'm Barb," she said finally, her voice catching, and focused on him again. Vic realized she was wondering if he brought bad news. Before he could say anything she hiked the toddler higher on her hip and said, "Nobody ever came out here before. You guys always call. Well, the one time anyone called."

"I realize that, but I'd like to ask a few more questions, if you don't mind. I thought it might be better to do it in person."

"Did you find her?"

"No ma'am. And we know that she's not working because she hasn't used her social security number."

"It doesn't make sense." A tear streaked unheeded over

her cheek. "Chrissie was a lot of things, but she loved Maya, her daughter." She glanced at the little girl on her hip. "I never thought she would just leave her behind. That she could take off without her." Something moved in Barb's eyes and she pushed open the screen door. "Come in."

Vic took the door from her and followed her into a living room. The floor was covered with a 1960s lime green shag carpet, most of which was hidden underneath a child's playpen, swing, and too many toys to count. The furniture predated World War I. Some kind of casserole was cooking in another room, and the smell competed with the tang of soiled diapers.

Barb swung her arm about the room. "See, she bought all this for Maya. Does a mother do that and then just leave?"

Vic replied gently that he doubted it, although he'd seen mothers guilt-buy their babies all sorts of things before they ran out on them. "How old is Maya?"

"Two." Barb let Maya slide down her leg onto unsteady legs. "We're going through potty training."

"The reason I'm here," he said carefully, "is because I checked your daughter's file recently. Then, as I said, we checked to see if Chrissie had popped up anywhere else. Started working somewhere. When that came back negative I thought we should look at things again."

Barb kept her eyes on Maya as she toddled over to a large fire truck and thumped down on her bottom. "I guess it's good you guys didn't lose the file." She turned her gaze to him. "It sure feels that way. I call you guys a couple of times a month and get the same answer. No new leads." She folded her arms, waiting.

"Well, maybe you could give me some background?" Vic nodded at a collection of five framed photographs hanging on the wall above the couch. "Is that Chrissie?"

She followed his eyes. "Yeah. The green dress is her junior prom. She got pregnant not long after that. Never finished school."

Vic nodded. Chrissie was stunning. A full head of red hair, high cheekbones and green eyes. The dress was cut low on her cleavage. On most young women the dress would have worn the girl. Chrissie pulled it off with a small, half-smirk smile as if she was the only one in on a joke. Vic guessed that three quarters of the guys in her class were scared to death of her.

"Out here," Barb said slowly, as if she could read Vic's thoughts, "the pretty girls go one of two ways. Get pregnant early or get married early. If they marry then they got to be lucky the guy is goin' someplace." She looked around at the house. "Otherwise you get stuck."

Vic felt an odd intimacy with Barb. It was something to do with the house and how she talked, as if she was being truthful all the time and expected the same from him. He liked her for it. He stared at a framed photo of a man in a military uniform. "You've lived here since high school?"

"No. My husband and I went to high school near here, but after we got married he joined the army, made it to Ranger. He was killed the first year we went into Afghanistan. Chrissie was a little older than Maya then. My Mom lived here, she was sick, so I came back to take care of her. No point staying in South Carolina on a military base. They would have kicked me out anyway. My mother died a few years ago. Now it's Maya and me."

Something hard and heavy pushed against Vic's stomach. He was stunned at how matter-of-fact Barb sounded. "Tell me about Chrissie," he said. "How she got to Pittsburgh."

"After Maya we needed money. She was always pretty and she kept the weight off while she had Maya. She's one of those girls who always looks young. When I was in South Carolina some of the soldier's wives were from Okinawa and Japan. I could never tell if those Asian girls were fifteen or forty. They all aged so well. Chrissie was like that. She told me she got a job waitressing in a restaurant in Pittsburgh. Long drive, but I could watch Maya at night for her. I answer phones and do record-keeping and payroll for a small company near here maybe three days a week, but it pays hardly anything and some weeks we don't cut checks. Just depends how much work there is. Anyway, I guessed what she was doing when I saw how much she was making in tips. She didn't seem to mind it. Apart from her boss they treated her okay, and a young girl like that wants a bit of excitement. So I didn't say anything."

Vic nodded. Anna stared at him, her eyes level. "Call me a bad mother. Go ahead."

Vic shook his head. "Not for me to say. But Maya is happy. The house is clean. There's dinner on the stove and you're holding it together. After some of the situations I've seen, I'd say you're doing a hell of a job."

Barb turned away and Vic couldn't tell if she was angry or disgusted with him. He waited a few seconds. "You said her boss treated her badly?"

"I didn't say that." She looked back at him. "Her boss was a pain, but I don't now what went on. Chrissie didn't want to do some of the stuff they were expected to do. The back room garbage. I understood that much. She said a lot of the guys were creepy. But this one boss used to give her a hard time about it."

"What was his name?"

"Who said anything about a guy? It was a woman. I don't remember her name."

"Okay. Tell me about when she went missing."

"Usually she drove to work, but this one day she got a ride with one of the other girls. She lives in Sharon and works two nights a week. I guess they like having different girls different nights, for the variety or something. Anyway, she went in and worked, but when the girl went to find her to come home, she was gone. So she just drove home. I guess she didn't think about it much, sometimes the girls go off with guys, although that was the first time Chrissie didn't come home. When I realized she wasn't here I texted her, but got no answer. I still don't." Barb stared at the photographs on the wall. "I call her every morning."

Vic let the silence gather for a few moments. "Could I have the name of the girl who drove her to work?"

Barb continued to stare at the wall for a moment before giving him the name.

"And that woman who gave her trouble at work. You don't remember her name?"

"I said I didn't." She looked at him. "What's your name again?"

"Vic Lenoski."

"Right. Vic. I appreciate you coming out here, but it's been more than a year now. I feel like you should have been here a couple of days after she went missing."

"Well, at the time we did investigate. The report says we sent a detective and she talked to Chrissie's boss, who said she'd seen Chrissie talking to a guy at the end of the night. She thought it was her boyfriend."

"Chrissie didn't have a boyfriend."

Vic let the statement hang. On the floor, Maya began making engine sounds. They both looked at her. She was on her hands and knees, pushing the fire truck about.

"So you want to know if this is connected to Maya's father, is that it?" Before he could answer she started talking again. "The guy who got her pregnant had no interest in the baby. He and Chrissie hadn't talked for more than six months before she disappeared."

"Maybe texted or something?"

"She would have said. Anyway, you're thinking they got back together and took off?"

Vic pressed the ball of his foot into the shag carpet. "I'm just working through the possibilities."

"Like I said. She wouldn't leave Maya. If he came back she woulda taken Maya with them."

"So where is he?"

"Last I heard up near New York State working for a fracking company. The guy can't handle responsibility but he was all-conference wide receiver twice. The girls always said he had good hands."

Vic heard the sarcasm. "His name?"

She gave it to him, and Vic slid a slim envelope from his pocket. Inside were the two sheets of paper that made up the entire police report on Chrissie's disappearance. Vic skimmed the second page. "So, Chrissie's boss, the one who said Chrissie was with her boyfriend, maybe the one Chrissie complained about, was her name Cora Stills?"

Barb's eyes narrowed for a split second as she shook her head. "I don't know. Like I said, I don't remember Chrissie mentioning her name. Maybe." She shrugged.

Vic folded the paper and slipped it back into his sport coat pocket. "Thanks, Mrs. Stutz. This gives me some things to work on."

She watched him for a moment, and then said slowly. "And I'll keep calling her number every morning. Because you never know, do you?"

Vic nodded. "You never know."

He hated himself for saying it.

CHAPTER 15

In his car Vic sat with one hand on top of the wheel. Barb had pulled the door closed as soon as he stepped outside. The house stood silent, the oak tree on the side shifting it's branches in the gusting wind, the leaves light green against the darkening grey sky. The seats of the swings swayed gently on rusty chains. He turned the key and listened to the engine idle. Around the house fields stretched away to a tree line almost a mile distant. From the size of the barn he guessed this was once a dairy farm, but the fields were now choked with weeds, the barn faded and drifting to rot. Everything seemed run out. Except Barb, he thought. Barely in her forties, getting up every day and raising her granddaughter. He wondered at that. How she lived in a creaking carnival of things missing, going or gone. The guts she needed to live every day among those overrun empty promises of fields, the rotting house, the yawning gap of her dead husband and missing daughter. He shifted the car into drive. What struck him was that Barb hadn't asked him for anything. She needed it the most, and yet she hadn't asked. She took care of the house, raised her granddaughter and worked where she could for money. Nothing ahead of her, except a granddaughter who one day would turn sixteen, seventeen and then eighteen and make her own choices, good or bad. The same way Barb and Chrissie had.

It took him fifteen miles to shake the mood, to shift his mind back to the case. What brought him back was the memory of the kid with the DUI. How he walked away free. It nagged at him, and he couldn't let it go even though he'd heard that kind of story before. He knew exactly how families with money made the law sing for them. He blinked it away, recognizing the next exit. Without thinking he cruised onto the ramp, then worked through suburban streets and stop signs until he reached Gretchen's burned house. Someone had shifted the crime scene tape to encircle the yard and property line, opening the street to traffic. He parked in front and stared. A notice that forbid access was taped to the front door. The hole in the roof above the second floor bedroom looked like the blackened entrance to a mine shaft. The roofline was etched against the grey metal-hammered sky.

For a moment he didn't do anything. Then he remembered Pokorny's statement about the back door being ajar and how that was different. He stepped from the car, glanced right and left and ducked under the tape.

Today the ground was firm, the dirt no longer saturated with water. He crossed to the driveway and mimicked the trip they had taken the day of the fire, around the side of the house to the back. The skin of water that once covered the back yard was gone. He crossed to the back door, staring at it. The screen door was closed now, as was the back door. Someone had placed a paper seal over the inside door explaining that he would be breaking several laws if he entered the house. He thought about it for a few moments, then pivoted on his heel and crossed to the edge of the brick patio. The far end of the yard was perhaps twenty yards away, defined by a narrow planting bed of shrubs above a blanket of mulch. Behind it was a small rise topped by young trees. Vic turned and studied the back door, then the far end of the yard. His mind turned. He studied the grass near the edge of the patio, stepped onto it and walked in a straight line from the back door to the rise at the end of the yard. Nothing. But during his first visit the grass was covered with water from the fire hoses. Anything there would have been washed away. He studied the planter bed.

And spotted it.

Them, actually, three footprints leading across the planting bed and onto the rise behind. He squatted down and stared at them. Everyone had assumed that the arsonists had arrived from the front and entered through the front door or garage, but it was the back door that was open. As if someone had come and gone from the back door, or at least left through the back door.

"Hey."

Vic rose and turned slowly. Pokorny stood fifteen feet away, his hand over his holstered service weapon. Vic gave him credit for being so quiet.

"Pokorny, right?" Vic asked. "Vic Lenoski from Pittsburgh. We met the day of the fire. I was driving by and thought I'd take a second look." Vic saw how the redness on Pokorny's face had faded and the whites of his eyes were clear. His uniform was spotless. "Seems you're doing better than the last time I saw you."

"I remember." Pokorny nodded slowly. "You and the fire chief sent me the EMT."

"That was mostly the fire chief, but I did say something to your boss about it."

Pokorny slid his hand from the butt of his gun and hooked a thumb over his belt buckle. "Neighbor called in that someone was skulking around the crime scene. Chief sent me over to check."

"Chief Dick?"

Pokorny tried to hide a smile but failed. "People call him a lot of things."

"I bet. And the caller said *skulking*. They used that word?"

"Oh yeah. Old lady a couple of houses down. I figure she's a book club person. So I decided I better be real quiet walking around the house. Because, you know. Skulking. Sounds dangerous."

"Smart move. But I have a question. I haven't seen your Chief's report yet."

"I sent mine to him the day after it happened."

"Does he know how to read?"

"He knows how to talk, I'll give him that."

Vic smiled, he couldn't help it. Pokorny was okay. "Yeah, so, look at this." He gestured him over and Pokorny gingerly crossed the distance between them. Vic pointed at the footprint. "Remember how you said the back door was ajar when you got here?"

"Sure. I put it in my report."

"That got me thinking if the person came from the back of the house or left by it. Not the front or through the garage. The back yard was covered with water after the fire and no one wanted to get their feet wet, so we didn't check back here."

Pokorny squatted and stared at the footprint, keeping his distance. After a moment he stood up. "Yeah, that makes sense. You told me to mention the back door in the report, which got me thinking. So I went back and checked all the canvassing reports. None of the neighbors saw a car parked out front or anyone go in or out from that direction. Even the lady who called when you showed up, although she did hear a car horn. She pays attention. She's called us three times since the fire."

"More skulkers?"

"More like the gas company, when they showed up to turn off the gas."

Vic pointed up the slope. "Where does that go?"

"I can show you."

"I tell you what, do you have a ruler or something in your car I can use for scale? I want to get a picture." He nodded at the footprints.

"I'll be right back." Pokorny turned and started for the front of the house. While he was gone, Vic walked carefully along the planter bed, searching for more footprints. Pokorny was back in a minute with a plastic zip-lock bag. Inside was a right angle expandable ruler for crime scene investigation. He opened the bag and handed the ruler to Vic.

Carefully, Vic laid it next to the clearest footprint and snapped several pictures using his phone. "Do you have a crime scene unit?" Vic asked, when he was finished.

"You're looking at it. So no, we don't."

"If you can tape this area I'll send one of our guys to get a cast made. We won't get much, it's too old, but it might help.

"Anywhere else? Are there footprints going toward the house?"

"No. But the water may have taken care of that. But tape the whole bed. May just be when they left they were moving faster and they were sloppy; they were more careful as they approached."

He nodded. "Follow me."

Pokorny led Vic on a circuitous root around the planter bed and up the slope. At the crest they overlooked a narrow strip of woods. On the other side of the woods the ground dropped in a short steep slope to an asphalt two-lane road. There was no center stripe on the road. Or traffic.

"What road?" Vic asked.

"Old Oak. To the right it leads into the next plan. To the left is Route 19."

"Think you could park a car anywhere along that road? Nearby?"

Pokorny pointed to the right. "See that corner? Just past there's a pull off for a pump station. Pipeline runs along there. I chase the high school kids out of there on Saturday nights."

"Let's take a car around and have a look." They returned to their cars and Pokorny offered to drive. Vic agreed, since he didn't know the way. A few minutes later, after they turned onto Old Oak, Pokorny pointed to a hillside.

"Back of the house is just over that rise. Pull off is on the other side of this corner."

Once they were around the corner he stopped on the road and flipped on the overheads to warn traffic he was blocking the road. Vic liked how Pokorny knew not to pull in next to the pumping station and possibly destroy the scene. They both got out of the car and walked the edge of the clearing, staring at the flat open ground.

"Somebody pulled in recently," Pokorny said after a moment. Vic could hear the excitement in his voice and guessed that he rarely got a chance to investigate.

"Yeah, drove past the entrance and then backed into place behind the pumping station."

"Not sure why'd you do that. I guess facing out so you can get away quickly?"

"One reason. The other is that your license plate is against the hill and can't be seen from the road."

Pokorny nodded, absorbing that point. Vic pulled out his cell phone and called their crime scene investigators. When he got through to the sergeant in charge he explained they needed casts made, both of foot prints and tire tracks. He gave the house address and explained someone would show them where the tire tracks were located. As he talked he glanced at Pokorny, who nodded. He then helped Pokorny put up crime scene tape blocking access to the pump station parking lot. "Tire tracks could be high schoolers," Pokorny said, stashing the tape in the trunk of his cruiser.

"Maybe," Vic said. "But I like the logic of this. They parked here and used it to get away. That way no one sees the car out front or spots them running from the fire. No skulking."

"Weird not to find footprints going toward the house."

"I have a theory about that," Vic said slowly, feeling the pieces line up in his mind. A car swung around the corner too fast and the hood ducked as the driver hit his brakes to avoid hitting Pokorny's cruiser. Pokorny folded his arms over this chest and started at the driver, who pretended not to see him. Pokorny finally glanced in the other direction, stepped into the road and waved the car around the cruiser.

"What's that?" he asked, when the car had disappeared down the road.

"We know the victim left her house and came back just before the fire. We know roughly where she went, or at least where her phone went. Suppose she brought someone back with her? She could pull into the garage and close the door before they both got out. So none of the neighbors would see a car out front or anything unusual. After setting the fire, the person she brought home cuts through the back yard to this vehicle and takes off."

"That makes sense. And if she already had a vehicle parked here, you got intent."

"She?" Vic stared at him, waiting.

"Size of the footprint," Pokorny said. "I doubt it belongs to a kid."

"Good spot," Vic said, although he had come to the same conclusion the moment he saw it.

CHAPTER 16

Back in the cruiser, Pokorny drove Vic down Old Oak Street to the traffic lights at the intersection with Route 19. As they waited for the traffic light to turn, Vic scanned the large convenience store and gas station across the street, his eyes stopping at the corner of the building next to the roof line. A CCTV camera was pointed directly at them. He turned to Pokorny.

"You said you gave your report to your chief the day after the fire?"

"Yeah."

"And you said not much traffic coming out of this road. We only saw one car the entire time we were down there."

"Well, and middle of the day is especially slow." The light turned green and he accelerated. "There's a cluster of five houses at the end of the road. They were thinking of extending the plan and maybe connecting to Reis Run Road on the other side, but I think the developer ran out of money."

"So not even a shortcut. Just access to those five houses."

"Right." They drove in a comfortable silence, the radio in Pokorny's cruiser squawking sometimes.

When he pulled in front of Gretchen's house Vic made no move to get out. "You don't mind waiting for the crime scene guys? Could be a couple of hours."

Pokorny thought about it for a moment. "I can wait, but can you give them my cell number? That way if I get called away

I can either come back when they get here or send someone."

They exchanged phone numbers and Vic texted the crime scene sergeant with Pokorny's number. He slid his phone into his pocket.

"One other thing."

Pokorny waited, although Vic guessed that he had an idea what the next question might be.

"Any way I could get a look at your report on the fire? I need to keep things moving and right now everything's too slow. Between us, I'm just saying."

Pokorny drummed his fingers on the steering wheel for a moment, then pointed at a soft-sided briefcase near Vic's feet. "Give me that?"

Vic handed it over and Pokorny dug inside for a moment and then handed him three sheets of computer printout. "I've been keeping hard copy of all my reports," he said quietly. "I can print another one for myself."

Vic took it. "You keep hard copy of all your reports?"

He shrugged. "Reports are kept on a general server. Everyone has access to everyone else's reports. Means anyone can make changes to other officer's reports. I just like to keep track."

Vic stared at him, surprised at what Pokorny was suggesting, and what it meant if someone was changing reports. "What did you do before this job?"

"Army for five years. Military Police."

"That's a unit that likes strict procedures."

"The procedures are there for a reason. They protect the integrity of investigations."

"Bit of a shock coming here, then?"

Pokorny turned his head and stared through the side window, his thumb tapping a slow beat on the steering wheel. "I've been here seven months. It was different when I first started here, yeah. But it wasn't until maybe a month ago I started keeping copies of my reports." He looked at Vic. "No particular reason." The gaze from his brown eyes was steady but a furrow creased his forehead.

Vic held his eyes. "If you feel you need to keep copies, you should. Trust your instincts."

"And that's where I am," he said. "Like I said. No specific reason."

Vic stuck out his hand and they shook. Pokorny's palm was warm. He was nervous, Vic realized, but he hid it well. He opened the door and climbed out, the report in his hand. Before he closed the door he leaned down, looked inside and held out his business card. "That's my number, if you ever feel the need to call. Okay?"

Pokorny took the card and nodded.

"And thanks for sticking around for the crime scene guys. Hopefully it won't take too long." He closed the door, started his car and placed Pokorny's report on the passenger seat. At the end of the road he turned right and worked his way to Route 19. Less than two minutes later he was inside the convenience store at the intersection with Old Oak Road.

It took half an hour for the manager to download footage from their security cameras for the five hour period around the fire. With the CD of the footage sitting in a properly annotated evidence bag on top of Pokorny's report he drove back to the north side. As he did he wondered about Pokorny printing out hard copies of his reports. He'd been clear that he had no special reason to do so, but Vic guessed that wasn't strictly true. Most likely Pokorny had seen changes made to his reports, and he wanted to know why and see if he could spot a pattern in the way his reports were changed. That put him in a tough position, but he liked the way Pokorny was handling it.

It was almost seven o'clock when Vic reached his desk. The room was quiet, with the exception of a detective playing music on his computer a couple of rows over. Vic caught up on his emails, noting that Chief Dick still hadn't sent in his final report. However the Fire Chief had forwarded the fire inspector's report. Vic opened it and skimmed the contents. As the Fire Chief had guessed, the inspector identified the fire as arson with two origin points, the bedroom and the top of the stairs. He also specified the likely accelerants, but paint thinner and gasoline were available anywhere. Vic closed the file, planning to reread it in the morning. It was almost eight o'clock when he slid Pokorny's report into a drawer. He then picked up the video surveillance CD, wrote a note for Craig and headed downstairs.

As he approached the door to the Tech department he heard two voices laughing and talking. He stepped inside.

Craig's workbench was diagonal to the doorway, halfway down the long room. He was bent over someone's laptop. Beside him, Crush's new secretary, Eva, peered at the laptop screen. They were both hunched on the high stools needed for the workbenches.

"Excuse me?" Vic called.

They both jerked around as if someone had set off a firecracker. At the same moment Craig hit a switch and the music gagged into silence.

"Sorry," Vic said. He nodded to Eva and remembered Liz's comment about how frequently Craig was visiting their floor. She slid off her stool, looking guilty.

"Didn't mean for you guys to stop the music." He held up the CD in it's evidence bag. "Craig, can I get your help on something?"

"Sure." Craig hopped off his stool, his chinos and shirt still in need of ironing and his flighty hair pointing in every compass direction. He wore square glasses, something Vic hadn't seen before.

"Little tricky," Vic said. "We don't actually have a case file in the system yet, although we probably will tomorrow. This is something out of our jurisdiction but the DA asked us to help. Anyway, I've got surveillance footage of an intersection. Can you go through it and track any vehicles leaving Old Oak Road between two-thirty and three-thirty on the time stamp? If you spot one, then check for the same vehicle turning into that road earlier in the day. You got it?"

"Yeah, no problem, Mr. Lenoski. Vic."

Eva shifted on her feet. Vic was close enough to catch just

the slightest whiff of alcohol from her. He looked at her and grinned. "You came back tonight to see this guy? Seriously?"

She rolled her eyes. "He's always working. He never comes out with us." She fell into a sharp silence, as if she realized she had given away too much.

Vic turned his grin on Craig. "No hurry on that, Craig. Like I said, we don't have a case file yet. No need to check it tonight," he added, hoping Craig would get the point.

"Oh, Detective Lenoski," Eva said. "Crush, I mean Commander Davis, was asking for you earlier." Her voice quickly grew more serious and Vic guessed she was trying to sound professional. "He told me to find you. I think he wants to talk to you."

"I didn't see an e-mail."

"No, he's got this new priority thing I have to follow." She started to roll her eyes but caught herself. "Red, yellow green. Red means I have to track you down right away, wherever you are, yellow means send an e-mail and arrange a time, green means he wants an informal discussion, catch you when I can." Vic heard the parrot tone in her voice, as if she was repeating something Crush had forced her to memorize.

"Thanks for telling me. I'll catch him in the morning." He nodded at the CD in Craig's hand. "You good on that?"

"Yes, sir."

"Okay, see you guys." Vic turned for the door but stopped as soon as he was through the door and listened. Inside Craig and Eva were giggling.

Vic smiled and started down the hall. Behind him the music thumped alive again.

CHAPTER 17

Vic was at his desk the next morning by seven. Something had happened overnight and several detectives were working, calling across the room and shouting insults at one another in the jagged way of people short on sleep. In a lull at about 7:30 Vic left his desk and checked Crush's office. Eva was already at her desk and smiled at him. Her hair was pulled back, her face pale. Vic thought her lipstick was a bit too red, as if she was compensating for something. He guessed a hangover. He jerked his thumb at the door and mouthed the question "Is he in?"

Eva hopped up and stuck her head in the door of Crush's office. Vic couldn't make out the exchange but a few seconds later Eva stepped away for the door and motioned him to go in.

"Thanks," he said as he passed her.

Crush was sitting behind his desk, his backbone as straight as a plumb line, his hands resting on his desk in front of him, fingers interlocked. The dark lines under his eyes looked like someone had placed them there with a branding iron. He gestured toward one of the two chairs facing his desk.

As he sat Vic asked, "Eva said you wanted to talk to me. You need an update on Gretchen's murder?"

Crush blinked as if Vic had suggested a new idea. "Sure." It almost came out as a question.

From Crush's reaction Vic knew he wanted to talk about something else, but he launched into an update, talking about the discrepancy in the location data in Gretchen's phone and how they'd connected it to a house on the South Side, thanks to their lunch with Dave Norbert. At the sound of Norbert's name Crush's forehead wrinkled like a turtle's neck. He then explained the footprints in Gretchen's back yard, the arrival of the fire inspector's report and how Chief Dick's report was still missing. He left out his conversation with Pokorny about the reports. He didn't know what to make of it yet.

"Good leads," Crush said, turning to the window. "Norbert," he said to the glass, and fell silent.

Vic waited, then said, "not sure what happened last night, but it's got the guys going."

Crush blinked again, disconnected his hands and waved one in dismissal. "Shooting in the Hill. Some kids playing gangster. Coupl'a teenagers wounded. Resource drain. Waste of everyone's time."

Vic wondered if it was a waste of time for the people wounded, but said, "Okay." He couldn't figure out why Crush had asked to see him. Even when Crush suspended him a few months earlier he'd been more direct and sure of himself. Vic let him stew.

Crush seemed to read his thoughts and turned his gaze onto him. "Was Liz with you yesterday when you found the footprints?"

Vic tightened. "No. I just decided to double check the scene after our lunch with Norbert."

"Why wasn't she there?" He grabbed a red rubber ball from his desk and began squeezing it rhythmically, his intensity back.

"At the end of lunch I think she said she was going to get a warrant going so we could get inside the house on the South Side today."

"She didn't say she was leaving early?"

"I didn't know she did." Vic was tight. He watched Crush try to flatten the red ball. "What's this all about?"

"She's been leaving a lot lately. Going out unexpectedly,

coming in late. Is she in this morning yet?"

Vic didn't like the feeling that he was in the principle's office. "No. But she doesn't normally come in until 8:30. She takes her son to school."

"I'm asking you, as her partner, to monitor her movements better. I need everyone on the team at work and putting in a full week."

"Look, you know she works hard. The hours we put in, if someone needs to take off unexpectedly, I'm not arguing with it."

Crush threw the red ball in the air and caught it one-handed. "You get to the bottom of it, get it to stop. You understand?"

Vic shrugged. "I'll ask her about it."

Crush was silent for a moment. "Are we gonna have a problem, you and I? Again?"

Vic stood up. "Only if you make it a problem. I said I'd ask her."

Crush stood, his shirt rippling and straining over his muscles. "You ask her and you get back to me. That's an order. You got me? This crap needs to stop. And we need to move faster on Gretchen's case."

He struggled to keep his voice normal. "I said I'll ask her." He turned and left the room. On his way out Eva gave him a guarded smile.

At his desk he checked the time. Liz was late, there was no question of it. He glanced down the aisle and saw a foot sticking out from Kevin's cube. Cold anger went through him like a sheet of rain. Only one person was always at their desk with a line of sight on Liz's movements: Kevin. He was the only explanation for Crush knowing that Liz was sometimes late to work or didn't return with him from the field. Annoyed, he walked to the small kitchen and poured himself a large coffee. Back at his desk, he found among his unopened e-mails a message from Richard Landry, the North Hills Police Chief. He opened the attached file, sipped his stale coffee and started to read.

He read the file twice, start to finish. Then, just to be sure, he pulled out the report that Pokorny had given him the day before and reread that as well. Finished, he sat back and stared at the ceiling then glanced at Liz's cube. It was empty, 8:55 a.m. by his computer clock.

"Any luck with those cold cases?"

Vic started. Kevin stood beside his cube and Vic realized that he must have come up behind him while he was thinking. "Uh, no," he said quickly. "You said there was no activity on their social security numbers, so that's it. Done."

As he talked, Vic saw Kevin do a quick scan of his computer screen and Chief Dick's report. "Well, if you have more let me know. Glad to help." He pointed at Liz's cube. "I guess traffic must be bad this morning."

"I talked to her this morning," Vic said quickly. "She's checking something on one of our cases before she comes in."

"Oh," Kevin said carefully.

"If anything comes up I'll let you know." Vic heard how harsh he sounded, but he didn't care.

Kevin hesitated as if he wanted to say something more but thought better of it and turned back down the aisle. "Sure," he called over his shoulder, as he headed to his cube.

Vic stared at his computer screen and Landry's report. He hit the print button and texted Liz from his phone, asking where she was. He collected Landry's report from the shared printer, placed it next to Pokorny's report on his desk and highlighted specific passages in both reports.

It was 9:15 when Liz arrived. She swung her shoulder bag into a corner of her cube with a thump and hung up her leather jacket, her movements quick and angry.

"Hey," Vic called across the aisle.

Liz glanced at him, her eyebrows furrowed.

"Got Landry's report. I'll forward it to you. We should get a cup of coffee." He held up his cup from the kitchen. "This tastes like crap."

"I gotta check my e-mails."

"When you're done. Made some progress last night."

"Good for you."

"You doing okay?"

Liz, already in the middle of signing onto her computer, stopped and dropped her hands from the keyboard. "What are you asking?" Her shoulders were tight, her face strained.

"Nothing that can't wait for coffee."

Liz turned to her computer but made no move to finish signing in. The line of her shoulders eased "Let me finish this," she said gently. "Just give me thirty minutes."

"Sure." Vic glanced down the aisle toward Kevin's cube. His foot was sticking out into the aisle, but this time the weight was on his toes, as if he was leaning over his desk, the better to hear their conversation.

CHAPTER 18

Half an hour stretched to two hours as they answered e-mails and sat through an emergency meeting called by Crush to review the night's shooting. His latest administrative program was nicknamed UPSTEC, for Update, STaff, Equip and Coordinate. To Vic it felt like more meetings and less time in the field, although he liked the idea of keeping all of the detectives aware of everyone's cases. It was almost noon before he and Liz settled into chairs at a sandwich shop near their offices.

"Did you read the report we got from Chief Dick, that North Hills Police Chief?" Vic asked, unwrapping his sandwich.

Liz finished uncapping the lid to her salad. "Yeah. I don't get it. He makes it sound like you can't tell what happened. Might be murder, might not."

"Right. Total bullshit. And he skated over Pokorny's report. He's whitewashing what happened."

"Yeah, but he's right." Liz speared some greens. "We don't have proof for a lot of it."

Vic swallowed a mouthful of sandwich. "So you know, I found footprints in the backyard leading over the hill to another road behind Gretchen's house. There I found tire tracks from a parked car. Probably a pick-up. He doesn't mention that because I found it last night, but his report shows up first thing this morning. Like he heard what I found and wants to get this case closed before any more information shows up."

"We can add the footprints to the report for Marioni."

"Right, but we have to send the report to Chief Dick before it goes to Marioni. We agreed to that."

Liz stared at him in anger until she got the joke and her eyes cleared. "Right. Like you're actually going to do that."

"In his mind we are."

"Is he that stupid?"

"Maybe. I have a copy of Pokorny's report. It's pretty clean and he is clear that the back door was ajar and that he heard screaming when he was inside. Chief Dick's report just says Pokorny gained entrance and suspected there was a person on the second floor. Leaves out the key details."

Liz stopped eating and watched him for a moment. "How did you get Pokorny's report?"

"I ran into him at the scene last night. And it turns out he prints hard copy of his reports and keeps them with him. He said they have a common server for reports and anyone can access them. As in someone might change them."

Liz forked some salad into her mouth and chewed slowly. "He thinks people are changing his reports?"

"He wouldn't say that out loud, but he thinks it."

Liz stirred her salad. "That makes you think. And that kid got off on his DUI through Chief Dick. But what's all that got to do with Gretchen's murder? Chief Dick doesn't say it was an accident or a murder."

"Right. Feels like he's trying to palm it off. Slide it by."

"So?"

Vic knew what she meant. "We wait for the forensics on the footprint. I saw you got the warrant to get inside Gretchen's secret South Side house. We'll take a look then send the crime scene guys through. Maybe we get lucky. As far as I can see Gretchen went out to her secret house, her phone records say that, came back with someone and parked in her garage. From the footprint, probably a woman. Somehow the woman got Gretchen upstairs and either drugged or tied on the bed, started the fire and then went out the back. She had a pick-up waiting for her."

Liz swallowed. "Too complicated. She'd need an accomplice. And we got premeditation out the wazoo. But what's the motivation? Why would someone go to all that trouble to kill her?"

Vic sat back. "Yeah, I'm lost on that as well."

They both ate in silence before Liz added, "And the Fire Inspector's report said two fire origins. Bedroom and top of the steps."

"Right. Even more complicated. Almost guarantees an accomplice."

"But you only found one set of footprints."

"Yeah. But that doesn't mean there wasn't one. Pot luck we found even one set after the way the yard was filled with water." Vic crushed his paper sub wrapper and stuck it in the plastic bag. He watched Liz picking at her salad.

She stopped after a moment. "Okay, what's really bugging you?"

"Finish your lunch."

Liz watched him, her eyes calculating. She put down her fork and carefully snapped the lid back on the plastic container. "What?"

"Crush called me in this morning. He wants to know why you keep disappearing and coming in late."

"Am I getting my job done?"

"Yes. This is Crush asking, not me." Vic felt his sandwich ball in his stomach. He hated these conversations. "You know how he feels about administrative crap."

Liz watched him and said nothing for a long few moments. "How would he even know my schedule?"

Vic nodded. "Yeah, I thought that as well. The only way is Kevin. He's always at his desk, he knows when you come in and leave."

Liz's eyes said that she had warned him about Kevin.

"I know," Vic said. "I was wrong about him."

"He isn't even a detective. What the hell is his grade? He

even sits in the UPSTEC meeting. I don't get that whole thing. Except that he's getting what white guys always get."

He ignored her last comment. "Here's the deal, Liz. Crush has asked, I need to give him an answer. Something. You tell me what to say, then we're past it."

Liz slid the plastic box with the remainder of her salad into a bag. "We need to get back."

"Liz, I need to go back with something. Anything. And so we're clear, I'd noticed it as well. There's something going on with you."

She stood and leaned over him. "You listen to me. I covered for you all last year. You know how many times you came in late stinking of booze? How many times you missed shit at the scene? You think Crush didn't ask me what was going on with you? Did I say anything to you? No. I trusted you. You want something for King Crush? Okay, I'm warned. But it's not an issue. Now we need to get back. I got shit to do. So do you." She walked outside.

Vic stood slowly, tossed the bag in the garbage can and followed her. As he slid into the car it occurred to him that Liz had mentioned covering for him, almost as if she was suggesting she needed the favor. As he turned the key he knew he would do exactly that. She didn't have to ask.

They drove in silence, Liz staring through the side window. Halfway back Liz's cell phone rang and she answered it, still looking through the window. After a moment she lowered her phone and said "Mendeloski, that North Hills fire chief." She put her phone on speaker.

"You guys there?" Mendeloski half shouted.

"Sure, Vic Lenoski here." He guessed Liz was not in a talking mood. "We're here. What's up, chief?"

"You got the fire report I sent, right? Two points of origin, accelerants used, all that?"

"Yeah, we got it, chief," Vic said.

"You read that garbage Chief Dick sent over this morning?"

Vic couldn't help but smile. "Yeah, we did."

"He left something out, I just want you guys to know about it, I mean actually left something out, instead of just saying what happened isn't a fact and doesn't matter. Like he did with everything else."

Vic stopped at a traffic light. "Yeah, we saw he'd greased the pig enough to stop anyone getting hold of it."

"Good way to look at it. But this pissed me off. He just left it out. I called him specifically about it."

Liz tilted her head so her ear was aligned with the phone. "What have you got?"

"Remember we had to use some guys to dig the body out for the ME? Meant we had to move a lot of debris. You're doing that and you have to bang on things, then crap slides onto you, stinks like shit, whole thing sucks."

"Isn't that why you guys wear helmets?"

"Wow, Pittsburgh cops, not much gets by you guys. Yeah, so we're banging away, we got this shower of shit coming down on us, and one of my guys almost gets his eye ripped out by some chunk of metal, about twice the size of a shoe box. Mini safe kind of thing. So anyway, we open it up, and mostly everything inside is burned, but we got enough left to know what it is. You guys ready? Cash. Hundred dollar bills. Mostly burned to bits and pieces. But there was a lot there. Enough to buy a car, maybe."

Liz craned her head. "Where was it before it fell," she asked quickly, before Vic could.

"I'd need a ladder to be sure, but I think it was in the floor between the joists. It was with a bunch of shit from the walk-in closet, so I bet they had a hiding place in the floor there."

"And Chief Dick left it out of his report." Liz said the sentence as a statement.

"Yeah. I've responded to a lot of fires. That was a first."

"Who has the box now?" Vic asked.

"Chief Dick sent his buddy over to collect it from us. You know, that tall skinny guy was at the back door when we went in, day of?"

"I remember," Vic said, picturing the man. "Yeah, that should go in his report. Anything else?"

"Wow, you guys want me to investigate the whole murder for you?"

"No need, chief, we got this, thanks."

"You guys take it easy. Good luck with it."

Liz disconnected the call. "Chief Dick," she said quietly.

"Yep. And we need to talk to the husband one more time. Have another conversation about his wife Gretchen. The saint." Vic turned onto the South Side street where Gretchen's second house was located.

"Can't wait," Liz said, to no one in particular.

"And I'm starting to think we need to talk to that kid who got off on the DUI. Maybe the whole family."

"Long shot," Liz said.

Vic glanced at her. "You win more money on the long shots."

CHAPTER 19

Gretchen Stoll's South Side house was on a long street at the foot of the South Side slopes, one in a row of old Pittsburgh mill houses that shared brick walls, peaked roofs and front doors three steps above street level as a prevention against Monongahela River floodwaters. On this particular street the traditional metal awnings over the front doors were gone, replaced by custom transom windows and colorful paint and trim. Vic stared at the three floors of the house. The brick pointing was flawless and covered with a fresh coat of paint the color of creamed coffee.

"I need a secret house," Vic said to Liz. "Especially one that smells of this much money. Maybe everyone should have one."

"It ain't the house, it's the secrets got you breathing hard."

Vic smiled. "Now that's the truth." He glanced at Liz, glad she was making jokes. He hoped she was past their lunch conversation, but understood his point. She was scanning the street, he guessed for the officer who was supposed to help them enter the house.

"Wonder if anyone's got a camera covering the street," he mused.

"Since when did we ever have any luck with something like that?"

"I guess not." He wanted to keep Liz talking but nothing came to mind. Fortunately a police cruiser pulled up next to them. "Detective Timmons?" called the driver from inside the cruiser.

"Right here." Liz pointed at the house. "That one."

He nodded and pulled farther down the street to a parking space. Vic and Liz crossed to the house and rang the bell. They both waited in silence. No one answered the door and they stood aside when the officer reached them. He wordlessly placed a small toolbox on the ground, bent over and examined the lock. He straightened up and almost as an afterthought tried the door knob.

The door swung open.

"Shit," Liz said, hopping off the steps to the sidewalk. The uniform retreated down a step, struggling to pull his weapon. Vic slid to his left so he wasn't directly in front of the door, peering into the entrance hall.

"Inside the house," he shouted. "Pittsburgh Police. Respond if anyone's there."

The uniform leveled his weapon, pointing it inside the house. Liz was to the right of the door, her back pressed against the house with her Glock in her hands.

"I got point," Vic said, pulling his Glock. The patrolman shifted to his left and Vic climbed the steps and angled through the door, stopping with his back to the wall on the left of the door. The hallway stretched ahead of him to an archway at the back of the house. Through that he spotted a kitchen counter. To his left a second archway led into a living room. To his right stairs rose to the second floor. A shuffling sound came from the doorway and he knew that Liz was near his shoulder. He called again, identifying himself.

Silence.

He pointed Liz into the living room and started down the hall, guessing that a second doorway led from the living room to the kitchen. A few moments later they met in a recently remodeled kitchen, the stainless appliances oddly flat in the filtered light of the mini blinds.

Vic glanced at her. "You told the uniform to cover the

door?"

"Course I did," Liz said. "Upstairs?"

"Yeah. Then we glove up, get a unit in here and sweep the place."

"With you."

Halfway up the stairs Vic thought he heard a shuffling sound above him and to the left. The first bedroom at the back of the house was completely empty except for carpeting. The second room, facing the street, was the master bedroom, and contained a king-sized bed, a chest of drawers and an armchair. The sheets on the bed were rumpled as if someone had hurriedly pulled the quilt over the mussed sheets. Through an open door Vic spotted a bathroom. From behind a second door he heard what sounded like a muffled sob. He motioned to Liz, but she was already moving to the closed door, her Glock held out in front of her. She flattened her back to the wall next to the door.

"You behind the door, open the door slowly and show us your hands!"

Silence, followed a moment later by a hoarse breath.

"Pittsburgh Police!" shouted Vic. "Open the door slowly and show us your hands!"

"Okay! I'm coming out! Don't shoot!"

Liz shifted her body so her shoulder was to the wall, her Glock pointed at the spot where the door would crack open, so she would have a sight line to fire as soon as the door opened even a inch.

"I'm turning the knob," came the muffled shout from behind the door. Vic frowned at the voice. He recognized it but couldn't place it.

The doorknob turned and a moment later the door gently swung open a foot.

"Show us your hands," shouted Vic. His heart pounded.

Two pale hands with long fingers protruded through the open door. In a quick movement Liz holstered her Glock, grabbed the wrists, pulled hard and let go.

A thin man lurched through the door and to his knees on

the carpet.

"Don't move!" Shouted Vic, staring at Mark Stoll.

Stoll tried so hard not to move that he shook. His stared at the floor, his scalp gleaming through his thin hair.

"Jesus," Liz breathed. With a quick movement she unholstered and pushed the barrel of her Glock around the doorframe and into the closet. "Clear," she called.

Vic stared at Stoll, then holstered his Glock.

"Mr. Stoll," he said slowly. "I'd appreciate it if you could stay on your knees for now. I guess the question is why the hell you didn't respond when we announced ourselves at the front door?"

Stoll nodded his head as if he was completely in agreement. "I don't know. I was scared. I just hid. I thought you would go away."

Liz came up behind him, a frown on her face. "Did you know about this house when we talked to you a couple of days ago?"

"No!"

Vic and Liz locked eyes for a second.

"Okay, Mr. Stoll," Vic said. "We're gonna need to talk about this. So we'll take this one step at a time. Stand up. Slowly. Then stay still."

Stoll rose slowly, his knees cracking. Upright he swayed slightly, his pale face drawn. Vic stepped to one side and pointed at the bed. "Have a seat."

Stoll shuffled to the bed and sat down.

"Let the uniform know," Vic said to Liz. While she was gone Vic and Stoll stared at one another. In the distance Vic heard an exchange of voices and a few seconds later Liz walked back into the room.

"Okay, Mr. Stoll," Vic said slowly. "Let's try it again. You said you were unaware of this house when we talked to you two days ago. How did you learn about it?"

"I was going through my wife's estate papers from her lawyer. It was listed there."

"And how did you get a key?" Liz asked.

Stoll reddened. "I was shocked the house existed. So I came down to find it. The front door was open."

"You mean unlocked?" Liz asked.

"Yes. So I came inside. That was why I hid from you. I didn't understand what was going on and I was worried you'd think I broke in."

Vic didn't need to look at Liz to confirm the story was ridiculous. "Could you empty your pockets. Mr. Stoll."

"Why?"

"I'm interested in what you're carrying."

Stoll hesitated, then slowly placed the items from his pockets on the bedspread. Vic hooked the keychain off the bedspread and handed it to Liz. Without being asked she took it downstairs.

"I need those back," Stoll called after her. "My car key is on that."

"You'll have them back in a moment. By the way, I didn't see your BMW outside. Where is it?"

"It's a block over. I couldn't find parking on this block." His eyes darted about the room. Vic thought about how easily the patrolman had found a parking space just a few houses down the street.

Liz returned and dropped the keys on the bedspread. She shook her head, and Vic knew that none of the keys worked on the front door. Their eyes met and Liz frowned and pursed her lips. He knew what she meant. While it was suspicious Stoll was in the house, there was actually little to hold him on until they checked with the lawyer who Stoll claimed had provided the address. More to the point, they had no leverage to prove that Stoll was lying to them. Vic hesitated then turned to Stoll.

"Mr. Stoll, what rooms have you visited in this house?"

"All of them, I walked around. I wanted to find out what was going on with this place."

Vic cursed his luck, or Stoll's cleverness. When Stoll said that he had visited all the rooms in the house, finding his prints or DNA in any of the rooms wouldn't change his story about this being his first visit. "I tell you what, Mr. Stoll. We're going to need a formal interview with you about this, but for now you can go. This may well be your house, at this point. I don't see how we can hold you."

"Do I need a lawyer?" His eyes jumped from Vic to Liz and back.

"That's up to you. We'll call you when we're ready to do an interview."

Stoll nodded, and after a few moments stood up, gathered the items from the bedspread and replaced them in his pockets. Vic called downstairs to the uniformed officer and heard him start up the stairs.

"You can go now, Mr. Stoll," Vic said quickly. "The officer will escort you out."

"If you find anything I want to know what it is."

"It'll be documented, Mr. Stoll. If it's important, we'll let you know." Vic nodded to the officer, who placed a hand on Stoll's elbow and guided him toward the doorway.

As the two men tromped down the stairs Liz turned to Vic. "You just never know what you're going to find, do you."

Vic nodded at the closet. "I'd like to find a front door key." They both stepped into the walk-in closet, which Vic guessed was about the size of his kitchen, but apart from a few blouses on hangars and a woman's work suit, it was completely empty.

As they waited for the uniform to return Liz disappeared through the door to check the other rooms on the floor. Vic entered the en-suite bathroom and checked the medicine cabinet and undersink cupboard. They were mostly empty, although he found several prescription drug containers in the medicine cabinet, all of them Gretchen's prescriptions. One was an antibiotic but the prescription date was from a year earlier. The other two were recent. He recognized Lorazapam, which he knew was for anxiety, but the other drug, BuSpar, he was unfamiliar with. He took pictures of all the prescription labels and returned them to the cabinet. When he stepped out of the bathroom Liz and the uniform were waiting for him.

"Anything?" Vic asked.

They both shook their heads.

"Apart from this room, ain't five pieces of furniture in this place."

"Didn't search the kitchen," the uniform said, so they followed him downstairs and along the hallway.

In the kitchen they all stopped and stared at the granite countertops.

"Custom cabinets and high end appliances," Vic said, more to himself.

"Just like my kitchen," the cop said sarcastically.

Liz's phone rang and she disappeared down the hall toward the front door. A few moments later she spoke sharply and then fell into a muffled monologue. Vic couldn't make out the words and guessed she didn't want to be overheard. He and the uniform exchanged glances and waited until Liz appeared in the archway to the kitchen.

"I gotta go."

"Not sure we're done," Vic said carefully, watching her, waiting for more of an explanation.

"I called a car. I'll see you tomorrow."

Vic tilted his head, watching her.

"Don't screw with me," she said quickly. "I gotta go, right now." Before he could say anything she turned and disappeared down the hall. The door slammed behind her. Vic stared at the empty space where she had stood a moment before.

"Okay," he said to no one at all. Then he turned to the uniform. "Can you wait for the forensics unit?"

"Sure."

Vic pulled open the refrigerator. Inside were several bottles of white wine, a six pack of craft beer and some half-filled take-out containers. He pulled open the freezer door and found two bottles of vodka, a full ice drawer and absolutely nothing else. The freezer air chilled his face.

"Okay," he said again, and shut the door. He looked at the

uniform. "I gotta go too."

"All overtime to me." The cop grinned. "You count those beers?"

Vic shrugged. "What beers?"

He walked down the hall to the front door, opened it and peered out. Liz was standing at the corner of the block, waiting for her ride. Vic watched her until she turned her back to him and searched the crossroad. He jogged to his car and slid inside. He adjusted the side mirrors so he could see her, turned the engine over and waited.

CHAPTER 20

I t was another five minutes before a grey Ford minivan with a small purple light on the dashboard stopped next to Liz. She bent over and said something to the driver, then slid inside. Vic cut the wheels, checked the road, pulled out into a sharp three point turn. When he reached the intersection he spotted the Ford a block away, moving toward Carson Street and its cluster of bars and restaurants. He felt dirty and didn't like what he was doing. He clenched his jaw tight and forced himself to follow the minivan.

When the Ford turned onto Carson Street Vic worked his way closer so he didn't get caught at a traffic light, but kept a few cars between himself and the Ford. He followed them over the Smithfield Street Bridge and onto the Fort Duquesne Bridge, headed to the North Side. For a few moments Vic wondered if Liz was returning to their offices, but that didn't make sense. Sure enough the Ford exited onto Route 65. Vic let the space between them open up, watching, until the Ford took the exit that dropped down by the U.S. Mail sorting facility. Vic wondered if she was headed home. He tightened up on the Ford as it worked through a series of back streets into the Manchester neighborhood, and a minute or two later pulled up in front of the Manchester Charter School. Vic knew instantly why she was there. Liz was out of the car quickly, strode up to the front door and disappeared inside. Vic pulled over half a block away, the minivan waiting at the curb.

It was about five minutes before the school's front door opened and Liz came out, followed by a shambling boy almost the same height as Liz. Vic tried to make sense of it, until his breath caught. It was her son, Jayvon. Vic tried to put it in perspective. He hadn't seen Jayvon in two years, if not longer. It was well before Dannie went missing. His last memory was of a compact and coordinated boy a foot shorter. He guessed Jayvon was in seventh grade now, his legs and arms gangly, and from his disheveled walk Vic knew he was still getting used to the length of his legs. His jeans were low on his hips, his white polo shirt torn down the front from the neck. His left hand was swathed in a makeshift white bandage. Vic guessed a fight. He watched Liz direct him through the minivan's sliding door and follow him inside. As the vehicle pulled away from the curb he followed.

The Ford threaded its way through the streets toward the North Side, and several minutes later turned onto Palo Alto Street in the Mexican War Streets. Vic knew then that they were headed to Liz's home.

Vic parked on the cross street at the far end of the block, hopped out and stood watching the minivan, his body hidden by the corner of a row house. Liz and Jayvon were clambering out of the minivan. As it pulled away Liz said something to Jayvon, who turned, searched his pockets and produced what must have been his key. As he climbed the two steps to the front door Liz swatted him on the back of the head. Not hard, but enough to make him turn and say something to her. She pointed at the door without replying, and a few moments later they were both inside. Vic exhaled slowly and returned to his car.

CHAPTER 21

Vic sat in his car for a few minutes, thinking about what he had seen, then checked the time. It was a little after four o'clock. Finally, he knew what was distracting Liz, but he didn't know if there was much he could do about it. He considered returning to the office, but knew that if he arrived alone chances were good that Kevin would tell Crush that Liz wasn't with him. He drummed the top of the steering wheel with his fingers for a moment, then checked the notes section of his phone. He studied the names and contact information of the people who had filed the missing persons reports on the three missing women and picked one. Moments later he turned the car around and headed north on Route 65 to the McKees Rocks bridge, waited through two turns of the traffic light, and followed the rush hour traffic across the bridge. Carole Vinney, the second name on the list, lived on one of the hills overlooking the bridge. As he drove, Vic thought about the disappearances of the women as a sequence. First Chrissie, followed a week later by Sue, three weeks later by Dannie and a few days later by Carole. The cluster was too coincidental to ignore, but he had no way to connect them and didn't want to fabricate links.

Across the McKees rocks bridge he turned left and worked through the town's confusing split main road arrangement before rising into the hills south of town. It took him another five minutes to find his way through the circling roads and irregular intersections to a small red brick house cut into a hillside.

The gravel driveway ran to a single car garage under half of the ground floor of the house. Cracked and shifted cement steps led from a tilted mailbox to the front door. The metal awning above the front door was rusted and partially disconnected from the wall. Vic parked in the driveway and climbed the steps. He heard music before he was halfway to the front door, the muffled thumping of the bass swelling through the door. As he knocked a guitar solo needled his ears.

He knocked twice and tried the bell but neither seemed to make a dent in the music saturating the door and walls. He was about to walk around back when the front door jerked open as if someone wanted to remove it from its hinges.

The man staring at Vic was in his forties, with a high percentage of his last meal splattered down the front of his wife beater T-shirt. His red-rimmed eyes struggled to focus as the music shoved a wall of pot smoke through the doorway. Vic forced himself to stay straight-faced and kept his ID and badge in his pocket. "I'm Vic Lenoski," he said steadily. "Does an Alberta Vinney live here?"

"You look like a cop." Hearing his own words the man rubbed a hand through his two week growth of beard and glanced over his shoulder. Vic guessed he was worried about what might be visible from the doorway. The music thudded through Vic's body.

"I am. But *all* I'm interested in is her daughter Carole Vinney. Alberta filed a missing person's on Carol. All I want to do is talk about that. And you are?"

The man frowned and it affected his whole face, lowering his forehead and unrolling creases from the corners of his mouth. "Wait."

He slammed the door.

A few seconds later the music volume dropped so fast Vic's ears hurt. From the other side of the door the man yelled "Berta! Berta!" A forceful, angry shouting match started from the back of the house and Vic couldn't make out the words. A moment later the front door opened. Holding the knob was a short woman, her black hair pulled back into a tight pony tail. She wore a peasant blouse with wide sleeves. Her face was plump, pale and round, her skin soft, and Vic saw right away that once she had been pretty, before age and hard living collapsed the soft skin and sank her hazel eyes into their sockets.

"Alberta Vinney?" Vic asked.

She nodded. "Well, Alberta Veerland, soon. Do you know something about Carole?"

"Not so far, but I'd like to ask you about the missing person's report you filed."

Berta stepped aside and motioned him into the small living room. Vic stood just inside the door, his eyes drawn to the top of a bong sticking above the arm of the couch.

"Have you found her?" The skin under Berta's chin quivered and she blinked several times.

"No, ma'am. I just wanted to ask you some questions, get a bit more background from the time when she disappeared."

She nodded hard and Vic knew the action was more about her trying to control her emotions than agreeing with him. The front door was still open and traffic shushed past, now that he could hear ambient noise again. He shuffled a few more steps inside and she swung the door closed behind him.

"Come in," she said, pointing toward the living room.

Vic looked into the room, at the gaping, grease-stained pizza box and the overflowing ash tray on the coffee table. The floor was littered with unfolded newspapers. The evening news was muted on a large screen television that took up most of the wall beside a doorway that led into the kitchen.

Vic stared carefully at the top of the bong and said, "I'm just here about your daughter, ma'am. I can stand here."

She followed his eyes, turned and shouted at the doorway to the kitchen. "Cal, please, can you clean up?" Her voice wavered, as if the idea of asking Cal to do something was too much.

"What the hell are you talking about, woman?" Cal shouted back from inside the kitchen. When he appeared in the doorway she nodded at the bong. Cal crossed the room and swooped it up. "Bad habit of hers," he said at Vic as he disappeared back into the kitchen.

Vic followed Berta into the living room but remained standing. She settled on the end of the couch near the side table.

Vic decided to start slowly. "We ran Carole's social security number. So far no one is using it, but that isn't suggestive of anything. It just tells us she isn't using it right now."

"But she should be using it. If she's working."

"Well, it would tell us more if she was using it, yes. But I'd rather hear about her background and the time she went missing. There isn't a lot in the report."

Cal's voice cut across the living room. "Why are you coming here now? She reported that a year ago. Longer." Vic turned to see Cal leaning against the doorway, his thumbs hooked into the waist of his sweatpants. He seemed cleaner somehow and Vic guessed he had splashed water on his face to pull himself together.

Vic turned back to Alberta. "We go back though unsolved cases on a regular basis. Carole hasn't been in touch during the time since you filed the report?"

"No." Berta seemed to deflate again.

"And is there anything you can tell me from the time she disappeared?"

"Yeah," Cal said. "She was working at one of those strip clubs. Wagging her butt. Stickin' her titties in pervert's faces."

"Cal, stop. Please." Berta's last word was almost a sob.

"Yeah? And why should I stop? Yinz tellin' me she wasn't doin' that shit? Yinz work those places this is what happens. I told her that."

A tear streaked down Berta's face. Vic cut in. "Which place was she working, exactly?" He watched Berta take a breath and wipe the tear from her cheek. When she did her broad sleeve fell back to reveal a bruise on her forearm. She hurriedly smoothed the sleeve back into place.

"It's in the report," Berta said, after a scared glance at

Cal. "That place near Shadyside. Bare Essentials. She got the job through a friend. She had time on her hands and she was a beautiful girl."

Vic started to ask, "Who was the friend—"

Cal broke in again. "Yeah she had time on her hands. Kicked out of high school her senior year."

Berta closed her eyes. "Cal, just stop. Please." She opened her eyes and turned to Vic. "She was friends with a girl a year older. They got into trouble a lot during Carole's junior year, they both got suspended a couple of times. Her friend got a job there and talked Carole into going. The money was so good." She looked at Cal. "First time she'd had money like that."

Cal stepped toward her and Vic shifted position so they faced one another. Cal saw Vic's movement, stopped and retreated into the kitchen, out of sight.

"The friend's name?" Vic asked, glaring after him. He turned to Berta. In the light from the window he noticed a discoloration on Alberta's neck covered with makeup powder. Vic guessed another bruise.

Alberta ran a hand through her hair as if she was holding herself together. "Theresa. Theresa Kartz."

As Vic wrote down the name Cal appeared in the doorway, beer in hand. "You want to find her, Terry strips by the name Mercedes. Carole used the name Tiffany."

Vic wrote down both names. When he was finished he looked up. "You know a lot of stripper names?"

Cal's eyes turned jumpy and he swigged his beer. "I might only be her stepdad but I looked out for her."

Vic suddenly felt lighter and awake. He was sure about Cal now, and knew where Alberta's bruises came from. "I guess that's why you signed the missing person's report."

Cal didn't answer, he just swigged his beer again and settled against the door frame, his eyes bright. Vic had the irrational urge to punch him but forced himself to turn back to Berta. "Do you remember anything she might have said or done in the time before she went missing? Anything different from her normal behavior?"

Berta blinked. Cal gave a long and drawn out belch that somehow came out sounding as if he was bored. Berta ignored him, as did Vic.

"Not very much," she said finally. "She worked the three nights before she disappeared. Two nights in a row and then some bachelor party the third night. She didn't like them. Guys are worse at those parties. It's like when they are in some hotel suite they feel like they own the girl. I guess the bodyguard who goes with them lets the guys grab them a lot more than in the club. She disappeared the next day going in to work. That was the how we found out something happened. Her boss at the club called."

"Do you remember who that was?"

Alberta frowned. "Yeah, some woman. I remember because Carole had complained about her. She was always in her face, trying to get her to mingle more and take more guys into the private rooms."

"And you remember her name?"

Her eyes lit up. "Kelly something. I remember because the girls called her Killjoy Kelly. Because she made them all sick with her complaining."

"Should'a been Buzzkill Betty," Cal said and snorted a laugh. Again Berta and Vic ignored him.

"And Kelly was the one who called to say she hadn't come in to work?" Vic wrote down Kelly and her nickname.

"Right. She was a pain about it. Actually asked if I knew someone who could cover for her, like it was my responsibility. Like we have a bunch of girls in the house we can ask to cover for her."

"Debbie?" Cal said from the doorway.

Alberta shivered like she'd touched a live wire. "No. Please."

Vic heard the crunch of the beer can being crushed and turned in time to see Cal push himself away from the doorway and disappear into the kitchen. A moment later came the suction sound of a refrigerator opening followed by the crack of a beer can pull tab.

"Debbie is my younger daughter," Berta said, her voice soft and apologetic. "She isn't his child either."

Vic just nodded. He didn't like to think about Debbie's chances with Cal in the house. "Do you have a picture of Carole I could take?"

"I do." Berta crossed the room and opened a drawer on the television stand. Inside was a white envelope with a photographer's name in cursive across the front. She slid out a photo and held it out to him.

Vic took it and studied it. Carole wore a graduation gown and a large smile, her teeth very white. She had light brown hair and the same hazel eyes as her mother.

"I thought you said she was suspended senior year?" Vic asked. "I guess I thought that meant she never graduated."

"She didn't. She worked at the club for six months, but she got her GED. Studied for it and everything. That's when we took the picture. Then she got into that Community College on the North Side. She was going to work another three or four months at the club to make money and then quit, take nursing classes."

Vic's jaw ached from the pressure of keeping his mouth closed and he didn't know why. But he did. Carole was someone else with everything ahead of her, gone. He was scared that if he let out his breath he would lose Dannie all over again.

"I'm very sorry," he managed to say.

"But she might be out there somewhere?" Berta asked, her face flushing.

"We plan to keep searching," Vic said. He knew it was a lie. The only reason he was talking to Berta was to find leads to Dannie. He felt sick. "We'll do the best we can." Every sentence sounded worse than the last.

"At least someone is looking," Berta said. She stood, as if she sensed the end of the visit.

Vic croaked out a thank you and let himself out the door. Halfway down the walk the music started again, pounding through the walls and front door. Vic sat in his car for a few moments before he turned the key. He felt like he had left part of himself with Berta.

Vic waited his way through rush hour traffic and arrived home just after six. The living room light was on. Instead of pulling down the short driveway into the garage he parked at the top, slipped out of the car and crossed the sheet-sized yard, his hand over the butt of his holstered Glock. A quick glance through the living room window confirmed no one was in the living room. He felt foolish, wondering if he had left the living room light on, but the knob of the front door turned under his hand and he knew he had locked it before he left. He eased his Glock out of his holster, held it against his thigh and pushed the front door open.

He saw no one, but as he stepped over the transom something creaked deeper in the house, from the direction of the dining room.

"Hello?" Vic called.

Anne, his wife, stepped out of the kitchen, a small frown on her face. "Vic," she said. "I'm sorry. I thought I would be gone before you got home."

Vic turned his body so she wouldn't see him holster his Glock. "No, it's fine. I didn't see your car outside." He closed the front door.

"I'm down the street. I was just dropping something off." She waved her hand in the direction of the dining room. "And then I went in there and ended up reading things. I'm sorry."

"It's okay." Vic was thrown by the sight of her inside the house. She looked like she belonged but it also seemed like she didn't. He flashed back a few months to her standing almost where he was, exactly at the moment when Lorna came down the stairs, her breasts spilling out of Anne's robe. "Can I get you anything?" he asked, wondering if he actually had anything in the house to give her.

She smiled briefly and glanced at the floor. "No, I dropped off some dinner. We made spaghetti and meatballs last night and we had way too much left over."

"Your old recipe?"

"Well, my sauce recipe was always my mother's recipe. She and I made it last night."

Vic had a moment's thought of Anne in her mother's small kitchen, the two of them moving back and forth. Her mother's hard eyes unblinking while the gold cross on her necklace glinted.

"Your Mom doing well?"

She shrugged. "I think she's starting to regret having me stay with her, what with my sister being there. But it's a good thing. She's starting to have trouble moving around and she's getting forgetful. Although she would never admit it."

Vic grinned. "Somehow I get that." He decided he liked having Anne standing in the hall. Her yellow crew-neck sweater appeared gentle and soft in the light, as did her faded blue jeans. He noticed that the gold cross on a chain that she normally wore under her clothes was now outside her sweater. Seeing her there made him remember what it was like living with her, with Dannie trotting from room to room. The memory forced an old habit back with a surge and he pulled open the drawer in the small table near the front door, unclipped the Glock and holster from his belt and placed it in the drawer, along with his badge wallet. He picked a tiny key from his keychain and locked the drawer. He nodded at the table.

"I still can't figure out how you found a table that size with a locking drawer."

There was a warmth in her face, and he knew it was from seeing the old routine acted out, the way he had done it every day when they were all living together. The act felt good to him in an odd way because he no longer used the drawer. Normally he took the Glock upstairs and left it on his bedside table. For several months he'd wanted it next to him at night, in case he ever built up the nerve to use it on himself.

"Well," she said. "I should go." She nodded toward the dining room. "Anything new there?"

"Not really. Those young women who disappeared around the same time as Dannie, they haven't shown up. At least none of them are using their Social Security numbers. I've talked to a couple of the mothers. One lives out in Portersville. I felt bad for her. Her husband died in Afghanistan, she came back to take care of her mother for a couple of years, then her daughter disappeared and left her with her granddaughter. I'd be surprised if she was much over forty years old."

Anne's eyes darkened. "All that, and the police never really searched for her daughter."

"Yeah. And I can't say she was that impressed by me showing up. Anyway, I'll check on the third woman in the next few days. Maybe something will fall out of it. But I still don't get the connection. They were all three or four years older than Dannie."

"Dannie matured quickly," Anne said. "I don't think you saw it. The father always sees the little girl, not the woman. I was starting to worry about it. She was only a few months from driving and could have passed for eighteen."

Vic didn't know what to say. He saw the hurt on Anne's face, the way it deepened the lines that ran from her nose to her mouth and hollowed her eyes.

"I'll keep at it," he said finally.

Anne's gaze turned thoughtful. Vic realized she was reacting to the gentle note in his voice. He was as surprised as she was to hear it.

"I know you will." She turned quickly and disappeared into the kitchen, reemerging with her windbreaker. She crossed to the front door.

"Looking forward to the spaghetti."

"There's a salad with it. I saw you didn't have any salad dressing in the refrigerator. Sorry about that."

"I'll figure it out."

They were close to one another and Vic sensed her warmth and the life in her. It was almost as if he could feel the blood in her veins and the pumping of her heart.

She smiled at him and ducked out the door. Vic followed her onto the porch and watched her skip down the walk and onto the sidewalk. Perhaps five or six parked cars farther down the street he spotted her car, saw the lights blink as she pressed the smart key. She gave him a small wave before she ducked inside.

He waited until the car's taillights were out of sight before he stepped back into the house. He closed the door, unlocked the drawer and removed his Glock. He couldn't quite understand why he had locked it in the drawer, but he knew it was something to do with trying to find some kind of normalcy.

In the kitchen, he lifted the foil over the plate and found a seal of plastic. Underneath was the spaghetti and four large meatballs, a mound that would feed him for two days. Parmesan or Romano was sprinkled over the top. He left the plastic in place, crossed into the dining room and flicked on the standing light in the corner.

He put his Glock and badge wallet on the table and crossed to the three photos hanging on the wall. He stared at the three missing women, his eyes lingering on Chrissie's red hair. She was real to him now. She had a mother and a daughter. If her mother was to be believed she had worked at the strip club to have money for her child. She had lied to her mother about the private rooms, he was sure of it, but that made her more honest somehow. More real. He crossed to the window and picked up the last photograph of Dannie from the line of photographs on the windowsill. It was a photograph taken perhaps two months before Dannie disappeared. He carried it to the wall of documents and held it next to Chrissie's photo. Studied the two faces.

The pit of his stomach turned. Anne was right. The two women could have passed for the same age. He didn't understand how he's missed it. Angry at himself, he returned Dannie's photo to the windowsill, picked up his Glock and badge wallet and went upstairs to change.

Later, in the basement, his boxing shoes laced up and his

gloves tied down, he worked the heavy bag again and again. The shock of each punch numbed his arms and ached in his hands. He didn't care. When it became too much he switched to the speed bag, forcing himself to move his feet, while the sweat plastered his hair to his skull and rolled over his cheeks. He counted out the seconds of each round and returned to the heavy bag when the round ended, his breath raw in his chest, his sweat salt stinging his eyes. He surged at the bag as the last round counted down, slamming it with all his strength, the thud of each punch overwhelmed by the guttural bark of his breath. As if getting Dannie back depended on enough pain, enough rage, enough hate.

When the round timed out he slammed a last punch into the bag and stepped back. He sucked in air, his throat raw and lungs gripped in a vice. He walked in small circles around the basement, his muscles numb and tendons aching with each step. His sweat sprinkled the floor with black dots.

But it wasn't enough to get her back. He knew it. It would never be enough.

Not even close.

CHAPTER 22

Ninety minutes later, stuffed on spaghetti, Vic was cleaning the kitchen when his phone rang.

"I think I've got something," Craig said when Vic answered.

"The tape from the convenience store?"

"Yeah." Excitement crept into his voice. "A pick-up truck. F-150."

Vic glanced at the oven clock. "8:30. You going to be there awhile or going home?"

"You kidding me? I got two hours ahead of me. You have any idea how much crap all you guys bring me?"

"I'll be down," Vic said quickly, glad for something to do. There was also something he wanted to check.

It was almost nine o'clock when he left the house. The air was heavy with rain but only a few small drops hit his windshield; the night lay over Pittsburgh like a salve. Humidity hung in small orange halos around the streetlights. Vic followed the parkway from Squirrel Hill toward the Point where the two rivers met to form the Ohio river. Pittsburgh loomed on his right, the neon company names glowing like afterthoughts from the tops and sides of skyscrapers. Traffic was light, the three lane highway almost deserted. For the first time that night, alone on the road, Vic started to feel comfortable.

Inside the offices on the North Side the lights were dimmed in their cube complex, although at the far end of the room someone was talking into a telephone and from another direction came the soft clattering of a Xerox machine. Vic placed his Glock in his desk drawer and walked downstairs to the Tech department. As he left the stairwell music greeted him and he followed the sound into the workroom. Craig was inside, sitting on his stool, hunched over a laptop.

"Craig," Vic called.

Craig bobbed upright and reached over his computer. A moment later the voice of the man singing sank to a whisper.

"Doesn't bother me," Vic said. "I like singing when someone has something to say. It's that techno dance stuff that does nothing for me. Makes me think someone's trying to hide something."

"You Dylan and Joni Mitchell? That kind of stuff?" Craig's unkempt hair seemed wilder somehow. With his square glasses he reminded Vic of a mad scientist.

"Can't go wrong with them."

"Try this." He played with his laptop and a moment later a vaguely hoarse voice started. Craig upped the volume. "Will Varley. English guy. Newer than your guys."

They listened through a stanza until the refrain began.

"He's talking about all of world history?" Vic asked.

"Yeah. Primordial muck until today. Same question the whole time. Why are we here? Meaning of life."

"I get that." Vic smiled. He liked the singer, but changed topics. "You said you had a truck?"

"Yeah." Craig lowered the volume and pointed at a flat screen TV above his workbench. His fingers worked his laptop keyboard and a picture jerked and wobbled onto the flat screen. Craig pointed at it. "Made a CD of the greatest hits. Not a lot of traffic in and out of that road, but about 2:15 p.m. a truck turns into the road." He paused the video. "Okay, so that's a Ford F150. Pretty sure. Now, watch this." He hit play. They waited as the truck disappeared down the road. There was a jump cut, then the truck reappeared at the intersection and at a break in the traffic, turned in the direction it had come from.

"How long?" Vic asked.

"Little over an hour. They had what, almost a mile to the place where we think the truck was parked?"

"And it's leaving at what time?"

He pointed and the time on the upper right of the screen. "Hits the intersection at 3:05. Original fire call was about three, right?"

"Right, the security service. Their smoke detectors picked it up. The first cop on the scene, Pokorny, he said he got there at 3:06."

"So that's it."

Vic was quiet for a moment. "I saw the same pictures you did. No chance of a license plate?"

Craig shook his head. "Nope. The camera is really pointed at those gas pumps." He waved at the screen. "Wasn't designed to monitor the intersection."

"How about the driver?"

"Too far away."

"Could you tell if the driver is male or female?"

Craig played with his laptop and the truck at the intersection suddenly loomed larger but blurred as quickly into thousands of pixels. "Best I can tell you is that coming out we have two people in the cab, one shorter than the other. Can't say gender."

"Okay. You got a best guess on color?"

"Black and white film, but it's daytime. I'd say the truck is black or dark blue. Could be a dark green. Best guess."

"Thanks." Vic slid off the stool. "That's better than guessing."

"Sorry I can't give you more."

Vic touched him lightly on the shoulder. "It's a start. And no other vehicles match the times the same way? No other suspects?"

"None of the others are even close, time-wise. From 2:45 to 3:05 the truck is the only vehicle to come out of the road. It's another twenty minutes before anyone else turns in there."

"Good. At least today we know why we're here, even if Will Varley isn't sure. Thanks, Craig."

Craig grinned. "Yeah." He tapped the volume key on his laptop and Will Varley's voice filled the quiet. Vic left him and stepped into the hall. As he did the stairwell door opened and Eva popped out. Her dark green wraparound dress clung to her. Her hair was free to her shoulders and her eye liner extended past the corners of her eyes. She jerked to a stop at seeing Vic.

"Just leaving," Vic said and grabbed the stairwell door before it could close. As he pulled it open, he nodded at the Tech Center doorway, "Craig's in there."

When the door banged shut Eva's embarrassment stuck in his mind. He smiled, climbing the stairs, inhaling the floral smell that lingered in the stairwell. He thought of her tight dress and make-up and wondered how Will Varley had missed that particular meaning of life. It was the second time Vic had seen her on the floor and he knew what it meant. As he exited the stairwell he also wondered if Craig was ready for what was about to happen to him.

His cubicle was in half darkness. Two people were now talking on the other side of the room and Vic saw that one of the Commander's offices was lit up. He dropped into his chair and pulled up the department record-keeping system. This was the second item he wanted to check. He entered the name Cal Veerland. A few moments later the system churned up two names. Vic tried the first one and rejected it, then clicked on the second.

Cal Veerland, Berta's soon-to-be husband and Carole Vinney's future stepfather, had a prior for grand larceny and two cases of suspected domestic abuse. The grand larceny earned him six months in jail. Vic did the math and saw that he still had two months of parole. He wrote down the parole officer's name, exited into his e-mail system and did a look-up. When he found the parole officer he addressed an e-mail to him and explained that in the course of an investigation he had visited Veerland's residence. He strongly suggested that the parole officer call in Veerland for a surprise drug test. He hit the send button.

All the way to his car he debated whether the e-mail was a cheap shot, but he knew it was.

By the time he was behind the wheel of his car he didn't care. If Veerland was sent back to jail for violating parole then Berta would have time to let her bruises heal and think about her situation. It would give her some distance. After that, he decided, it was up to her. But he owed Carole something, the whole damn police force did following their puny search for her. He was dead sure about that.

CHAPTER 23

The next morning Vic beat everyone into the office, but was at his desk only a few minutes before Kevin sauntered in. He made a point of saying hello to Vic, and Vic knew from the tone he wanted to call attention to himself. Vic gave him a few minutes to settle in, then dragged Liz's chair from her cube, placed it next to his cube and called Kevin over.

"I could use some help," Vic said, as Kevin sat down.

"Sure. Cold cases?"

"No. The Gretchen Stoll case. So here's the deal. Gretchen Stoll was the victim, right? We've finished interviewing her colleagues and we got some interesting things going on. For starters, some of her colleagues felt she gamed her workload so she didn't have to work that hard. Could be a million reasons for that, all legitimate, but I'd like you to review her cases from the last few years."

Kevin's eyes widened. "Like how many?"

"Don't know, but you don't need to go through all of them. She had three kinds of cases. The ones that fell apart, the ones that were resolved by a plea deal, and the ones that actually went to court. I don't care about the plea deals, at least not yet. That's what usually happens. I do care about the ones that fell apart or went to court. That'll be a small percentage."

Kevin frowned but his eyes were bright and Vic knew he was hooked. "What am I looking for?"

"I don't know yet, but I want to know anything different

about those cases. For starters, there was one DUI case, a young guy from the North Hills suburbs got drunk and hit another car. The guy driving the other car died, he was a vet and father. The suburbs kid never saw the inside of a court room. That file I want to see. Otherwise just search for patterns."

"Like what made the cases fall apart?"

"Right. And how the ones that went to court ended up. I'll e-mail the DA and tell him you're coming over. You'll need access to the court systems and we don't have that here."

"Sure. How much time do I have?"

Vic sat back, thinking. "Tell you what. Go look at the cases and see what you have, then let me know how long you'll need to get through the files. We go from there. But I need the name of that kid with the DUI as soon as possible. I want to talk to him."

Kevin stood up. "Great."

"I'll let you know when the DA answers."

As soon as Kevin returned Liz's chair to her desk, Vic typed and sent an e-mail to DA Marioni explaining why Kevin needed access to the court records. Finished, he timed out another journey in his mind and guessed that he might be able to squeeze it in before Liz arrived. He rose, and a few minutes later added his car to the rush hour traffic headed downtown.

It was a little after eight o'clock when he found the address of Paul Kim, the person who filed the missing persons report on Susan Kim, the third missing dancer from Bare Essentials. He shoehorned the car into a space farther down the block and walked back to the house along the ruptured sidewalk. He guessed that Paul was Susan's father and perhaps Korean originally, knowing from the photograph of the missing woman that she was Asian.

The address was a small Victorian house with a front porch. Three mailboxes were attached next to the front door and Vic was about to press the button under the name Paul Kim when the front door opened and a tall Asian man in his mid-twenties stepped onto the porch. He wore tan chinos, a button-down shirt and tie and carried a small briefcase. They stared at each other.

"I'm looking for a Paul Kim," Vic said.

"Who are you?"

Vic showed him his badge. When the man nodded, Vic said, "I'm following up on a missing person's report for a Susan Kim. The report was made by a Paul Kim. Was that you?"

"That's me." The man shifted back half a step as if he'd been stung. It was a natural reaction to the expectation of bad news, Vic realized, as he worked through the options and wondered if Susan Kim was the man's wife. "I'm sorry, what is your relationship to the missing?"

"Do you have any information on her? Has something happened?"

Vic stared at him. Paul's backwards step gave Vic a better view of him, and he was struck with how young Paul looked. "I'm sorry," Vic repeated, "Your relationship to the missing?"

Anger flickered through his eyes. "Her brother."

Vic nodded. "Just trying to understand, it wasn't clear on the report. We don't have anything new at this point, beyond the fact that she hasn't been employed anywhere recently, at least not anywhere that requires her to pay taxes. Do you have a few minutes?"

"I'm on my way to work." He shifted on his feet, his briefcase bumping his legs. He was thin, but Vic didn't get the feeling he was weak. When he moved it was as if his whole body shifted in a coordinated way, arms, legs and torso together. His dark eyes drilled into Vic. "I can give you five minutes, if it's about Susan. Someone's picking me up and they're not here yet."

"Thanks. I just want some background. Why did you file the report?"

He frowned. "Because she was missing. No one had heard from her. I still haven't. You guys didn't understand that? I thought that's what the report was for."

"And her parents?"

He smiled the tight smile people give to bad jokes. "When

my parents figured out what she was doing they disowned her. I'm not even supposed to talk to her, but the hell with that. I was the only one who would file a report. They weren't going to."

Vic shifted on his feet. "I guess that's the kind of thing I'd like to know. What her situation was like when she disappeared."

"Why are you doing this now? Kind of late, isn't it?" He hefted his briefcase in irritation.

"We always review open cases. Anything else you can tell me about her?"

"Sure. She has a masters degree. Statistics. She also has a boatload of school debt. She was dancing two nights a week to work it off. On a good night she'd make four hundred dollars in tips. And she was three weeks away from quitting when she disappeared. She'd got a job at Carnegie Mellon, something in robotics for one of the professors. He had some DoD grant. That job's up in smoke now."

Vic felt rooted to the spot. "Did she have a boyfriend or anything?"

"You kidding? All she did was work at Pitt, the university? She was a TA, but she had too much debt."

"So she got this job dancing?"

He shrugged. "Yeah. She did a lot of Tai Kwon Do when she was a kid. We both did. But she also liked to dance. She used to watch all these YouTube videos and dance to them when Mom and Dad weren't around. It was her thing. Mom and Dad hated it. If she got caught my mother used to say what she was doing was *jeosoghan*."

"Still," Vic said, thinking out loud and not bothering to ask for a translation. He had a pretty good idea what the word meant.

Paul rotated his shoulders and tilted his head. "What? Asian women don't strip? Yeah, we never had prostitutes in Korea. This is weird to you somehow?"

"No." Vic felt the need to apologize and he wasn't sure why. "I'm just saying, someone well educated like that. You'd think she wouldn't need to."

Paul was silent for a moment, watching him. "Welcome to America. You want to get ahead you gotta pay, pay, pay."

Vic tried to focus. "So, no boyfriends. Did she ever complain about customers or anyone at work?"

"Yeah. She hated the customers. I mean who are these guys who show up to watch? What is going on with them? She attracted military guys who'd served in Guam or Japan or the Korean DMZ. Bunch of jerks who thought Asia women are these quiet do-anything-for-you types. They didn't have a clue. She was smarter and better educated than any of them. They'd have freaked out if they knew what she was really like. But she never had a big problem with them."

"You said she did Tai Kwon Do. Could she defend herself?"

"You kidding? She could kick your ass. She's got a ton of tournament hardware at home, unless Mom and Dad threw it all out."

Vic noted that as well. "Black belt?"

"Fourth degree. Her weapon was short sticks. She used to spar the guys. She could take three-quarters of them. She loved it. Nobody scared her."

Vic thought about that. "So maybe she took off voluntarily? Doesn't sound like someone could force her to go. Sorry, how tall was she?"

"Like five four."

A car slid to a stop in front of the house and its horn sounded.

"That's my ride," Paul said. "Look. When my parents disowned her, she and I started talking a lot. More than we did when we lived at home. I even went to the club at closing sometimes to make sure no one hassled her on her way home. No way she took off without telling me."

"How did your parents find out what she was doing?"

"Because she had an asshole boss. Everyone working there called her Killjoy Kelly, or something. She wanted to know if Sue could take another shift, but I don't think that was it. I think she wanted her to have problems at home. I mean she called my parents on their land line, she didn't call Sue's cell. No way that's an accident."

The car horn sounded again.

"Did she have a stripper name?" Vic asked quickly.

"Yeah. Jade. And don't start about it being typical Asian shit. She liked it was because she said when guys were staring at her she felt like stone inside."

"Doesn't sound as if you liked her dancing either."

Paul shifted to the edge of the porch and started down the steps. Over his shoulder he called, "Of course I didn't. Who would? But throwing her out of the house made no sense. Look." He stopped at the bottom of the steps and faced him. "I have to go. But if you find anything, call me. And if you need to spend more time, text me, my phone number is on the report."

Vic nodded. "Thanks. I'll do that. Did you ever catch her boss's last name? You said Killjoy Kelly and someone else mentioned that name. But did this Kelly have a last name?"

"Not Kelly. That was her nickname. I met her a couple of times when I picked up Sue. Her boss' real name was Cora Stills." Paul turned for the car.

"Thanks," Vic called after him. He meant it. Because just like that, he had a lead. Cora Stills. Her name was listed as the supervisor of all three missing women, and all three people he'd interviewed had said she was disliked by the missing women.

CHAPTER 24

As Vic returned to the office he thought about Cora Stills. The question was how to find her. He would check arrest records, but if she was clean there was no easy way to track her down. He couldn't ask Kevin to do it because Crush would know in a heartbeat, and that could lead to a reprimand for doing personal business during his shift. He'd already risked that once. He switched lanes on the Fort Duquesne Bridge and took the North Side exit ramp. Slowly, he accepted the idea that he had another option: the gangsters Bandini and Thuds Lombardo. Originally, they had given him the names and photographs of the missing women and Bare Essentials was one of their businesses. They should have Cora Still's employment records, or at least her social security number. But going to them now was different than when they handed over the names of the three women. Originally, it was a thank you for saving Bandini's estranged daughter. Now, he would be asking a favor, and he didn't want to owe a favor to gangsters, even if it appeared that all their current businesses were legitimate.

He turned the problem over in his mind as he walked into the Bureau's North Side headquarters. It was a little after nine o'clock and Liz was at her desk, her fingers clattering on her keyboard.

"You late?" she called over as he stripped off his sport coat.

Vic looked at her for a few moments. Liz stopped typing,

and Vic guessed that she understood her joke was in poor taste given her own attendance. Vic stripped off his sport coat and checked that Kevin's cube was empty.

"No. I was out checking on something. I was in at seven. So was Kevin, so I sent him over to the courthouse to go through Gretchen Stoll's court cases. I want to track down that kid who got the DUI and walked. I want to talk to that family."

"Tell them what assholes they are?"

"If it comes up. But I want their take on Gretchen. I also told him to go through all of the cases Gretchen didn't plea deal. The court cases and the ones that fell apart."

Liz sat back. "Does Kevin know how to read?"

"Yes. And he comes in at seven."

They stared at one another for a long few seconds, then Liz said, "Well, guess what. I need to leave early today. Two-thirty."

"Related to what made you leave Gretchen's south side house yesterday?"

"Pretty much."

Again neither of them spoke for a few seconds and Vic took the moment to sit down. "Is this going to happen a lot from now on?"

"Might. I don't know." Her neck was stiff, her eyes wide, ready for a confrontation.

Vic stabbed the space bar on his keyboard to wake up his computer. He knew Crush was going to ask him if he had resolved Liz's absences, and he needed a way to talk about it. He dug his heels into the carpet and wheeled his chair over to her.

"Then we need a cover story for the times you have to go. I told you Crush asked what you're doing, why you keep taking off. If you aren't going to tell me what's happening then we need to cover for it."

"So we cover."

"Yeah, but I'm gonna tell him we talked and you said you would minimize the absences. Okay? And whenever you have to take off we agree on a cover story."

Peter W.J. Hayes

Liz shrugged. "Sure."

"Then this afternoon you're back at Gretchen's house rechecking shit."

"Just like I planned." Her tone was almost insolent.

They stared at one another. Vic wasn't sure what to do. It was the first time since their partnership started that Liz was so aggressively secretive. He turned to his computer screen and spotted an e-mail from Marioni giving permission for Kevin to source the court record system. Liz started typing again. He refreshed the screen and an e-mail from Kevin appeared. He opened it to find the name and address of the man who had avoided the DUI charge. He forwarded it to Liz and a few moments later she stopped typing.

"I'll call rich boy and say we need to meet." Her tone of voice had softened.

"Might be good to meet the whole family. Father and mother as well."

"I'll see what I can do." A few moments later he heard her talking into the telephone.

Vic caught up on his e-mails and forwarded Liz the report on the truck Craig had found on the convenience store video, so she was up to date. His thoughts wandered back to Cora Stills, and suddenly he knew of a way to avoid asking Bandini and Thuds Lombardo about Cora Stills. He checked his cell phone and made a call. A moment later a receptionist at Monahan Investments answered in the hushed tones of too-much money.

"Is Mrs. Monahan in?" Vic asked. "Tell her it's Vic Lenoski."

"Yes sir," the receptionist answered, recognition dawning in her voice. "Just a moment." Vic was gratified she knew him. Six or seven months earlier Mary Monahan had inherited the company from her husband, following his stabbing death. Solving her husband's crime had required him to save her life as well, and, by coincidence, Mary was Bandini's daughter from his first marriage. Mary might be able to track down Cora Stills without Vic owing favors.

"Vic." Mary Monahan's voice was almost a purr. "I sin-

142

cerely hope you are well."

"I am. Even lost a few pounds."

"That was perhaps more information than I needed, detective."

"City policy. Always be completely open about information."

"Clearly I need to vote out some politicians. And Vic, knowing you, this isn't a social call."

"You're right." Vic strained his neck, trying to find the right way to start. He decided to just dive in. "Do you remember that your father gave me the names of three women who disappeared about the same time as my daughter?"

"I do. I pushed him to do it."

"Well, I've been following up with their families and one thing has come out of it. Everyone talks about someone named Cora Stills who apparently was the manager at the club and not a fan favorite. Is there any way I could get some information about her?"

A soft chuckle came over the line. "And I assume you don't want to reach out to my father directly." The line fell silent for a moment. "Well, you came to the right place. You may remember that I ended up with ownership of a number of my father's businesses?"

"I do."

"As we discussed once, he wasn't very happy about it, especially after I forced him to give the women medical care and pension benefits."

"I remember." Vic grinned. Mary had made the workplace benefits a condition of returning the profits of the businesses to her father.

"The upshot is that my father decided to get some revenge. He dumped all of the personnel files for his workers on me. Said if they were going to get benefits he wasn't equipped to manage the HR side of it, and since I now owned this business, I was the right person to handle it. So I have all the employment records of the people who work in his businesses."

"Wow." Vic sat back, staring at the ceiling. "And it sounds like your Dad got a little bit of payback."

"My father has that way about him."

"Any chance I could get information on this Stills person?"

"For you, Vic, I'm willing to bend some privacy rules. But you will need to come over here to review the files and you can't copy anything or take anything off premises. Do you agree?"

"I can be there this afternoon."

"Then it'll be good to see you."

Vic hung up, staring at the phone. He smiled. When he first met Mary Monahan he'd thought she was a trophy wife, as beautiful as a sunrise, but he'd soon learned that her curves hid the strength of a longbow and a business sense sharper than an arrow. But what he liked most was her fierce loyalty to her friends.

"What you got going, Vic?" called Liz from her cube. She was leaning back in her chair, watching him. Vic realized she had probably heard most of the conversation, or his side of it.

"Following up on those three women *you know who* gave me."

Liz nodded. "Anything I can do?"

"Not right now, still wading through it."

"Good, and I got that DUI kid set up for tomorrow morning. Him and his parents. I didn't need to ask for them. I called the kid, he put me on hold and when he came back on he said his mother was going to sit in as well. Didn't give me a choice. So I told him we also needed his Dad there. He seemed relieved about that. Which was real interesting."

"Good deal."

Liz was silent for a few moments, then crossed her arms on her chest. "We need something to break, here, Vic. I don't know if you noticed, but we ain't got much. You can bet Crush is gonna be on us soon. We got a truck in a road, one of about ten million out there, but we got diddly for forensics. Nothing came of that footprint in the back yard or the cast of the tire tracks. And Freddy sent me a message this morning. You remember how he said he was gonna look at the tox screens to see if Gretchen Stoll was drugged? Turns out no go. She didn't have anything in her."

"So she must have been tied to the bed."

"Right. No question she was murdered, but after all this we got a lot of nothing. Although I'm still checking her husband's alibi."

"No, we do have something." Vic scratched his head. "We got a lot of weird shit going on with Gretchen. Our Magic Mary."

"You know what they say about weird shit?"

Vic nodded. "Yeah. It's weird. And it's shit."

Liz watched him, her eyes flat. "Like I just said."

CHAPTER 25

Late that afternoon, after updating the on-line case system and sitting through Crush's weekly staff meeting, Vic drove to Mary Monahan's office building, a squat four story building between the Allegheny River and the restaurants, night clubs and grocery stores of Pittsburgh's Strip District. When he reached the top floor he was met by a receptionist who almost sprang out of her seat at the mention of his name. She led him through the doorway into the collection of cubes and offices that made up most of the floor.

The hum of activity surprised him, until he remembered that he had only visited the floor during off hours, shortly after the murder of Drake Monahan, the company founder. Automatically he glanced at the doorway that had once led to Drake Monahan's office, but the doorway was now a wall and from the nearby glass he saw that new offices were in place, shutting off the area where Drake Monahan was murdered.

"Vic."

Vic turned to Mary Monahan. She was standing in the doorway of the largest of the new offices, wearing a form-fitting blue dress with large white side panels. It was striking, and in the way Mary Monahan had in choosing her clothes, somehow elegant at the same time. Her posture was perfect, and Vic had the fleeting sense that she had called his name from that distance to give him a chance to look at her. He already knew that she used her figure to effect. As he crossed to her he thought that her shiny black hair, which fell to her shoulders, was a bit shorter. She offered him a cheek to kiss.

"Looking great as always," Vic said as he straightened up. He'd caught just the slightest whiff of a floral perfume when he was close to her.

She smiled at him, her brown eyes light. "Men are easy to please."

"I think you have men pretty much figured out."

She arched her eyebrows at him, at once innocent and skeptical, "Were they ever that complicated?"

"Only when they try to hide stuff."

She laughed softly. "I should know better than to banter with a detective. Especially one who boxes."

Vic angled his head, thinking. She was too young to know about his years boxing golden gloves, and then he remembered. "You've been talking to Thuds."

"Once in a while. He respects you, did you know that? That's rare."

"Is it a good thing?"

"It's better than when he doesn't. Come in."

He followed her into her office, recognizing that part of it had once been the conference room she first used as an office.

"I guess you renovated this entire side of the floor?"

"We did." She gestured to the window. "The view of the river is too good to lose." Mary lifted her phone, dialed four numbers and asked someone to join them.

Vic remembered his first view from those windows, how the water was brown and swollen with spring rain. Now the water was grey-blue and cold. A young man appeared in her doorway.

"John," Mary said, "Meet Vic Lenoski. He's a Pittsburgh detective and a dear friend. He's the one I told you was coming. Did you pull the file on Cora Stills?"

"I did." He held out the file and Vic thanked him and took it. John trundled out of the office.

Liz nodded after him. "Interns. I can't find anyone willing to keep those files up to date. Everybody thinks the work is below them. It's annoying. But I guess everyone applies here thinking they're going to be titans of business."

"Isn't that how it works?"

She shook her head and smiled. "I have no idea how it works. I just keep reading balance sheets and hoping for an idea or some kind of insight." Her smile was unguarded and Vic knew she was being honest with him. He hefted the file and she caught the movement.

"You can sit outside my office in the cube right there. No photos of the file. I'm sure I'm not supposed to be showing it to you without a warrant or something."

"I get that and appreciate it." Vic crossed to the cube. The file only contained a few pieces of paper, but from Cora's original employment application he learned that she had graduated from the same high school as his daughter, enlisted and spent seven years in the army, then worked her way through a couple of minor management jobs at restaurants until she was hired to manage Bare Essentials. She had left the job about four months earlier. The file contained the forwarding address for her last paycheck. Vic copied that down as well as her social security number. The process took him less that five minutes, but as he crossed back to Mary's office an idea came to him. He placed the file on Mary's desk and waited for her to finish a phone call.

"All finished?"

"Yeah, and I have a thought. You said you need someone to take care of these files, keep them up to date and stuff?"

Mary settled back in her chair. "I do." She looked at him as if he was the most interesting person in the world, but he knew it was another of her techniques with men.

"This might be worth a try. When I was interviewing the people who filed the reports on the missing women from the strip club, I talked to Barb Stutz, she's the mother of Chrissie Stutz, one of the women who went missing. Barb's raising Chrissie's daughter, Maya. Before that she raised Chrissie after her husband died fighting in Afghanistan, and while she was raising Chrissie she moved back here and cared for her mother as she died. I get the feeling she's rock solid. All she has for work is some part-time stuff for a construction company, doing filing and payroll. I think that if you offered her the job taking care of those HR files, she'd give you the shirt off her back. She'd need help relocating from Portersville, and you'd need a way to make it look like part of the job, because I don't think she would ever ask for help. She's that type."

Mary stared at him for a second, then pushed a pad of sticky notes over to him. She placed a pen beside it. "Her name and phone number."

Vic worked through his phone until he found Barb's details. He wrote them down.

"If this works out I'll owe you another one, detective." She smiled.

"Just doing my job, ma'am." He winked at her. "Thanks for the Cora Stills background, I think I have what I need." He hesitated. "She left her job a few months ago, but it doesn't say why. I thought that was required."

Mary shrugged. "The files are what I was given. When my dear father made me take them that's what I got. It doesn't surprise me much." She arched her eyebrows to tell him she was about to pull his leg. "You would have to ask him."

"Yeah, thanks a lot."

They said their goodbyes and Mary told him to stop by more often. Vic knew she was being polite. She was a friend, in her own way, but they moved in completely different circles. He guessed that her next marriage would be to a congressman or a senator, if not a future governor. As he reached his car his phone trilled.

"Yeah?" he asked, once he was settled behind the steering wheel.

"Vic? It's Kevin. Listen, I've been through all of Gretchen Stoll's cases. They have this indexing system that made it real easy. They just list the case names by lawyer and the resolution of the case. I don't have to go through every single file. I just printed the screens out."

"What does it look like?" Vic tapped his key on the steering wheel.

Just the last two years, she had eighteen cases that were dismissed and nine that went to court."

"Good. I need names and contact information related to the defendants in both groups so we can interview those people, or at least some of them. And do a description on each case saying why it was dismissed or went to trial and what happened at trial."

"Sure, got it."

"Nice work, Kevin. About how long until you have it all?"

"End of day should be good."

"Good, and one last thing. Gretchen Stoll's husband. Can you run down his alibi? He said he was at work at the time of the fire and that about twenty people can confirm it. I want to be dead sure about that because something doesn't sit right with him. We found him in that second house Gretchen Stoll has on the South Side. I want to be sure about him."

"Doesn't Liz usually chase that stuff down?"

Vic squeezed his eyes shut, concentrating. She had promised to, but he'd received no e-mail about it, and he guessed she hadn't got to it before she left work. He chose his words carefully, knowing he might as well be speaking to Crush. "Normally, yeah, but I forgot to tell her and sent her back to the South Side house to check on some stuff this afternoon. I figure she's already on her way. So I'd appreciate it if you could help."

"Sure!"

Kevin's enthusiasm jarred him. He disconnected the call and realized an itch had started in the back of his mind. It was something to do with the forwarding address Cora Stills had provided on her employment record. He looked the address up on his phone, started the car and headed there.

The street was perhaps five minutes from his own house, but in the wealthier Squirrel Hill neighborhood. When he turned onto it his stomach lurched and he pulled into the first parking spot he saw. The street led to Dannie's high school. Vic was sure that on school days it was one of the streets Dannie walked on her way to school. He gripped the steering wheel and steadied his breathing. His eyes searched the sidewalks, he couldn't help himself, but there was no sign of her. He climbed out of the car and walked along the sidewalk, wondering if Dannie had preferred that side of the street, if he was following in her footsteps. When he reached the intersection he stopped, breathed and turned around. He stared at the block and then searched house numbers. The home was on the other side of the street, a wooden two story wedged between two larger Victorian houses, a sagging porch on the front. All the lights were out and there was no car in the driveway. He crossed the street, forced himself up the front walk and onto the porch, the wood creaking under his feet. He rang the doorbell and heard it ring inside the house, the two-part tone gradually swallowed by the silence.

He waited and then knocked, to no answer. A metal mailbox was attached to the wall next to the door and when he checked inside, he found among the junk mail an electric bill addressed to Cora Stills. He breathed again and felt as if he was reconnecting inside. He gathered himself and returned to his car. As he slid behind the steering wheel he thought about tracking down her phone number and calling her, but he decided he wanted to meet her in person, before she had time to prepare herself.

CHAPTER 26

It was a little past nine o'clock the next morning when Vic and Liz turned off Route 19 and made their way through a series of suburban neighborhoods to Maid Marion Drive. As they passed Friar Tuck Road and Robin Hood Avenue the houses and yards swelled in size. When they turned onto Prince John Court the house sizes almost doubled. They stopped in front of a rambling two-story with high windows and a Tudor façade.

"If I say I'm moving to a place like this just shoot me," Liz said. They were her first words since leaving Pittsburgh.

"Seems kinda nice, Sherwood Forest-ty."

"Just shoot me." Liz got out of the car.

Vic followed her down the flagstone walk to the front door. When he pushed the doorbell the chimes in the house played London Bridge is Falling Down. Liz looked at him. "If I ask for your gun you give it to me."

"Stays with me," Vic said, as the door opened.

Vic guessed that the woman who held the door open was in her late forties, and she projected so much nervous energy that Vic almost stepped back. She wore a Ralph Lauren polo shirt and tan Capri pants over tanning-bed skin. Her brown eyes darted from Vic to Liz and back again.

"You're the police officers who called my son?"

"That was me." Liz showed her badge and ID and Vic did the same. She peered at both badges and Vic had the feeling that she wore reading glasses but was vain about using them.

"We're not in Pittsburgh." She dropped her hand from the door handle and stepped back, but not enough to let them in. Vic noticed that she didn't really have a waist, but she wasn't plump, either. Solid was the way Vic categorized her, although he still wasn't sure what to do with her energy. Right now her fingers were decimating a hangnail on her thumb.

Vic felt the need to lead the conversation and not answer her questions. "We're investigating a murder, the victim was Gretchen Stoll. I believe that at one point she represented your son, Thaddeus Miller?"

"My son goes by Thad. If you knew anything about that ridiculous case you would know that."

"Mom!" called a voice from farther inside the house. It carried a warning note.

She glanced back in the direction of the voice and stepped back, dropping her hand from the doorknob. "I suppose you had better come in."

As Vic and Liz stepped into the house a tall, blond-haired young man appeared. He had a strong jawline and high forehead, but came across as if he was unsure of himself. He offered his hand.

"Thad Miller?" Vic asked.

"That's me." He shook hands with them both but barely made eye contact. He seemed happier to stare at the floor.

"This way," his mother said, waving them through a wide archway into the living room. She shot ahead of them and plumped some of the couch cushions so hard it was as if she was practicing CPR. Liz and Vic sat on one of the couches while Thad and his mother settled onto the facing couch. "Where is your father?" she asked.

"He texted, he's coming."

"He's always late."

"If I could," Vic interrupted. He slid his notebook out of his sport coat pocket and balanced it on his knee. "Thad, you probably heard that one of our Assistant District Attorneys, Gretchen Stoll, died in a house fire recently. It actually wasn't that far from here."

"What a dirty little suburb she lived in," the mother said.

"Ma'am, if you don't mind. I'd like Thad to answer the questions." Vic turned back to Thad, who was staring at a square of carpet near Vic's feet. Vic purposely didn't ask how Thad's mother knew where Gretchen Stoll lived. "Anyway, Thad, if you could just take us through how you met Gretchen and what happened from there."

He nodded, his eyes still locked on the carpet. "You probably know the charges?"

"We do, but we'd like to hear it from you," Liz answered. Thad's mother flinched just a bit, as if she was surprised Liz could talk.

"Okay, I got arrested on McKnight road for DUI. It was a car accident and the other driver was killed." He took a breath as if his lungs hurt. "Anyway, my Dad felt I should go through the process, own up to my mistake."

"Your father is an idiot. And you hadn't made a mistake. You weren't guilty. That came out."

In the silence that followed the mother's loud statement the doorbell rang, chiming through a stanza of London Bridge falling into the Thames River.

"That'll be your father," Thad's mother said, but made no move to answer the door. Vic wondered why Thad's father didn't have a key. Thad rose and slouched to the front door. In the distance they heard the father and son talking, and Vic thought that Thad's tone of voice was lighter.

He turned to Thad's mother.

"Mrs. Miller, I'm going to ask you to stop interrupting. If you can't stay quiet I'll have to ask you to leave the room."

Her face flushed. "I'm in my own house, and all I'm doing is correcting factual mistakes."

Liz cut in. "We'll decide what's factual and what isn't."

Before she could answer Thad entered the room with a man the same height. Vic and Liz stood to meet him. The man had the same jaw line as Thad and the same blond hair, although he was bald on top of his head. They shook hands all around and the man disappeared through an archway and returned with a chair that Vic guessed was taken from the dining room. He placed it between the two couches and sat down. Vic noted that he didn't acknowledge his wife and that she was concentrating on something outside the window, as if she didn't want to look at him.

"Thanks for joining us, Mr. Miller," Vic said.

He nodded.

Liz turned to Thad. "You were saying?"

He nodded, a bit more energy about him. "Yeah, well, like I said, my Dad said I needed to take responsibility, that I needed to face what came up on my own. I'd just got out of college and didn't have a job back then, so I had to use a public defender because I didn't have the money to pay a lawyer."

Vic glanced at Mr. Miller, who was watching his son with steady eyes, his jawline set. He sensed a toughness, and he wondered if it had come about in response to being married to Thad's mother, or if it had always been there. Thad's mother shifted on the couch as if she was getting ready to say something and Liz held up a finger to stop her.

"Anyway," Thad continued, "I met Mrs. Stoll like twice after it happened, and that was it. Then like three months later I got a letter from the DA's office saying his case was dropped."

"See! He wasn't guilty of anything."

Vic looked at Thad's mother and she collapsed back into the couch.

"He got off on a technicality," Mr. Miller said. He sounded tired, as if this was an old argument.

"And those were the only times you spoke to her?" Liz asked.

Thad tried to hold her eyes as he responded. "Yes. And both meetings were very short. At one of them there was another lawyer there from the DA's office, but I don't remember his name. He didn't say anything."

"And what did you talk about?" Vic asked.

"She laid out what charges they were going to file against me, what was likely to happen, that kind of thing."

"She took your statement?" Liz asked.

"No, she had planned to do it but she cancelled the appointment."

Vic clicked his pen. "And when was that?"

"Maybe two months after the accident."

Vic wrote down the sequence of events, more to let the silence fester. He'd noticed that Thad's nervousness was growing, if that was possible. "And that was the last time you saw her until the letter arrived?"

"Yeah."

Vic glanced from Thad's mother to his father. "And did either of you see her at any time between the accident and the DA's letter?"

"No," Thad's father answered. "This was up to Thad to sort out."

"I did," Thad's mother said. Vic knew from the ADA interviews that Thad's mother had talked to Gretchen and he was relieved that she didn't lie.

"Okay, can you tell me about that?"

"Of course. I made an appointment and went in to tell her that we would engage our own counsel. We wouldn't need her."

"And that's all you talked about?" Liz asked.

Thad's mother stared at her. "What else would there be?"

Vic saw that Thad was staring at the carpet, chewing his lip. His eyes were fragile, somehow. His father stared at Thad's mother as if he expected her to say more. Thad's mother pointedly kept her eyes on a spot on the couch between Liz and Vic.

Vic sat back and glanced at Liz. She tilted her head slightly, as if to say *I got nothing*. Vic flipped his notebook closed and stood up. "Thank you Thad, and thank you Mr. and Mrs. Miller. We'll be in touch if we have any more questions."

Thad's mother was off the couch in an instant. "I'll show you to the door." She darted ahead of them. Vic remained still, watching Thad, who seemed as embarrassed as someone caught with their pants down.

"Anything you'd like to add?"

Thad looked up, startled, and glanced at his father. "No, I think that's it. I didn't see her except for those two times."

"I understand that." Vic shifted his gaze to the father. "It's tough for us, sometimes. We ask a lot of questions, but we never know if they're the right ones. Sometimes we need people to guide us there."

The father considered Vic for a few seconds, and Vic knew he'd hit a chord, he just didn't know which one. The father turned back to Thad and stared at him, waiting. They all did, and Thad shifted in his seat, his eyes wide and still locked on the carpet.

"I thought you were leaving?" The way Thad's mother asked the question it sounded like a question and a command at the same time. Thad visibly tightened.

Louder, his mother said, "I thought you were finished?"

Vic gave it a moment, watching Thad, and then turned for the door.

"Thank you," Thad's father said.

Thad's mother stepped closer to her husband, leaning over him. "You're thanking a police officer who's asking your son about an arrest that should never have happened?"

The father ignored her and extended his hand. Vic shook it. He and Liz said their goodbyes all around and Thad's mother shepherded them through the front door. She closed it so quickly it was almost a slam. Liz and Vic walked down the sidewalk and slid into the car.

"Nothin' goin' on there," Liz sneered, once the car doors were closed. Vic strung on his seatbelt. "We need to separate them. Or just get the mother out of the way. I might have got that wrong. I thought it would make more sense to see them together."

"No, you were right. Now we know the kid is caught in the middle. Father wants him to take responsibility, the mother is pretending it never happened. I don't get her. Her drunk son kills a hard-working vet with two small kids and the mother thinks he did no wrong."

Vic started the car. "I liked the Dad, but it's Thad we need to get to."

"And who the hell names their kid Thaddeus? Something like that I gotta look up." Liz tugged out her smart phone and tapped on it.

"Not a common name." Vic was still thinking, trying to make sense of the interview.

"Means courageous heart." Liz put her phone away.

Vic started the car. "Maybe he needs to grow into it."

CHAPTER 27

Vic and Liz spent the rest of the morning working through Kevin's list of Gretchen's court cases. Liz focused on the ones that fell apart while Vic developed a list of interviewees from the cases of people who had gone to trial, lost, and received heavy sentences.

"I still don't get why so many of these cases are plea-dealed," she said at one point.

"Keeps the wheels of justice moving." Vic's list was shorter than Liz's, but he liked the possibility of finding motive within the group. The families of the sons and father's sent to jail would be angrier and more vocal, he just had to be careful of them carrying a grudge. He looked for similarities across the cases but didn't find any, beyond the fact that all the people sent to jail were men. He made a list of family members and by the end of the day had found and interviewed two families. Both were sullen, tight-lipped, and convinced of the innocence of their family member. During the first interview he explained that he was just reviewing Gretchen's cases. In the second interview, sitting in a small kitchen warm from the oven and the smell of an Italian sausage casserole, he mentioned that Gretchen Stoll was dead.

"Well thank god for that," the mother said sharply enough to split the table. She grasped a small gold cross on her necklace between a thumb and finger.

"What happened?" the husband asked, a smile breaking

out on his face that he didn't bother to hide. He was a large man wearing a MOPAR baseball cap with a dirty brim. Car grease was driven so far into the wrinkles around his knuckles that Vic wondered if it might be tattoo ink.

"House fire," Vic said.

"May she burn in hell." The mother almost spit out.

The father reached out a large knobby hand and laid it carefully over his wife's forearm. As his smile dissolved he patted her forearm, a quick couple of taps as if he was sending a message. Vic wondered about that.

Something in the mother's eyes moved and she said, "Well, you can understand why we might wish ill on her. I might even say it's God's will. This was our son she sent to jail."

"Not for me to say." Vic watched their interaction. "We just arrest and detain. What happens afterwards is all in the courthouse."

The father patted his wife's forearm and moved his hand to his lap. "Well, we wish we could be more help."

Vic thought about their reaction as he drove back to the North Side, but he didn't know what to make of it. Maybe they just didn't want to be seen gloating about the death of someone they felt had failed them. When he reached his cube Liz was sitting in hers, typing. Vic almost said something about her not having left early but chose to leave it alone, in case Kevin was listening. He stripped off his sport coat and sat down. "How did your interviews go?"

Liz stopped typing and sat back. "They were different."

"How so?"

"I got through three of them. I ain't saying they were tight lipped, but they were tight lipped."

"Same happened to me."

"But there was one thing that was different." Liz hesitated, a frown on her face, "I was expecting them to be real happy to talk about the case, wanting to say how they got off, that kind of thing. Bragging, kind of. But I didn't get that. It was like they were scared to talk about the case." She stared at the ceiling for a moment. "You know how your kid comes home and you say how was your day, you hungry, but they don't want to talk about it? Like they got something going on they don't want you to know about, and they don't want to talk to you because they don't want it to slip out? That's what it was like. Same feeling."

"Did you tell them Gretchen was dead?"

"They already knew from the news. And that was the other thing. Instead of being sorry she died, they all asked what would happen to her cases. Would they be reviewed, like they were real worried I'd shown up at all. Everybody's acting different than you would expect."

"Right."

Liz tugged at the cuffs of her blouse. "I can get through the rest of the interviews tomorrow."

"Same here."

"Then, I'm leaving." She stood up.

Vic made a point of not saying anything and turned to his computer. He faced a long string of unopened e-mails, and starting at the bottom, began to work his way up the list.

It was well after six when he merged his car into the rush hour flow heading across the bridges. He didn't think about it much, but he knew where he wanted to go. It still took forty minutes to work his way down route 28 to the Highland Park bridge, cross the river and take the left up past the zoo. A few minutes later he was at the top of the hill among the Victorian houses of East Liberty. He parked in front of Anne's mother's house, crossed the walk and rang the doorbell.

For a few moments nothing happened. He was alone on the wood porch, the wind pressing on him and searching around the house, as if it didn't have a care in the world. From behind the door he heard a muffled exchange of angry words, and then the door opened. Anne stepped to the glass of the screen door and waited.

"Sorry to just show up. But I wanted to thank you for the spaghetti. Also, I've talked to all the people who filed missing person reports on those three women we learned about? Thought you might like an update."

Anne cocked her head slightly, something he had seen her do when she was angry with Dannie, and the memory turned inside him. "Vic, you're supposed to call before you come. You know the deal." She softened her tone. "It's my sister's rule, yes, but it's still a rule."

"Next time. I promise."

She watched him, her blue eyes still. She brushed a strand of hair away from her face and tucked it behind her ear, turned the screen door handle and stepped onto the porch next to him. She let the door slam, something she didn't usually do, and Vic wondered if she was sending a message to someone inside the house.

"So tell me." She moved to the porch railing, staring at the street. She folded her arms.

Vic joined her and they stood side by side without looking at each other. His fleet car was parked at the bottom of the walk and he stared at it. "I talked to all three. Two mothers and a brother. No one has heard from them. All three of the women were working because the pay was good. That Asian woman? She was paying off school loans. Chrissie, the redhead, she was raising a daughter."

Anne sucked in a short breath.

"And the brunette," Vic continued, "she needed the money, but I get the feeling she was more into the fun, but she'd finished a GED and was thinking about community college. Kim, the Asian woman, she'd just got a full time job and was going to quit in another week."

"And no one's heard from any of them?"

"Nothing at all. So I'm down to one lead. All three women worked for a woman named Cora Stills. I haven't talked to her yet, I'll try and do that tomorrow. But here's the coincidence. Cora Still lives on one of the streets that Dannie took when she walked to school."

"Is it one of the streets on her way to her friend's house?"

"No." Vic knew what Anne was getting at. When Dannie was abducted she was on her way to a friend's house. "If she did, Liz and the team would have interviewed her. They talked to everyone along the route."

Anne nodded. The wind pushed at her hair. On the road in front of them a pair of cars hummed past.

"So that's it. The fact Cora Stills lives on one of the streets where Dannie regularly walked is weird, but probably a coincidence. I just can't figure out how Dannie connects to the three missing women and Cora Stills."

Anne nodded a single time. Vic recognized her distracted air and knew she was thinking. Then, slowly, she said, "Does it have to connect?"

"What do you mean?"

Anne looked up at him. "Do you know what I was thinking about when I first saw the photographs of those women?"

Vic waited. In the sunlight the crows feet at the corners of her eyes reminded him of past years and laughter. Or the scars of those things.

"Their hair."

Something moved inside him. "What do you mean?"

"A redhead, a brunette, a black-haired woman, and with Dannie, a blond."

"You're saying it's what's different about them that matters." The fact felt significant to him, but he didn't know why.

"Right. I just don't know why."

He almost laughed out loud at how they mimicked each other's thoughts, but he caught himself. "I need to think about that. I've been looking for connections. I hadn't thought about what makes them different."

"Something to think about." Anne turned to him. "You're doing better Vic. Better than three or four months ago."

"I feel better."

"Good." She reached up on her toes and kissed him lightly on the cheek, her hand on the crook of his elbow. It was how she had kissed him for years to say goodbye when he left for work and the memory welled up in him. "Call next time." She turned and let herself back into the house.

Vic watched her close the door and turned back to face the street. The porch felt as empty as the sky. He crossed to his car and sat behind the wheel, thinking, the touch of her still on his elbow. He had noticed the differences in hair color, but he hadn't considered that it might be significant. It rankled him. Craig's father—his first commander after he made detective—had routinely dropped hard-learned aphorisms about how to conduct investigations. How many times had he told Vic that any angle not thought through was a lost clue?

He started the car. Before he could pull away from the curb his phone rang and he slid the call button.

"Vic? It's Kevin here."

"Yeah. What's up?"

"You know how you told me to check the alibi on Stoll's husband?" Excitement electrified his voice.

"You found something?"

"I checked with a bunch of people at his law firm. They remembered seeing him all morning, but no one remembers seeing him during lunch and the early afternoon. His door was closed. He'd told his secretary he was working on some contract language."

"Nothing big there."

"So then I thought, if no one saw him when his door was closed, how can I check he was actually in his office? That's what took me so long. I had to get building security to give me the ID card swipes of people going in and out of the building."

"Okay."

"Day of the fire? Mark Stoll was out of the office from about noon to four."

CHAPTER 28

On his way to work Vic drove by Cora Still's house, but the windows were dark and the driveway empty. He was back at his desk at eight a.m. and five minutes later Kevin stopped beside his cube, a wide grin on his face.

"I was thinking. You want me to get a warrant on Mark Stoll's phone records? Location ID might tell us where he went."

Vic hesitated. His plan was to have Liz do that, but he also wanted to keep the case moving and Liz wasn't at work yet. "Sure. Talk to Craig down in Tech. He can handle it."

He saw a thought process play out on Kevin's face and he wondered if Kevin didn't want to bring Craig into it. But he continued down the aisle to his cube and called "on it," over his shoulder.

Vic turned to his computer and sent Liz an email telling her of the development with Mark Stoll and how Kevin was chasing the phone records. He then let her know he was headed out to interview more families. As he worked his way through the buildings more detectives and support staff passed him in the halls and offices.

The third family on his list lived north of Pittsburgh in the outlying suburbs. Vic picked his way down Route 19, past the roads that led to Gretchen Stolls' house, until the strip malls fell away and either side of the road shifted to farm fields, car dealerships or muddy construction sites. He turned left onto a secondary road and ten minutes later left again onto a gravel driveway.

The driveway led to a square farmhouse and three out-buildings, including a small barn. Someone had repainted the clapboard of the house a bright yellow and the window trim in white. The house shone in the morning light, offset by the dull brick-red paint of the barn and outbuildings. A small Ford sedan was parked near the front door of the house. Vic pulled up next to it and let himself out. Behind a split rail fence, fields stretched away to a low rise. They didn't look as if anyone had planted them in years. As Vic crossed to the front door he saw a curtain move in an upstairs window. There was no doorbell, so he knocked.

The woman who answered wore tight jeans and a sweat-shirt. Her hair was platinum white and her skin spray tanned such a deep brown it almost matched the door. Vic guessed she was in her early forties, but it was hard to tell. Her face tended to the square side, her brown eyes bright and she carried herself like a woman used to being looked at. Her right hand was behind her waist.

"Yes?" she asked. "You understand this is private property?"

"Yes ma'am." Vic showed her his badge. "Pittsburgh Police. I know I'm outside my jurisdiction but we're investigating a case that took place in Pittsburgh. Is your name Lily Bauer?"

"Yes."

"Could we have a few words?"

"What's the case?"

"It involves your son, John Bauer. As I understand it he was represented by a public defender named Gretchen Stoll."

"He was. Not that it did much good."

"Could we talk about it?"

She hesitated and glanced at the barn. "Yeah, sure. So you know, I have a weapon behind my back. I'm gonna put it on the hall table, okay?"

Vic stepped back and placed his hand on his Glock. "That would be a good idea. Why don't you turn around so I can see the weapon, then place it on the table while you have your back to me."

They stared at each other for a moment until she turned slowly so Vic could see the weapon, a small black SIG. Vic guessed a woman's model. Lily let her fingers loosen until she held it only by the butt, moved it away from her waist to arms length, then placed it gently on the hall table. She turned around with a small smile and moved backwards from the doorway. Vic stepped inside and nudged the weapon farther onto the table.

"Can't be too careful out here," Lily said.

"Understand. No need to explain. Thanks for telling me you had it."

Her eyes searched his face. In the smudged light of the house she seemed younger and Vic was suddenly aware of her as a woman, as if putting down the gun had made her more vulnerable, and more available. Her sweatshirt was baggy, but not enough to hide the roundness of her breasts. The tight hallway pushed them together.

"Is there somewhere we could talk?"

She nodded to her right and walked through a narrow doorway into a small living room, her movements liquid. From behind, Vic couldn't help but admire how well her jeans fit. Lily sat on the couch and crossed one leg over the other so precisely it reminded Vic of scissors cutting. The sharpness of the movement dissolved his attraction to her. He sat in a nearby armchair, aware of a small smile on her face, as if she understood the effect she'd had on him.

"Gretchen Stoll," he said, more to ground himself than anything else. "She represented your son, John, about a year ago. The case went to trial and the prosecution won."

Lily's square face hardened. "Yes. She screwed him. Us. No way he should have got that kind of sentence for a first time drug possession."

Vic was tempted to point out that her son was arrested with three pounds of marijuana in his possession, which was more than anyone could claim was for personal use, but he let it go. "Did you meet with Gretchen at all?"

"Apart from seeing her at the trial? Once. It was not long after he was arrested."

"What did you guys talk about?"

She settled farther back into the couch with the slightest of wiggles. "Call me Lil, everyone else does. She told us the charges he faced. What was likely to happen."

"Did she suggest a plea deal?"

Lily hesitated. "Not really. She said it was a possibility but unlikely. County was cracking down on drug dealers, that kind of crap. That the DA had a hard on for him."

Vic knew she had brought sex into the conversation on purpose and wondered why. "Where was he arrested?"

"He was living in Braddock then."

Outside a vehicle surged by, the tires crunching on gravel. Vic glanced at the window but from his position only caught a glimpse of something dark passing by.

"My boyfriend," Lily said. "He parks in the barn. He's headed to work."

"What's his name?"

She frowned. "Does that matter? We only started going out a couple of years ago."

Vic waited. After a few moments Lily waved her hand. "Jesus. Denny Halpin. He owns this place."

"Thanks. And you are aware that Gretchen Stoll has passed away?"

"I watch the news."

Somewhere in the back of the house a mobile phone rang.

"Can I get that? It's probably Denny wondering who you are."

Vic nodded and Lily hopped lightly from the couch and disappeared toward the back of the house. A moment later he heard the distant sound of her talking. Vic stood, crossed into the hall, lifted the pistol and carried it into the living room. He tugged the slide back far enough to see that a round was in the breach. He looked around, spotted a side table near the doorway Lily had used, crossed to it and placed the pistol on the table. A small framed photograph sat on the table, a picture of Lily and another woman, a selfie, the background some kind of nightclub. As he turned back to his seat he heard Lily say urgently, her tone low and sharp, "Don't worry. It's not what you think. We'll talk when you get home."

Vic returned to the chair. A moment later Lily appeared in the doorway, her phone in her hand. She sat on the couch and placed her phone on the coffee table.

"All good?"

"Yeah. He just didn't see you come in but he knew from the car you're a cop. He wanted to know what was going on."

Vic nodded. "We're about done anyway. So if I get it, you met Gretchen Stoll once, not long after your son was arrested. And that was it?"

"I saw her at the trial. Not that she was doing anything"

"Right. And what was your reaction to the sentencing?"

Lily leaned forward. "Are you kidding me? It's complete bullshit. First offense?" Lily's face reddened. "And she hardly talked during the trial. I mean she sucked as a lawyer."

Something moved in Lily's eyes, as if she realized she was getting too worked up and should pull herself back. "I mean, he's my son. Yeah, he made a mistake, but to have that kind of crap lawyer? She should be disbarred." Her voice trailed away.

Vic gave her a moment. "Do you have other kids?"

Lily stared at him, a question on her face. "No."

"Was John's father involved in the trial in any way?"

"No. Last I heard he was in North Dakota. He had a job fracking north of here, but the company moved him out there. He seemed real happy to go. That was like four years ago. We were never married anyway."

"How old is John?"

"He was eighteen when he was arrested."

Vic found himself clenching his teeth. He breathed out slowly. "Okay, Mrs. Bauer. I think that's everything I need. I guess one last question. Did Gretchen Stoll ever do anything you thought was inappropriate while she was defending your son?"

"You mean apart from being an asshole and useless?"

Vic waited. "When you say asshole, what do you mean?"

Lily waved her hand. "Like I said, I asked her about a plea deal. She just laughed at me. End of story. Asshole."

Vic let the statement sit in the air, then stood up. "Thanks, Mrs. Bauer. I put your gun on the side table there. I appreciate your time."

She rose as well, her movement fluid. "I'm sorry. I think my son got a raw deal and it makes me mad. Hey, also, do you think this affects his chances of parole?"

"No need to apologize, and I don't know about parole. That's a question for the DA's office and the parole board."

They shook hands and Vic let himself out. Inside his car he sat for a moment, then started the engine, turned around and started down the driveway. He hit the brakes almost immediately. Blocking the way was a black pick-up truck. A lean man lounged against the cab, arms folded over his chest, watching him. Vic cut the engine and stepped out of his car.

"Denny Halpin?" he called, staying a good ten feet from the man.

"Yeah. My property." He pushed off the truck and moved to the edge of the driveway, his tan work boots crushing the weeds.

"Lily told me. I'm Vic Lenoski, Pittsburgh Police. I'm looking into the death of Gretchen Stoll."

"Lily told me. See some ID?"

Vic removed his badge wallet slowly and held it up. Denny stayed where he was, silent, and Vic was aware of the wind pushing across the field and bending the weed stalks.

"So are you done?" Denny asked. The wind picked up and lifted his black hair. As Vic slid his badge wallet back into his pocket he placed Denny in his mid-forties. The gauntness of his brown eyes and the baseballs of his cheekbones were hard to forget.

"You know how it goes. We're done when we decide we are."

"John got a raw deal. Shoulda got a plea deal. Lily's still pissed about it."

"I got that."

Denny patted his open hand against his jeans. It struck Vic that while Lily was controlled and moved her body as if she knew what she was doing, Denny was nervous and unsure of himself. "Nice truck," Vic said, to change the subject.

Denny glanced at it as if he had forgotten it was there. "You need to come out here again you call first." His eyes narrowed.

Vic decided that if Denny was a nervous guy, then he might poke at that a bit. "Depends on the circumstances."

Denny swung his hand at the surroundings. "Private property." As quickly, he turned for the truck, opened the door and climbed into the cab. He gunned the motor and pulled away so quickly that a handful of gravel ticked against the front of Vic's car. Dust drifted up from the driveway and was snatched away by the wind. Vic turned back to his car, thinking about Denny. As he settled into the drivers seat he decided that not only was he a nervous guy, something made him insecure about Lily. He started the car and followed the truck down the driveway.

CHAPTER 29

V ic reached the North Side headquarters a little before lunch. He was finished with his list of families to interview and he guessed Liz was as well. So far he had nothing, but the interviews had unsettled him somehow.

Liz was waiting for him when he reached his cube. "How'd it go?" she asked.

"Same as yesterday. Nobody is saying anything and I feel like I need to ask different questions. Everyone says Gretchen was the worst lawyer ever, but they all lost their cases and they've got a family member in jail, so I wouldn't expect it any other way."

"Everyone's real tight-lipped for me."

"Although," Vic said quietly, as the thought came to him. "Every single one of them asked me if this would help with the opportunity for parole."

"That's got nothing to do with Gretchen."

"It shouldn't," Vic said, thinking. "But they all asked. And you're right. Tight lipped. It's like no one wants to talk about it."

Liz stretched back in her chair. "So what's next?"

"Get ready to interview Mark Stoll. Although I want to find a receipt or something that says he was out of the office. We need a warrant for his phone's location data but that takes too long. And we need updates for Crush and the DA."

"I'll put Kevin on it." She hunched over her keyboard.

Vic watched her, still worrying over the question that

had nagged at him on the drive back to the office. He opened the report Chief Dick had sent and skimmed it, then dug out his phone and found Pokorny's number.

When Pokorny answered he said, "Hey, Pokorny. I got a question for you. You got a second?"

"Yeah. Haven't left for my shift yet."

"Your chief's report doesn't mention you guys finding any gas cans or anything to carry the accelerant used to start the fire. Is that right?"

"Sounds right to me. I know I didn't find anything."

"Thanks." Suddenly, he didn't know why, he said, "so you know, I was out near you today. Visited a Lily Bauer past Cranberry. You guys cover that area?"

"No, but the combined North Hills units do. We back them up when they need it."

"She answered the door with a handgun behind her back, real different than how people usually answer a door. I didn't ask if she had a permit. I bet she does, but so you guys know."

"I can check the permit registry."

"Ah, don't bother. Low priority. I'm not even sure why I'm telling you."

Eva appeared next to Vic's cube. She held out a post-it note gummed to her finger so Vic could read it. It said: *Crush wants to see you now.*

"Thanks, Pokorny. I'll talk to you. And like I said, don't worry about that gun thing." He hung up and looked at Eva. "Liz and I?"

She nodded. "Right away. He's been angry all morning."

Vic glanced across the aisle to see Liz roll her eyes and stand up. Vic followed her to Crush's office. Crush was at his desk, the only things in front of him a computer monitor, keyboard, and a coffee cup with the words 'Bring the Hammer' printed on the side.

As they sat down Crush said, "I hear you guys have a suspect."

Liz frowned. Vic guessed at what Crush was talking about.

"If you mean Mark Stoll, Gretchen's husband, yeah, we have an inconsistency in his interview. His alibi was that he was at work, but his ID card walked out the front door of his offices between noon and four day of the fire."

"When do you bring him in?"

Liz broke in. "Vic and I talked about that just a little while ago. We want to confirm it was him who was outside before we question him."

Crush glanced from Liz to Vic and back again. A bead of sweat stood on the top of his head. "Why not bring him in now? Get his statement, then check it against his phone's location data later. Why wait?"

Vic studied the coffee mug, thinking about Kevin. "Well, there's a problem." He looked up and met Crush's gaze. "Kevin asked for the card data from the law firm's security guys and they just gave it to him. I'm not sure they can legally do that without a warrant. If that's true, any half decent defense lawyer will get the card swipe evidence thrown out of court and the case will go with it. So we need to go back and do it right, and get a warrant for the card swipe data. But to get that warrant we need other proof he was out of the office, we sure can't use the card swipe data to get a warrant to get the card swipe data. So we're going to check his credit card and financial records. If we're lucky he bought something while he was out of the office. We then use that transaction to get the warrant for the card swipe data and then we got him on obstructing an investigation."

Crush slammed his fist on his desk. "So get it! We got our guy. We need to close this. And why the hell is Kevin the only one solving this case? I thought that's what you guys were here for?"

Vic checked his anger. "Yeah, Kevin showed some initiative, but he overstepped."

"Don't give me that kind of talk. Initiative is initiative. Now solve it. Get out!"

As they rose Crush stabbed a finger at Vic. "You stay."

"Bow wow," Vic said under his breath, just loud enough for Liz to hear as she passed him on her way out of the office.

Crush held up broad hand. "Did you say something?"

"No."

"Close the door."

Vic pulled it shut, turned and waited. He purposely didn't sit down.

"Where are you with solving Liz's problem?"

"We talked, I told her I need to know when she is taking off. She got it."

"I said she needs to stop taking off, did you not get that? I hear she's still leaving work."

Vic silently cursed Kevin. "Not that I know of. If she's out of the office it's because she's with me or working on some other aspect of the case."

Crush looked him up and down. "I hear different and I will be all over you. You get that?"

"Sure."

They eyed one another for a moment until Vic pointed at the door and tilted his head in a question.

"Yeah. Get the hell out," Crush said.

Vic let himself out, winked at Eva and walked back to his cube. Liz was standing beside it, waiting for him.

"What was that all about?" she asked.

"You." He nodded at Kevin's cube, took her elbow and drew her away from it. "Kevin is still telling Crush that you're skipping work."

Her eyes darkened. "I'm gonna rip him one."

"Pick your time. Not now. But we know for sure he's blabbing to Crush about us, so let him. We just control what we tell him."

Liz swayed and Vic knew she was fighting with herself about it.

"Excuse me?" someone said from behind Liz.

Vic stepped to once side to see who it was. Eva stared back at him, her cheeks flushed. Vic knew she understood she was interrupting something and was embarrassed about it.

"Yes?" Vic asked.

"The front desk called. There's someone down there wants to talk to you. A Thad Miller, or something. He says you guys talked to him yesterday?"

"Is he by himself?"

"I think so."

Vic and Liz exchanged glances.

"Okay," Vic said. "Can you put him in one of the rooms downstairs? We'll be down."

Eva nodded and twirled as if she was glad to get away.

"Official interview?" Liz asked.

Vic shook his head. "No, let's just hear what he has to say. Maybe he wants to get something off his chest. If we do an interview we need to give him his rights and that might scare him off. And don't record it."

Liz nodded and turned back to her desk. Vic slid into his sport coat, wondering what made Thad drive from the North Hills. He turned to Liz. "Let's run out and get coffee. Let him stew. We'll bring him something back so he's not pissed at us."

Twenty minutes later Vic opened the door to one of the interrogation rooms to find Thad slouched down in a chair, leaning to his right, his knees tight together and his hands, palms pressed together, jammed between his thighs. He straightened up when they opened the door, his eyes swimming in tears. Vic carefully didn't say anything and placed a cardboard coffee carrier on the table.

"Sorry, Thad, we were out getting coffee when you got here. We brought you some if you want it."

Thad rearranged his hands and legs as if he had just realized that he looked awkward. "Sure." He rubbed his eyes with the backs of his hands.

Vic worked one of the cups out of the carrier and placed it on the table in front of him, then dropped a pile of sweeteners and creamers beside it. "Didn't know how you like it."

Thad nodded, popped the cap on the coffee cup and

dumped in cream and sugar. As he stirred Liz left the room and returned with a small garbage can, which she put next to the table so he could dump the used creamer and sugar packets. Vic tugged one of the chairs from behind the table and set it across from Thad for Liz, and then dragged another chair around from behind the table. They settled across from him as if they were all sitting around a campfire. Vic sipped his coffee.

"Didn't expect you to show up like this, Thad. What can we do to help?"

Thad glanced about, his eyes settling on a microphone on the table.

"We're not recoding anything," Liz said. She pointed at a small red light set into the wall. "If we were it would be lit up."

"The way you just showed up today I thought you might just want to have a conversation," Vic said. "It's just the three of us. Unless you want us to get you a lawyer and make this official. We can do that if you want."

"No. This is fine." Thad sipped his coffee.

Vic heard a distance in his voice, as if he was trying to draw himself out of somewhere deep inside. He waited. Thad sipped again and Vic noted the tremor in his hand.

"You came to us," Vic prodded gently.

"Right." Thad carefully placed his coffee cup on the table. He gripped the fingers of his right hand with his left hand and then dropped them, as if he didn't know what to do with his hands. "It's complicated," he said quietly. He looked around as if he was seeing the room for the first time.

"Just take a run at it," Liz said. "Doesn't matter how it comes out."

Vic added, "sometimes things that seem complicated are really pretty easy, it's just that thinking about them makes them seem more complicated than they are."

Thad nodded. "Well, so you can tell, my Mom and Dad are pissed at one another."

"It looked that way," Liz agreed.

"They're separated. Mom changed the locks on the

house."

"Okay," Vic said into the pause.

Thad raised his head. "It's my fault."

Liz smiled at him in a friendly way. "Why don't you tell us about it?"

Thad stared at the wall for a moment, his breathing shallow, and Vic knew he was building up to something.

"That night of the accident?"

"The car accident?" Liz asked. "Yes, that was bad luck."

"No it wasn't." Thad shook his head slowly and stared at a spot between them. "I'd drunk too much. No question. And then I wrecked." He stared up at the ceiling. "I got put in jail." He shivered. "My Dad drove down the next morning and posted my bail. As we were driving home he told me I had to own up to it. That bail was all I was getting from him and he expected to be paid back. He kept saying I had to take the consequences. I'd got myself into it, I had to get myself out."

Thad looked around, saw his coffee cup, picked it up and took another swallow. As he put it back on the table his hand started to shake so hard that he almost knocked it over. Vic waited, not moving, knowing Thad needed to explain everything in his own way.

"So when I got home, my Mom said we were going to get the best lawyer, take care of things, there was no way it was my fault. That the other guy must have driven into me. Mom and Dad were arguing straight away. He said he'd talked to the cops, he knew what the situation was, that I'd probably go to jail. He kept telling her I had to take the consequences. I'd never seen them like that. My mother started screaming, she threw a plate at him."

He gulped down a breath, his eyes wide, and Vic knew he was back in the house again, watching the argument.

"Anyway." He closed his eyes for a moment and opened them. "So my Dad wouldn't move on it. Said I had to own up to it, that he wasn't paying for anything. I didn't have any money, and when I went to my hearing I didn't have a lawyer, so they assigned me Mrs. Stoll."

"We know that much," Vic said.

"Like I said yesterday, we met a couple of times, the first time she just told me I was screwed, that I'd probably do time in jail, at least a few years. She told me to tell my parents that. Anyway I did, and my Mom completely freaked. For days after that she was after my Dad all the time. Saying we needed to hire a lawyer, had to make everyone understand that I couldn't go to jail. My Dad hardly said anything, but he was always clear I had to own up to it."

He reached for his coffee again, his hand not shaking as much. Vic knew he was into the groove of telling the story now. Vic had seen it before. The hard part was getting started, after that it was a relief to be telling someone.

He sipped and returned the cup to the table. "Anyway, I'd been looking for a job, going to interviews and stuff, and one day I came home and my Mom is all happy. She told me she talked to Mrs. Stoll and they were working something out. It was all good. She stopped yelling at my Dad, but whenever he asked her what was going on she would smile and tell him the adults were taking care of it. He didn't need to worry. She kept acting like she had some big secret. I hated that more than her screaming at him." Thad glanced at a corner of the room but Vic could tell he was committed now, that he was fine telling them whatever he had come in to tell them.

"So anyway, I was supposed to go in and give Mrs. Stoll a statement, but she e-mailed me and told me to forget it. And then a few months later the letter showed up from the DA saying they'd dropped the case."

"Do you know how that came about?" Vic asked.

"Yeah." Thad started to take a sip of coffee but thought better of it and put the cup down. "A couple of weeks after the letter came I heard my parents arguing again. Really loud, like the early days. It was late and I'd come in through the garage, I don't think they knew I was home. Anyway, it came down to my Mom saying she paid Mrs. Stoll fifteen thousand to make the case go away. My Dad was really pissed. I mean hoarse from shouting so loud. So I snuck off to bed and the next morning my Dad comes into my room and says he's moving out, it's not working with my mom. He left that afternoon."

The room was silent. Vic felt as if dominoes were falling in his mind, one after another. All the things that were different about the case, how Stoll's workload seemed to dissolve, the metal box of burned cash, why the people whose cases were dropped were so tight lipped. He finally knew the right question to ask when he and Liz talked to them. One simple question: *Did you pay Gretchen Stoll cash to make your case disappear*?

"Thad, this is very brave of you," Vic heard Liz say. "But you're absolutely doing the right thing by telling us this."

After a few seconds Thad asked, "Does this mean I'm going to jail?"

"I don't know," Vic said, "that will be up to the DA. But keep this in mind. There's enough guilt to go around on this one. It's not just you. And I think that you need to make this official, in a statement. You'll want a lawyer with you when you do that. And Thad," he studied the young man, who finally looked him in the eye, "I want to say this as well. You are doing the right thing here. You'll make your dad proud."

"It's too late." He shook his head slowly. "He filed for divorce."

"But you've picked the right side, Thad." Vic hesitated. "Can you tell me something else?"

Thad nodded, watching him.

"After your case was dropped the family of the man who died brought a civil suit against you. What happened there?"

He shrugged. "My mother hired some big shot lawyer. She paid them like one hundred and fifty thousand dollars and they were fine with that."

Vic thought about the size of the house Thad lived in, guessing at how much it was worth. At the same time he knew how fast one hundred and fifty thousand dollars would disappear after all the lawyer fees, and as the weeks and months sped by as the widow cared for her two children. He felt a drumbeat of anger inside him, saw again Thad's mother and her nervous energy. "I tell you what, Thad. Let's set a time for you to come back in with a lawyer and give a statement. Are you okay with that? If you need a public defender just tell us and we'll get someone for you."

Thad nodded.

"Thad, tell me something else," Liz said. "Did you tell your mother or father you were coming in here today?"

"No."

"Good, and can I suggest that you keep it that way? At least until you've made your statement. Can you do that?"

Thad's mouth was tight. "Yeah. I can do that."

Vic watched him and made a bet. He was sure Thad wouldn't tell his mother, but he would tell his father immediately. He'd put money on it.

"Actually," Vic said carefully, "do you want to make the statement now? I mean since you're here. Save a trip later. We can arrange everything for you. You don't need a lawyer unless you want one, and we are glad to provide one. No pressure, but maybe it's time to make this official."

Something shifted in Thad's eyes. Vic thought for a moment he'd scared him off, but Thad nodded. "No. Let's do this. I don't need a lawyer."

"Good man." Vic patted his knee. "You sit here and we'll get you set up. If you want anything just say so. Just give us ten minutes."

He stood up and nodded at Liz.

CHAPTER 30

"Jesus," Liz said, when the door was closed behind them and they'd walked a few steps down the hall.

"Yeah, but we have to be careful." Vic's mind was racing. "Getting just Thad on record isn't going to do it. We still don't know who the hell killed Gretchen. So we've got two problems here."

"And the people who paid her aren't gonna testify if they can avoid it. They don't want this opened up again."

"You sure about that? We know the right questions to ask now. We just have to get them under oath. Someone will fess up and confirm this." Vic stopped as they waited for the elevator, his mind still racing. "And maybe we got a motive. One of them got scared Gretchen would get caught and their case reopened, so they took her out. We need to depose every single one of those people."

"Depose everyone? The DA will never go for it. It's an election year. Even if public defenders don't report to the DA, that mud is going to splatter everyone."

They stepped into the elevator and fell silent as a uniformed officer hurried in just before the door closed. When they reached the ground floor they stepped out and Vic touched Liz's arm to guide her outside to the parking lot. The air was warm and humid, the sky grey. They moved down the curb several feet so they were by themselves.

Liz turned to him. "We have to tell the DA this."

Vic stared at the sky. "You think?"

"We can't sit on it."

"And what do you think the DA is going to do?"

Liz shifted away from him. "Not our problem."

Vic stared across the parking lot toward the river. He knew she was right, but he hated going to Crush and the DA before they had everything they needed to make the case.

Liz faced him. "Vic, I know you want to see it through, but this is too big. If there's more than Thad involved, the whole DA's office gets sucked in."

Vic pulled his eyes from the place where he guessed the river was. "Okay. But, before we go to Crush I want to do one thing. Double check Thad. Confirm it."

"How?"

"If Gretchen was taking bribes to drop cases, there's one group of people who will know. Guys in jail. If she was making the offer regularly, someone will have said no. She represented people who couldn't afford council, for Christ's sake, and fifteen thousand is a lot of money. I have to believe the people who said no ended up in jail. And they'll be bitching to their cell mates that they were screwed by their lawyer."

"Every con says that."

"Yeah, but this is different. This will have the part about how they couldn't come up with the money to pay her so they got screwed. And I know a guy who hasn't been out of jail that long."

"Am I gonna like who you say?"

"No. I'm thinking Mike Turcelli."

Now it was Liz who turned and stared at the casino and the Steeler's stadium. "You're gonna talk to Thuds and Bandini again, a couple of gangsters, just so you can ask their goon some questions?" She looked at him. "You know that can get you fired."

"No one needs to know. Levon can set it up. Fifteen minutes in and out. But if Turcelli's heard scuttlebutt about it, or knows someone it happened to, we confirm Thad. Then the DA can't bury it and he has to do depositions."

Liz kept staring across the parking lot. Vic guessed she was thinking about the Ohio River. He always felt good knowing it was there, even when he couldn't see it. He'd never understood why he felt that way, and he wondered if Liz felt the same. There was something certain about it, something about how a river of that size and length started right there, you could see it come to life, and if you followed it far enough, you could go anywhere in the world.

Vic collected himself. "You and Levon are still going out, right?"

Liz's eyes snapped back onto him. "And what's your point?"

"I'm just planning to have a beer with my old friend Levon. If we happen to bump into his old client Thuds Lombardo and his buddy Mike Turcelli, wasn't anything I planned."

Liz took a deep breath. "You got more stories than the bible, Vic. But you're gonna owe Thuds after this. You want that?"

Vic thought about that. He had already talked to Mary Monahan to avoid Thuds, just for that reason. He also knew that if he asked his questions, Thuds would figure out what they were investigating. That did matter, because Thuds and Bandini could figure out a way to make money from—or use—any kind of information. But he needed to be sure that Thad's statement was confirmed.

"Do we have a choice?" He said finally. "Let's go take Thad's statement, but I'll tell you something. When his mother finds out she's gonna show up with a hot shot lawyer who screams Thad wasn't read his rights correctly, he didn't understand them, or something? That'll bottle up his testimony, at least for awhile. But if we have a second source, an informer, saying the same thing, we're covered. Anyway, just because Thuds comes back later and wants a favor, it doesn't mean we have to give it to him."

Liz smiled, the first smile Vic had seen from her in days. "Vic, you and I know you ain't built that way. You're a guy who pays his debts. Always. Okay, we better get in and get Thad going before he changes his mind."

Twenty minutes later they had read Thad his rights and he'd officially turned down a lawyer and made his statement on tape. When Thad left the room, Vic could have sworn he moved like he was five years younger.

Before he sat back down at his cube Vic drifted down the aisle enough to see if Kevin was in. He wasn't. He then sat down at Kevin's desk and used his telephone.

"Levon Grace," came the gruff reply after the fourth ring.

"Levon, Vic Lenoski. You busy?"

"Not damn enough. You got a case for me?"

Vic smiled. After a military career Levon had drifted back to Pittsburgh. Not long afterwards the parent of a college friend asked him to find his son. The job hadn't gone well, but Levon had liked the work and soon afterwards hung out a PI shingle. However the work was spotty and he was always hustling for his next case.

"Wish I did. Dinner good enough? I was hoping you could set me up with one of your old clients for a quick talk, then we could have dinner."

"Which client?"

"Take a guess. I really need to talk to his guy Mike Turcelli, but I bet Thuds will want to be there. I need it in a hurry. Maybe tonight?"

"I doubt it, but I'll call. What it's about?"

"Tell Thuds this is just gathering information. All clean for him. Nothing to worry about. And apologize for the short notice."

"Let me give it a shot."

After hanging up Vic put in the requests for Mark Stoll's financial records, flagged Liz and asked her to review them for any usage between two and four on the day of the fire. As he finished his phone rang.

When he answered, Levon said, "You got lucky. We're on."

CHAPTER 31

I t took Vic forty minutes to work through the rush hour traffic from the North Side to Bloomfield, the neighborhood where Thuds Lombardo had agreed to meet. One of his legitimate businesses was an upscale hamburger place where they had met before. Vic and Levon agreed to meet half an hour earlier at a coffee shop nearby.

Vic was fifteen minutes late, but Levon seemed unperturbed. He was sitting low on a chair, his fingers flicking across the screen of his cell phone. When he saw Vic he rose to his full six feet. They shook hands.

"You got lucky," Levon said. "Thuds usually pushes everyone out a couple of days."

"You told him it would be short, right?"

"Yeah." Levon smiled. His mother was African American and he had never met his white father. Levon had told him that his father was the oldest son of a family where his mother once worked as a maid. Somehow, out of that, Levon had grown up well adjusted and well educated, thanks to his father's family paying his tuition to a local private school. His skin was the color of creamed coffee, his high forehead and well-spaced eyes a combination that made people instinctively trust him. There was another side to him that included two tours in Iraq, one as a sniper and another in Marine Intelligence, but somehow the difficulties of his life didn't seem to bother him.

Vic didn't order coffee, knowing he wouldn't have time to

drink it. "Dinner afterwards?" he asked.

"Sure. Good deal for me for just a phone call."

"I got a question for you, we can save it for then."

"I don't know Vic, you're usually a come out and say it kind of guy."

"This one is trickier."

He shrugged. "Yeah, no problem, but let's head over. Can't hurt to be a bit early."

They walked down the street, side by side, and entered the restaurant. People were three deep at the bar, and in the back left corner a large glass window showed the grill where the burgers were cooked. Next to the window was a narrow hallway leading toward the back kitchen and the rest rooms, and leaning back against the wall next to the hallway stood Mike Turcelli, his back to the wall. His arms were folded on his chest, the muscle so thick it looked like he regularly bench-pressed pianos. His neck was as thick as an elephant leg. They made eye contact and Mike tilted his head toward the hallway, turned and lumbered down it.

"I'll get a beer," Levon said, turning toward the bar.

Vic followed Mike down the hallway. He knew that the last door on the right before the kitchen led into a small office that Thuds used for meetings sometimes. When he reached it he tapped twice, lightly, and the door was opened immediately by Turcelli. He held it open and Vic stepped inside. When Turcelli closed the door the racket from the bar collapsed into a distant thunder.

"Vic Lenoski."

The tall, lean man standing behind the desk wore a dark grey suit over a black T-shirt. Vic decided that was all Thuds ever wore. His full head of hair was flecked with grey and the cords on his neck might have been hawsers. He held out a large, knobby hand. Vic crossed to him and shook the hand.

"I appreciate you doing this on short notice."

"If we can do it in ten minutes we're good."

"It's Mike I had the question for." Vic glanced at Mike, who was standing beside the door, his arms folded once again. "Mike looks a lot healthier than last time I saw him."

Thuds gave the slightest of nods. That last time they met Mike was new to his job and had broken one of Thuds' rules. It had cost him a broken nose and eight weeks of recovery.

"Go ahead." Thuds nodded at Mike.

Vic turned to him. "You spent three years in Somerset, I remember your record."

Mike nodded carefully, his head wobbling on top of his thick neck. Worry twisted in his eyes like a worm.

"This is nothing that's going to come back on you, Mike. I just want to know if you heard something while you were there."

Mike glanced at Thuds, who tilted his head as if to say go ahead.

"I was wondering if you ever heard anyone talking about one of our public defenders. Anyone saying they could pay her off to make a crime go away."

Mike frowned, but Vic was more aware of the way Thuds tightened. It was as if his entire body flexed in one movement. Vic waited.

"Nah, don't remember nothing like that."

"Nobody talked about it?"

Silence sifted around them, until Thuds said slowly, "interesting case you must be working on."

"You never know where stuff leads," Vic said, still watching Mike.

Thuds turned to Mike. "Mike, think about that question every way, did you ever hear *anything* related to paying off a public defender?"

The frown was still in place on Mike's forehead, but something shifted slowly in his eyes, as if he was waking up from a long sleep. "Uh, yeah. Not about paying a public defender to get off, but about getting sent to jail for *not* paying her off. Yeah. Couple of guys said they were in there because they didn't have the money she wanted."

"Was there a standard price to get off?" Vic asked.

Mike shook his head slowly, as if it was heavy and needed a lot of effort to move. "Yeah, I don't know. I just heard people bitching about not being able to pay."

"You remember their names?"

"Just their yard names. Crispy and Trunk."

Vic knew that most of the cons fell into nicknames in prison, and those rarely showed up in their records. It wasn't going to help. "Thanks, Mike. if you think of anything else you let me know." He looked at Thuds and another thought came to him. "Do I have time for one more question?"

Thuds waited.

"Cora Stills," Vic said. "I know she worked for you guys at one time. She left after a couple of years. Can you tell me anything about her?"

Thuds' grey eyes didn't move and he stayed silent. Vic knew immediately that Thuds remembered her. But he also knew that Thuds didn't talk his way out of situations, he thought his way out, using his fists as a last resort. Finally Thuds asked carefully, "How'd her name come up?"

"Through the three women you gave me to check, the ones who disappeared?"

"Yeah. I get that." He relaxed. "She managed one of our clubs for a couple of years. I took a chance on her, thought she might be good with the girls. When guys are the boss they can get too hands-on, if you get it. Wanted to try a woman. Didn't work out."

"Why not?"

"She free-lanced. Turned out she was setting up private dances for the girls at bachelor parties, that kind of thing, and didn't tell us. Stole the money. That doesn't work."

"You fired her?"

"Oh yeah." Vic understood why there was no note in her work file about being fired. Those kinds of private parties skirted the law and Thuds and Bandini didn't want anything written down.

"Thanks. Like I said at the start, I appreciate you seeing me this fast."

"No problem." Thuds' eyes narrowed just slightly. "Your DA there, Marioni, must be worried sick about shit like this around Gretchen Stoll, what with an election a few months off."

Vic wasn't surprised Thuds had put together what he was investigating. He was too smart to bluff so he decided not to answer the comment.

He and Thuds shook hands. When Vic turned he held his hand out to Mike, but he seemed unsure if he was allowed to shake hands with a police officer. Instead he opened the door and the noise from the bar crashed in.

"Good luck," Thuds called, and with a nod Vic slid into the hallway.

CHAPTER 32

Vic and Levon left the restaurant and walked down the street two blocks without talking. As they approached a Thai restaurant on the same side of the street Vic pointed at it.

"Good?"

"Beats Ritters."

"I don't know," Vic said as they stepped into the cool interior. "Ritters has them on breakfast."

"And anything else at three a.m. Except maybe Primanti's."

Inside, the restaurant was the opposite of the one they had just left. It was dim and the conversations muted. They were shown to a booth, and once they had ordered, Levon studied Vic's face.

"You look better than a few months ago."

"I just said the same thing to Mike Turcelli."

"You had the hangdog and haggard look going for you last time. From what you told me Mike had the two-fist-tattoo thing going. Looks like you're sleeping better."

"Less drinking."

"Good place to start."

Vic waited as the waitress put down a glass of water for each of them. After she left Vic said quietly. "So I have a question about Liz."

Levon waited, watching him.

"What's going on with Jayvon? I get the feeling it's a mess. She's distracted at work and keeps taking off."

"What did she tell you?"

"Nothing. Our commander noticed it, he's told me to fix it. Which is the usual bullshit from him because I outrank her but she reports to him, not me. We're partners, not boss and employee. I talked to Liz and she's not saying what's up. She just says she'll handle it. Gets pissed at me when I bring it up. Jayvon's what, in seventh grade, now? I'm guessing being a cop's son isn't helping him in school."

"What makes you think it's Jayvon?"

Vic sat back. He didn't want to say that he had followed Liz. "Just makes sense. It's clearly something personal and it's getting to her emotionally. I'm guessing that she doesn't want to let on at work, because it's hard enough for a woman to be a cop, and a detective, and a lot of guys would use it to say women shouldn't be detectives."

"Especially black women."

"There's always a few of those people, yeah."

Levon sipped his water. Vic waited, knowing it was possible that Liz's moodiness had to do with Levon, since they were dating, but after seeing Liz pick up Jayvon at school, he doubted it. He also knew that Liz was a private person and wouldn't want Levon telling him what problems she was facing. He stayed quiet, interested in how Levon would work it out.

"Okay," Levon said finally. "I'll give you my take on it. It's up to Liz to tell you the details and what she thinks." He stopped as the waitress arrived at their table and placed steaming dishes of food and a bowl of rice between them.

After she left Levon spooned vegetables from one of the dishes onto his plate. "Some of it is Jayvon's age. He's thirteen. Part of it is he doesn't have his father and doesn't even know what happened to him. Liz told him about Katrina hitting New Orleans and what happened to the force down there afterwards, but he's too young to really get it. And yeah, part of it is the school he goes to and the fact everyone knows his mother is a cop and his dad was too. I'd bet the bad boys pick on him, try to make him prove he's not a snitch. Right when teenage boys start wanting to fit in with everyone, his classmates are pushing him out. At that age it's tough to know what to do."

"She said this to you?"

"No, I just heard about what he did and what happened. That's my read on the causes, and my opinion only. I've told Liz the same thing, but put yourself in her shoes."

"No easy answer."

"None. You don't fix this with a couple of sit-down talks, not that I can see. And it's all too big for a kid that age."

They fell silent, and in the pause Vic spooned Pad Thai onto his plate. Levon did the same.

After a few mouthfuls Vic asked, "What kind of kid is he?"

"Pissed off. Some of that comes from not knowing his Dad. I know that feeling. It's like you're missing something and can't find it, 24/7. You can't have fun at anything. And some of it comes from his situation right now. Like the world is out to get you. But from what I hear he doesn't lie or try to bullshit anyone. He seems to be a straight shooter."

Vic swallowed, heat from the spices in the food moving with it into his stomach. "That sounds good."

"Yeah, and he also doesn't snitch. People put him up to stuff, he won't tell the school what's going on."

"Good again."

"Yeah, but it's not helping him. When you act that way but the situation stays bad, you start looking for something else to get you out of it."

Vic nodded. "I bet Liz is telling him to snitch. She'd want to catch the people who are really creating the problems. That's how she's built."

Levon swallowed. "You know, Vic, sometimes you surprise me. It's like there might actually be more than a cop under there. But yeah, that's my guess too. So his head is all twisted around. He's doing all this shit to prove he isn't a snitch, so people at school trust him, and his mother's telling him to snitch."

"Good luck telling Liz that."

Levon pushed some vegetables around his plate with his chopsticks. "Yeah, and that's the size of the problem."

"Any drugs in the picture?"

"Not so far. That we know of."

They ate in silence for a time until Vic asked, "How'd you handle it, being mad? You didn't know your father."

Levon glanced at him, his brown eyes soft. "I didn't. It doesn't go away, it doesn't get smaller. It's like all the friends I lost in Iraq. They were my brothers. Same thing. Each one is a hole inside you. When it happens it's a huge hole, almost all of you, and you keep falling into it. But over time you meet more people, do more stuff, learn shit, and while the size of the hole doesn't shrink, that new stuff builds out around the edges until you've got safe walking space and can avoid falling into it every five minutes. You still fall in it sometimes, but you have more ways not to. And you just keep going."

Vic stopped eating. A memory of Dannie hit him like a wave, Dannie riding her bike, her hair streaming behind her, the blurred purple of the bike and its white wheels, the streamers fluttering from the hand grips.

From somewhere he heard Levon's voice. "See, now I got you going."

Vic yanked himself back from the abyss, heard himself say, "The problem is that Jayvon doesn't have time." He brought himself all the way back. "He needs something now."

"Yeah." Levon put down his chopsticks. "I found lacrosse. Gave me a bunch of guys to hang out with, taught me to work hard and that working hard gives you something. That's what got me through."

"Lacrosse? I keep forgetting you went to that rich kid's school."

"You need to pay attention. Almost every high school in Pittsburgh has a team now."

"Doesn't change where you went to high school. But that's

helpful. At least I know Liz isn't disappearing from work for bullshit reasons."

"She never would be. Isn't that type."

"And we aren't going to solve Jayvon sitting here." Vic put down his chopsticks as well. He felt bad for Liz. "Maybe a change of school?"

"I've been telling her that."

"How would that work?"

Levon sat back and smiled. "She moves to Sewickley with me. Levon goes to the Quaker Valley schools. Fresh start."

Vic laughed out loud. "You dog. You asked her to move in with you?"

"Well. Tried to. We started to talk about it but she changed the topic. I'm hoping she just wants some time to think about it."

"I hope that works for you guys."

"Me too."

But what Vic was thinking about was Liz's comment from a few days earlier. How there was something in Levon he wouldn't give up or tell her about. That it defined him. How it was the one thing he carried from Iraq that wouldn't let go.

And how she didn't trust it.

CHAPTER 33

As Vic drove home he planned his workout, wanting to keep himself distracted from the memory of Dannie on her bicycle. The memory wrapped him up like a blanket he couldn't push away. But he didn't want to push it away, either. He turned onto the street where Cora Stills lived, and he knew that, without thinking about it, he had picked a route home that took him past her house.

A car sat in her driveway and lights glowed from the ground floor. Vic was alert, suddenly, and slid his car into a space about half a block down from her house. With the engine turned off and headlights doused, he aligned his notebook under the beam of the courtesy light. He skimmed the notes he'd taken during his meetings with the family members of the three missing women, then checked his sport coat pocket for the envelope containing the photographs of the missing women. As he finished, the quiet of the street bore down on him, and when he slid out of the car he felt as if something loomed in the darkness. He glanced about and strained to hear, wanting Dannie's footsteps to materialize out of the air, but only black silence pressed back. He hiked down the sidewalk, the only sounds his own footsteps and the occasional whir as a car or truck sped down the nearest cross street. The porch creaked under his feet as he approached the front door.

The woman who answered his knock was medium height and wide shouldered, her auburn hair cropped short against her head. Her eyelids were low on her eyes and her lips tight, as if she was peering into a sandstorm. There was something about her that Vic recognized, but he couldn't understand why. She reminded him of someone, or he had seen her before. It made him wary.

"Ms. Stills?" he asked. "I'm Vic Lenoski with the Pittsburgh Bureau of Police." He showed her his badge and ID, taking his time with it, trying to put the feeling of the walk to the house out of his mind. She studied his ID, her eyes sharp.

"That's me. What do you want?"

"As I understand it you used to be a manager at Bare Essentials? I just had some questions about a few of the women who used to work there at the same time you did. I believe you were their boss?"

"I haven't worked there in months."

"I understand that. But ten minutes would be helpful." Vic noted how she held the door, blocking his entry, and how she had arranged her foot behind the door in case he tried to push his way in. The fact he was a police officer hadn't made her any less cautious. He watched her process his request. It didn't play out on her face, but rather in a softening of her body posture. In a single motion she moved her foot, dropped her hand from the door and stepped back so he could enter. "Sure, can't hurt."

The way she said it made Vic think that she was speaking more to herself than to him. He followed her into the entry. On his right a staircase rose to a turn and then disappeared into the darkness of the second floor. A small table was pushed against the wall below the stairs. Perched on top was a brown ceramic dish holding a ring bristling with keys. Above it hung a red rug with an African design.

"In here," she said, and led him into a living room. Above the fireplace were two African masks, and what looked like a cowskin Zulu shield hung on the wall beside an archway that led into the dining room. She reached down and pressed a couple of buttons on a remote control and the television ducked into darkness. She scooped up a half-full water glass, led him into the dining room and pointed to a seat at the dining room table.

"Unusual artwork," Vic said, as he sat down.

She hesitated, then sat across from him. "I was Army for seven years. One of my posts was Somalia, I was also in Johannesburg for a while. Picked them up along the way."

Vic nodded, unsure where to start.

"I doubt you wanted to talk to me about the stuff on my walls." She took a quick swig from the glass and Vic caught a whiff of white wine.

"Yeah, I swung by the last couple of days but I kept missing you."

"I was away."

"Anywhere interesting?"

Her mouth tightened and Vic knew the question irritated her. But he'd done it on purpose, and her reaction made him tingle.

"North Dakota," she said finally. "Friends. Okay, so what is this about?"

"Sure." Vic made a show of taking out his notebook. He decided to play dumb, to see if she tried to take advantage of it. "Well, let's see. Just some cold cases we're chasing down."

He flipped through the pages and back again, slowly, as if he was unsure of the case and his notes. "Yeah, here it is." He said it as if he was surprised to have found it. "We have some missing women reports. Let's see. A Chrissie Stutz, Susan Kim and a Carole Vinney. We just have to follow up, you see. The reports are still open."

Cora sat unmoving, waiting.

Vic gave her a moment and then asked, "Do you remember any of those women?"

"We had a lot of girls come and go. Can't say I remember any of them specifically. How did my name come up?"

Vic took his time writing down her answer. "Oh, we talked to the people who filed the missing person's reports. I guess your name came up with them. You were their boss?"

"Well, my job was taking care of all the girls. Making sure they showed up on time, that they weren't too drunk or stoned to dance, make sure they got on stage at the right time. Off stage at the right time. I mean none of them were rocket scientists. It was like a goddamned babysitting job. And then you had the headliners who came in, the porn stars and all that shit. They were a pain. Thought they were movie stars or something." She hesitated a second, then added, "Just because they gave some guy a blowjob in front of a camera."

Vic chuckled and rearranged himself in his chair, knowing she'd made the comment to test how seriously he was taking the investigation. He lightened his tone. "So you don't remember any of the three?"

She smiled at him. "Not offhand. Maybe if you had a picture or something."

Vic shot back his response, letting a sharp tone come into his voice, "Not Carole? Her stripper name was Tiffany. Her mother said you were the one who called to say she hadn't showed up for work."

Cora blinked at the precision of the question and covered it by settling back as if she was thinking. "Offhand I don't remember," she said finally. "Like I said, I was babysitting. A lot of the girls didn't show up when they were supposed to. Most of 'em were dumber than fence posts." She took a slug from her glass.

"Uh huh." Taking his time, he slid the envelope from his sport coat pocket and rummaged inside. Carefully, he lined up the three photographs on the table, facing her. He fiddled with them, to make sure the row was even and neat. "I guess too bad your job didn't work out."

She stared at him for a moment. "Look, I don't know what this is all about. I don't know what that has to do with these girls you say are missing. Are we done here?"

Vic could tell she was avoiding the photographs. He tapped his finger above the row. "You wanted photographs, here they are."

Anger coursed through her eyes and he watched her fight it. After a moment she bent toward the faces. He could almost see her counting to herself, trying to figure how long she needed to look at them to come across as giving it an honest try. She made it to six seconds.

She sat up. "You need to understand. I worked at Bare Essentials for less than two years. It was a stupid job babysitting a bunch of stupid and mostly screwed up girls. I was glad to get out of there."

Vic leaned toward her. "But you made a few bucks out of it. I mean, tricking out the girls to bachelor parties and stuff without telling management."

Cora stood up so fast her chair bumped the wall. "We're done. Get out of here."

Vic stayed in his seat. "You need to understand something. I interviewed everyone who filed a missing person's report. Your name came up every time. Every one of the missing women talked about you, your name was everywhere. You're the common denominator."

"Goddamned right I was. I was their boss."

"So you do know them."

"Sure. Fine. Now, I'm supposed to be somewhere. I can't do this right now."

Vic took a long look at the half empty glass of wine, letting her see him stare. "Is that a fact?"

"Yes. That would be done and I'd be on my way out if you hadn't shown up."

"But we aren't done here."

Cora folded her arms over her chest. "Okay. All right. Tomorrow."

Vic rose. "What time? And I'm assuming your memory will be better tomorrow."

She grabbed the back of her chair with both hands and for a split second Vic thought she might hit him with it. He held her gaze. "I get you don't want to talk about it. Who would? But you knew these women and I guarantee you know more about it than you think. But they left behind families. I want to know what made them go missing."

Her hands flexed for an instant and her eyes shifted, as if she had just spotted the exit in a burning building. She relaxed. "Fine. Tomorrow. Seven o'clock. But I don't guarantee I'll remember anything. Like I said, a lot of girls came and went. There was a lot of turnover. End of story."

"One more thing." Vic collected the photographs from the table, slid them into the envelope and pulled out another. Dannie. He held it up for her to see. "How about her?"

"No." the word was so quick it could have been part of Vic's question. "Door is that way." She pointed.

Vic returned the photograph to the envelope, crossed to the front door, opened it and stepped outside. Once he was off the porch he cut across the grass to the car in the driveway, aware of her watching him through the window inset in the front door. Standing behind the car he fished out his cell phone, and, taking his time, lined up a shot of the car's license plate. He took a flash photo, stared at the result, then slowly lined up another shot. Finished, he gave her a quick smile and wave as he turned for the sidewalk.

He slid into his car, convinced Cora Stills knew something. It worried him. He'd realized years earlier that when he interviewed witnesses and suspects they tended to fall into three groups: the ones who talked his ear off, the liars, and the ones who didn't want to talk. The talkers were usually innocent, and if they weren't, often accidentally admitted their crime. The ones who lied were almost always guilty and it was a matter of untangling their falsehoods. But the ones who didn't want to talk always worried him the most. Usually it meant they were stalling, that they needed time to cover their tracks or get away. He started the car, wondering which it was with Cora Stills.

CHAPTER 34

Vic was in a river. It was black, the current swift, and he couldn't breathe. Again and again things bumped against him as they swirled past, he couldn't identify them, he only knew they were different things, branches, flotsam. The suck of the current drew him faster and faster downstream, his breath aching in his chest. He felt himself giving in to the pull of the current, accepting it, glad for the blackness, to being drawn away. Something turned inside him and the ache in his lungs was a friend. He felt himself give up. It was enough. He'd done enough.

The voice was clear, the tone like a bell. "Dad?"

He wrenched awake, Dannie's voice in his ears, the way she got his attention before she asked a question. He gagged air into his lungs, sat upright on the bed, and swung his feet to the floor. His whole body shuddered. He grabbed the sheets in his fists, breathing, willing his heart back into a normal beat. The tightness fell from his body. Somewhere in his mind, the tone of Dannie's question lingered like the last spoken word of someone leaving.

He stood up, swaying slightly. It was almost four a.m.by the red numbers of his bedside clock. He padded through the darkness of his bedroom, the only light the orange glow of the outside streetlight. In the bathroom he soaked his face with cold water. Back sitting on the bed he waited, wondering if he could sleep again.

He already knew the answer. He lifted his Glock from his bedside table and weighed it in his hand. Brushed the trigger with his finger. He felt as if he had crossed something, reached another place. He didn't understand how or why. He rose, slid on a pair of sweatpants, lumbered downstairs through the darkness and sat facing the dining room wall. The night hid the words on the documents, all he could see were pale rectangular shapes. He waited, for a voice, for something. Slowly, the memory rose of the times Anne had dragged him to church when Dannie was small. The waiting was the same.

And yet.

This time it was different. He sensed something just past what he could see, feel or hear. Something was there. Curled among those pale shapes of the documents. Something living.

The last lingering note of Dannie's voice seeped away. But it wasn't just her voice that faded, it was an entire world, a way of speaking, a philosophy of life. A full breath of memories.

A restlessness rose in him. He didn't understand if it had to do with Gretchen Stoll, or Dannie. Or both. It waited with him, searching for whatever was among the documents. He wondered what Gretchen felt when an envelope of cash was pressed into her palm. He wondered what had gone through Dannie's mind the instant she disappeared.

By seven Vic was back at his desk, his energy deep and rushed. The night shift detectives were shouting and calling to one another a few rows over. None of the lights were on in the offices. He worked through his e-mails, searching.

At 7:30 Kevin passed him, headed to his desk. Vic gave him a few minutes, then rolled down to his cube on his chair.

"Kevin," he called, as he got close, to give him time to close any computer windows he didn't want Vic to see. "How's your schedule?" He looked into Kevin's cube.

Kevin had his e-mail program open on his computer. Vic noticed his paleness, as if he'd had too many beers the night before.

"Good," Kevin said, a bit too quickly, as if he felt the need to make the point.

"I could use some help. You know when Liz had you write up our last report, that part about the house that belonged to Gretchen Stoll on the South Side?"

"Yeah. Husband said he didn't know about it."

"Yeah, well, we'll see. Since we found him in it. But here's the deal. I want to canvass the neighborhood. See if anyone spotted anyone going in or out, and maybe we'll even get lucky with some video. I want that before we interview Gretchen Stoll's husband. If he's been seen going in or coming out earlier than the last couple of days, I want to catch him in the lie."

Kevin's eyes widened. "Okay."

It occurred to Vic that Kevin might never have run a canvass before. "I'll talk to Sergeant Wroblewski, he handles that kind of stuff. I'll tell him what we're after. Just do what he says and you'll be fine. He'll get you the manpower."

Kevin sat up straight. "Great! When do we do it?"

"Soon as we can. I'd like you to start today, if you can. Remember, the key thing is that we need to know who might have gone in or out of Gretchen's house. The house address is in the report you did."

"Sure."

"And one other thing. After you do that, can you go back to the courthouse? Remember those case files you went through? I had another thought. Can you go through all the ones where the suspect either got off or got sentenced, and tell me the location of their crimes. I want to know the neighborhoods where the people were arrested."

"Yeah, that won't take long."

"Thanks." Vic rolled his chair back to his desk and sent Sergeant Wroblewski an e-mail, copying Kevin. When he looked up Liz was hanging up her leather jacket. Anger radiated from her.

"Hey," Vic said. As he did Kevin shot down the aisle, struggling into his sport coat. Liz watched him go and then turned to him for an explanation.

"I sent him to canvass around Gretchen's house on the South Side."

"You trying to teach him how to actually do police work?" She dropped heavily into her chair.

"Never hurts."

She stared at him for a moment and then smiled. "But it does get him out of the office."

"Oh yeah. I also asked him to check some of Gretchen's case files. If we're lucky we get two days."

"Vic, sometimes you're a genius."

"Never feels like it."

"And we talk to Crush today about our boy Thad?"

"Yes we do." Vic's phone rang. Liz rolled her eyes and turned to her computer. When Vic answered the phone Officer Pokorny's voice came over the line.

"Just thought you might be interested," he said without preamble.

"Depends what it is."

"You remember last time we talked you mentioned that person out here you interviewed? The one with the gun? Lily Bauer?"

"Yeah."

"So. Last night their barn burned down."

Vic sat back. "No shit. Anyone hurt?"

"Nah. But the fire chief says it's arson. They're gonna have an inspector out there today."

"Probably just a coincidence."

"Yeah." Pokorny laughed. "The leprechauns did it."

CHAPTER 35

It was ten o'clock before Eva could arrange for Vic and Liz to meet Crush. At 9:45 Liz leaned back, her face still drawn and her gaze distracted.

"Anything new before we talk to Crush?"

"No." Vic rose slowly. He'd twinged something in his back while working out the night before and every time he stood up or sat down it reminded him. Liz rose with him and they walked to Crush's office in silence. Liz still seemed distracted, the feeling of it radiated from her.

Eva waved them inside Crush's empty office and they sat down facing the desk. Liz stared out of the window. Thirty seconds passed before they heard Crush shouting at someone and a moment later he appeared in the doorway.

"You guys," he said, walking around his desk. He didn't sit down. His shaved head gleamed in the fluorescent lights and Vic wondered if he'd had it waxed.

Liz didn't say anything and Vic realized she was leaving it up to him. "Had something big happen with Gretchen Stoll." He glanced at Liz but she was still staring out of the window, and Crush was studying her behavior as if he didn't understand her. "Do you want the long or short version?"

Crush snapped his head in Vic's direction. "Short."

"Looks like she was taking money to mess up her cases so people could get off."

Crush blinked and lowered himself into his chair. "Long

version," he croaked.

Vic walked him through Thad's confession and Gretchen's reputation among the public defenders for having her cases collapse. "I think she kept her eyes open for likely candidates, I'm guessing people who had no trouble making bail. Then she fished for money. If it got so far that they talked her fee and the person didn't pay, then she took them to court and made sure they had the book thrown at them by the judge. That was her leverage. I'm guessing she told people that if they ratted her out she would kill any chance of parole. But that's a guess. We're going through the cases that collapsed and the cases that went to court now. Kevin is doing it," he added, to make sure Crush knew they had involved him.

"But you only have the one case." Crush had trouble speaking, as if his mouth was dry.

"So far. I want your permission to depose the people whose cases fell apart and see if they fess up."

Crush raised the palm of his hand toward them. "No. Don't do anything yet. Marioni needs to know."

"I figured, but we could start setting up the depositions now. No need to wait."

"I said you wait!" Crush shouted. He looked distracted. Vic could see him doing the mental arithmetic about how the DA's office and the County Commissioner might react to their findings. "Jesus," he said to no one in particular, "we were just doing them a favor by helping out. This isn't even our jurisdiction."

"Makes you wonder why he wanted us involved." Vic realized he was enjoying himself.

Crush slammed the palm of his hand flat on the desk. "Don't go there. We need to talk to Marioni, today if we can. You do not work on the case until we do. He needs to call the shots." He glanced at Liz. "Liz, you solid on this?"

Liz didn't answer until she turned her face from the window. "Yes," she said finally. "I saw the same evidence Vic did. The guy who came in yesterday had no reason to lie. He seemed relieved to tell us about it."

"That means he'll go to jail. He understood that?"

Vic shrugged. "He knows it's possible. His mother may end up there as well. But we read him his rights and offered six ways to Sunday to bring in a lawyer. He wanted no part of it."

"Shit. Okay, I'll get us over to see Marioni. All three of us go. Vic, you'll do the update. He needs to hear it from you."

Vic nodded, knowing that Crush didn't want to give the bad news to Marioni himself. Rule number one of getting promoted: don't deliver bad news. Vic stood. "Call us when you want to go over."

"Yeah." Crush waved his hand in a distracted way and Vic left, Liz shuffling behind him.

"That went well," Vic said when they were back at their desks.

"You really think Marioni knew about it?"

Vic lowered himself gingerly into his seat, feeling the twinge in his back. "Beats me, but he never really explained why he wanted us on the case. Maybe he thought we wouldn't look that hard since we were doing him a favor. But I would sure like to know."

An hour later they were sitting in Marioni's office, Vic explaining what they had found. Marioni's hands were on his desk, his fingers interlocked, thumbs tapping together. When Vic finished he glanced at Crush, intrigued that his skull could shine even in Marioni's dim office.

Marioni blinked a couple of times. "You guys dug in."

Vic shrugged. He wasn't sure what to say and he had a feeling that Marioni made the comment to buy himself time to think. All he knew was that he wanted to get at it, to start the depositions and uncover whatever Gretchen Stoll was up to.

Marioni's thumbs stopped moving and he looked at Crush. "I appreciate what your team has done here."

"I thought you needed to hear this as soon as we discovered it." Crush gave Marioni an apologetic smile.

Marioni nodded. "Thanks for that." He turned to Vic.

"We'd better take it from here. I'll get my detectives on it. Just send over your notes and anything related to the case. And I don't have to tell you, none of this gets out, right? I need my guys to work it before everyone and his brother finds out."

Adrenaline tingled in Vic's arms and legs and he started speaking before he could stop himself. "Are you kidding? We're into this now. We know the leads to follow." Vic guessed that by 'everyone and his brother' Marioni meant the media.

Marioni sat rock still, watching him. His hair was slicked back and it made him look streamlined somehow. His eyes had narrowed, as if there was too much sun.

Vic couldn't let it rest. "I need to ask a question."

Marioni unlocked his fingers and showed him his palms in a go ahead gesture.

"When you asked us to investigate you said you needed an objective third party investigating. You need it now more than ever. So why take us off?"

Crush jumped in before Marioni could say anything. "Vic, the DA gets to make this call." A tinge of desperation buoyed his voice.

"I'm just saying," Vic said. "We already have leads to follow."

Marioni rose and walked around his desk. He sat on the front edge, directly in front of Vic, one knee jutted toward him. Concern shrouded his face, but Vic saw right through it. "I appreciate that Vic, but this is home cooking. We need to take care of it. You can understand that, right? If you want to help, pass along your notes and case files and keep this confidential." Before Vic could answer he shifted so his body faced Liz. "All good Liz? You guys did outstanding work."

It was as if Liz woke up, but again, before she could respond Marioni popped upright and stuck out his hand for Vic to shake. Vic rose to take his hand, and the moment he did Marioni clamped his other hand down on top of their handshake and guided him toward the door. "Outstanding work," he said, and glanced back at Liz, who was following them, her eyes blank.

"You too, Liz." With a quick pump and flick of his wrist Marioni propelled Vic through the doorway. When Vic turned around to argue Marioni was guiding Crush through the doorway with a sharp slap on his back. "Great work, Commander. Outstanding team." Moments later the door thumped shut and the three of them were standing in the hallway. None of the ADAs or support staff noticed them.

"You guys got it?" Crush asked. A half smile twitched on his lips and Vic saw relief in his eyes.

"Oh yeah," Liz said, as if she was waking up. Vic couldn't bring himself to say anything but followed them as they crossed to the office door. As they approached it swung open and Dave Norbert stepped in and shifted sideways to avoid running into them.

"Vic," he said, watching Liz carefully. He kept moving, across the offices to Marioni's door.

"I guess we know what that's about," Vic said. He felt displaced, as if he'd been angry and now wasn't, but didn't know what to do with the space where the anger had been.

"Not our problem." Crush sounded almost happy. "Best scenario for us. Marioni takes care of his own business." Crush led them through the door.

Thirty minutes later Vic was back standing behind his desk, staring down at it.

From across the aisle Liz said, "So we're off the case."

"Yeah. Send copies of everything to Marioni." He drifted down the aisle and checked Kevin's cube. Empty. When he looked at Liz again she held his gaze.

"But keep the originals here?"

Inside him, Vic felt the same restlessness he had felt the night before. It tried to climb up his throat. "Goddamn right," he said. He walked back to his desk.

Liz sighed. "You aren't going to stop, are you?"

Vic lightly punched the flimsy wall of his cube. "No."

"Crush told you to stop."

"Yeah." He turned to her. "And I always listen to Crush.

You know what's going to happen, right?"

Liz's mouth was tight. "Sure I do. Nothing at all."

"Exactly. Nothing. And then after the election they'll re-organize the DA's office and call it a day. It's bullshit."

"And Gretchen's dead."

"Damn right. Whoever killed Gretchen is on that list Kevin put together. So I'm going through it again one asshole at a time. And I'm gonna depose those people. One way or another. And I know exactly how to start and which lawyer I'm asking for help. You can walk away from it if you want."

Liz's laugh could have shredded metal. "Screw you. I'll print out the list."

"And we need to find something on Gretchen's husband. Blow up his alibi. Mark freaking Stoll. He's got less spine than Crush."

"If he's got something out there we'll find it."

"But we do that tomorrow. I got something much better to do right now."

CHAPTER 36

Before he left Vic shot an e-mail to Hanna, Gretchen Stoll's colleague and the first of their interviews to identify problems with Gretchen's workload. He remembered her as young and disillusioned with the public defenders office. He bet himself that her disgust with the office would motivate her to uncover Gretchen's corruption. She'd be the perfect person to depose Gretchen's clients.

But he needed a back-up plan in case she said no.

The road to the North Hills was choked with traffic. At each red light he talked to his windshield, reliving the conversation with Marioni and throwing out ways to keep the investigation going without him knowing. It didn't work. Every scenario ended with Marioni discovering his investigation and Crush landing on him harder than an aircraft carrier. He didn't really care, but he didn't want to drag down Liz as well. Then, somewhere along the endless string of red traffic lights, he remembered Dave Norbert passing them on his way to Marioni's office. He slid out his phone and dug through his contacts until he found Norbert's number.

He was about to press dial but stopped, breathing slowly, and tossed the phone onto the front seat. He needed to be calm when he called, and he needed leverage. Two red lights later another thought came to him and he scooped up the phone and pressed dial.

"Figured you might call," Norbert said, as the third ring

disappeared into an electronic black hole.

"I'm guessing Marioni wants you on point to investigate Gretchen."

"Something like that."

"So we send you our files?"

"I'm writing the official request now."

"Did he tell you to slow walk it?"

The line stayed silent as Vic finally pulled away from a traffic light that didn't have another directly in front of it. He accelerated, the road opening in front of him. Carefully, he said, "C'mon, Dave. What's going on? You and I both know that sleeping with Gretchen means you shouldn't be investigating her death. Officially you're a person of interest. So start talking. If Marioni finds out he'll bounce you out of the DAs office. You know it and I know it. You'll be lucky to work security at Kennywood Park. You work with me and maybe I see past telling him."

"Asshole. And what about your partner? Liz? She'd tell Marioni just to piss me off."

"She'll go along with this. But you have to play ball."

Silence, but somehow the air between them was electric. Vic smiled for what felt like the first time in a week.

"Fine," Norbert said. "Yeah. Investigate but go slow."

"Nope," Vic shot back. "You're going to get it in gear. You're gonna do exactly what I tell you to do and keep it moving. The first thing we need are depositions from some of the people Gretchen represented. Marioni told you Gretchen was taking money to make cases go away, right?"

"He said that rumor was out there. He also said it was just a rumor. He said that like three times."

Vic shook his head. "As in make damn sure you don't find it to be true."

"If I was reading between his words, yeah. But if I schedule a deposition he'll see it on our system and tell me to drop it. That's a no go."

Vic gripped the steering wheel. He hadn't considered

that. "Then let me worry about them. I might know someone who'll do it. I just need to talk to them first. I'll call you tomorrow and give you a name."

"Jesus. Who died and made you god?"

"You did, the second you hound dogged Gretchen. So quit complaining. We'll get this done and you keep your job. Good?"

"What the hell happens if it turns out she was taking money? You go to Marioni with it?"

"Probably the County Commissioner. But one step at a time."

Vic slowed as the road split and he followed the exit ramp north.

"Fine," Norbert spat into the phone just as it went dead.

Vic dropped his phone onto the front seat. A rush of energy shot through him and he laughed out loud and banged the steering wheel with his palm. It might just work. He scooped up the phone and dialed another number.

"Officer Pokorny," came the reply, a few rings later.

"Pokorny, it's Vic Lenoski. I'm headed out to Lily Bauer's place. I want to see that barn. You around or busy?"

"You want to see a burned down barn?"

"I want to ask Lily Bauer some questions about her son. Remember Gretchen Stoll put him in jail. The whole situation struck me as weird when I was up there."

"I can meet you."

"I was hoping you would."

Vic hung up and dropped his phone on the front seat again. He didn't know what to make of Lily Bauer yet, but the way she answered her door with a gun, how her boyfriend worried about the meeting and the barn fire immediately afterwards was a lot to swallow.

When Vic pulled up in front of Lily Bauer's house Pokorny's cruiser was already there. Vic spotted him standing near the charred remains of the barn, staring at what was left of the foundation. Vic parked and Pokorny turned and waited for him, his arms folded.

"Still smells," Vic said, when he drew close.

"Yeah. Fire inspector said the origin points were far corner and next to the door. Flames went up the sides and met at the roof."

"Truck wasn't inside?"

"You know about that? Yeah, Denny Halpin usually parks his truck inside but that night he didn't. And you'll like this, although I don't know if it matters." Pokorny paused, and Vic knew he had found something. "Accelerants were the same as Gretchen Stoll's house."

"Interesting, but those are pretty available." Vic studied his profile. "You compared the two reports, huh?"

"Seemed logical. She knew Gretchen Stoll."

Vic liked Pokorny all the more. He turned and studied the remains of the barn. Charred debris littered the scorched earth of the barn floor. He pointed to the far end of the barn, where the blackened corner of a concrete pad stuck out from underneath some debris. "He had a real floor on that part?"

"Yeah. I thought that was different too. Halpin said he had a workroom in there and needed a concrete floor for his table saw and some other tools."

"Pretty big for that."

"Yep."

Vic wiped his mouth with the back of his hand. "You guys arresting him?"

"For burning down his own barn on his own property? We might get him for destroying the barn without a permit, but I'm not even sure that would stick. Chief is chewing on it."

Vic headed for the house, Pokorny beside him. As he did Denny Halpin's pick-up ground up the driveway, its wheels kicking up dust and gravel. They all reached the front door at the same time.

"What the hell do you guys want now?" Halpin asked. His chest strained his t-shirt and his fists were clenched.

"Came to talk to Lily Bauer," Vic said evenly. "Pity about the barn."

Denny glanced at the barn as if he'd forgotten it was there. "It was old."

"Nowhere to park your truck now," Vic pointed out.

"Why the hell would you care?"

Vic was interested in why Denny was so antagonistic. As he thought about it the front door opened. "Denny," Lily Bauer called. "Don't get worked up. Again."

Vic heard a message in the way she said it, a warning maybe. Today Lily had changed the sweatshirt for a red checked cowboy shirt and blue jeans that clung to her curves. With her hair pulled back Vic thought she looked younger.

"Ms. Bauer, I was wondering if I could ask you a couple more questions about Gretchen Stoll?"

She stared at Vic, her brown eyes set. Vic couldn't read her thoughts, but from the set of her mouth he knew she wasn't happy. "About John, my son?"

"Yeah. I was hoping you could clarify a thing or two. Shouldn't take long."

She stepped aside and led them into the living room. As the men crowded into the small room she remained standing, her arms folded over her chest. She stared at Vic, waiting. Vic glanced at the table where he had placed Lily's pistol on his last trip to make sure it was gone. Only the framed photograph sat on the tabletop.

He turned back to Lily. "I was wondering when John has a chance for parole?"

Lily tilted her head. "You came all the way out here to ask me that?"

"I was wondering what you were told."

"Stoll said we'd be notified. I know it isn't for a few years yet."

"Okay. And I guess I have another question." He hesitated, wondering where it would take him. "Did Gretchen Stoll every suggest to you that a cash payment might lighten your son's term, or make it go away completely?"

Vic felt the corners of the room tighten. Denny shifted

position. Lily's eyes didn't move from Vic's face.

"No," she said finally. "Why?"

"Just wanted to ask the question." He sensed tension between Lily and Denny, but wasn't sure what to do with it. "And you'd be willing to state that under oath?"

Lily loosened her posture and a small smile crossed her lips. "Sure. Why not?"

Vic watched her for a second, then glanced at Denny. He too had his arms folded over his chest, but his shoulders were tense and his eyes narrow as he stared into a corner of the room. It was as if he didn't want to see any of them.

"We may ask you to do that," Vic said slowly. He was disappointed. "We'll let you know. I appreciate you answering the question directly."

She shrugged. "Sure."

"I guess that's it," Vic said. "We'll get going."

Denny relaxed, the tension sliding out of his shoulders. As Pokorny turned to leave the room Vic stepped aside to give him space. Closer to the table, he glanced at the framed photograph and stopped dead. He turned back to Lily.

"I saw that photograph last time I was here," he said.

"Yeah. So?"

"How do you know Cora Stills?"

Lily glanced at the photograph as if it might answer for her. At the same moment Vic knew that was why he'd recognized Cora when he met her. He'd seen her face in the photograph, he just hadn't connected it.

"We used to work together," Lily said.

"Where was that?"

"Bare Essentials. She was my boss for a while, but we got along. We partied sometimes."

Denny turned sharply and left the room. A second later the front door slammed.

"You were dancing there?" Vic asked carefully. His heart beat faster.

Lily dropped her hands to her hips and pushed out her

chest. "With this you think I wouldn't be?"

Pokorny backed up a step but Vic held his ground. "I saw Cora last night. Going to see her again."

"Good for you." She held her pose, her head tilted back, as if she was looking down on him from a stage.

In the silence Vic couldn't think of another question. "Okay. We'll leave you to it." He pointed toward the barn. "Too bad about the fire." He searched his memory, trying to find a way to lighten the mood. "What the heck is Denny going to do with his table saw?" He smiled so she would know it was a joke. He didn't know why he felt like he needed to make the effort.

"In his dreams he has a table saw," Lily said. "We can't afford something like that, even if we still had a barn to put it in."

Pokorny stiffened and Vic knew he had caught the inconsistency as well. He cut Pokorny off before he could say anything. "Thanks, Ms. Bauer. We'll get out of your hair." He turned and grabbed Pokorny's elbow to move him.

As soon as the front door closed behind them Pokorny said, "That's not what Denny said." Vic scanned for Denny, who wasn't in sight. His truck sat beside Pokorny's cruiser.

"Right," Vic said, turning back to him. "But we don't know enough yet. Never let them know we've caught them in a lie until you're ready."

Pokorny was quiet for a moment. "I get that."

But Vic was thinking about Cora Stills, and how her photograph ended up with Lily Bauer. It was something else to ask Cora.

"And anyway, the way things are going we'll be back here," Vic said to Pokorny. "I guarantee it."

CHAPTER 37

As Vic drove back to Pittsburgh his phone rang and Liz's name splashed on his screen.

"What's up?" he asked.

"Got him."

"Who?"

"Mark Stoll. Remember we needed something that put him outside the office so we could get a warrant for the card swipe data? We got him."

"He wasn't at work when he said he was?" Vic slowed for yet another red light.

"Not the whole time. No phone data yet, but we got a credit card transaction outside the office. Guess where?"

"Gretchen's house on the South Side?"

"Close enough. After he told us he was in the office all day and didn't know about the house until the day we found him. So I set up an interview. He's coming in tomorrow. And guess what? Now he wants a lawyer with him."

Vic glanced around the stopped cars beside him. He could tell from the way the driver on his right was concentrating straight ahead that he'd identified Vic as a cop. "Good. Let's hit him with everything. How he lied to us about being at work. The cash in the metal box the fire chief found, the receipt that says he knew about Gretchen's South Side house after he told us he didn't."

"Already got it lined up."

"Good, and I talked to Norbert. Marioni did tell him to slow-walk the investigation into Gretchen. I made him agree to keep it on speed."

"How'd you do that?"

"I'm a charming guy."

"Oh sure, that's what everyone says about you. What do I need to know? With you there's always a leg trap in the middle of your deals."

"Yeah, so, it would be good if you could forget about that whole Norbert sleeping with Gretchen thing, at least for a while."

The phone went silent, apart from the sounds of their office: someone in the distance calling to someone else, a telephone ringing.

"You want me to forget he planted evidence as well?" Liz's voice was tight.

"No. I just need you to look the other way on the affair for a while."

"He shouldn't even be investigating her."

"Right, but it's better this way. We watch what he investigates, and we'll see if he skips something. He'll give himself away by what he doesn't investigate. We just watch for what he does different."

"Jesus, you got more honey on your tongue than the devil. You remember he never gave us an alibi?"

The traffic light switched to green and Vic pressed the accelerator. "Fair enough. So we ask about that. Make him cough it up."

"And then we check it."

"And then we check it."

The silence stretched out again. "Okay. I can live with that." The tension left Liz's voice. "How about the depositions?"

"Yeah, you remember that young lawyer we interviewed right at the beginning of going through the public defender's office? Young woman with country club hair? Hanna?"

"Yeah, every time I see a woman's hair shining like that I

want to rub dirt on it. Your Mrs. Monahan always had that hair."

"Right. But Hanna was the first one to talk about Gretchen's workload being funky, told us she was called Magic Mary, and she is totally disgusted with the public defenders office. I bet she goes for something like this in about one second. She'll probably use it to find another job. But she agreed to meet me for coffee in about half an hour."

"She can set up the depositions?"

"That's what I want to ask her." Vic glanced at the dashboard clock. "When are you leaving today?"

"Soon. I got something with Jayvon I gotta work through."

Vic fought down the urge to ask what. It was the first time he could remember her saying Jayvon's name related to leaving early. "Okay. Good luck with that. I'll see you tomorrow and we go after Mark Stoll."

"Sounds good."

Vic slowed at a traffic light. Ahead rose a steep hill. On the other side of it, he knew, was an adult store immediately followed by a church. The ramp onto Route 279 followed that. Somehow, sequentially, the order made sense to him at that moment: sex, church for the guilt and then a quick exit. It made him think about Lily Bauer saying Gretchen never asked for money to free her son. He decided it felt like the truth, it was something in how quickly she said it and how she laughed at the same time, as if the whole idea was stupid. But the photo of her with Cora Stills was odd. He didn't know how, or why. He decided to ask Cora about it when he saw her. He thought about that as the church slid past and the exit onto Route 279 appeared. He guessed that Lily would call Cora Stills and tell her he'd spotted the photograph. He didn't know how that changed anything, but it was something to watch for when he talked to Cora.

CHAPTER 38

Hanna was waiting for Vic when he arrived at the Starbucks in the William Penn hotel. She had some kind of drink in a large, see-through plastic cup in front of her on the table, but she was intent on her phone, typing with her thumbs. She nodded to Vic without slowing and with one eye still on her screen. Vic pointed to the cash register and she nodded, her eyes locking back onto her phone. When Vic joined her she placed it next to her drink and waited.

Vic settled into the chair across from her. "I appreciate you meeting me."

She smiled, and Vic was surprised at how it made her look younger and perhaps a bit vulnerable. "Ah. I think I owe you one after I unloaded on you guys during my interview. I don't know what got into me."

"Or maybe what caught up to you?"

"Yeah, something like that. How's the investigation going?"

Vic guessed she already knew how the DA had warned them off the case, but he liked the way she played dumb to get information. "Well, as you know, he put us off the case."

She didn't bother acting surprised. "Makes me wonder why."

Vic liked that as well. She didn't care he'd seen through her, she just kept plowing ahead. He sipped his coffee. "Yeah. See that's the thing. She was a different type, your Gretchen Stoll."

Hanna smiled again. "So don't keep me waiting." She dropped her eyes and raised them again. "And how do I fit in?" She said it with exaggerated importance, making a joke out of it.

"I guess I have a favor to ask."

"On the case the DA told you to stop investigating?"

"Exactly that one."

Hanna sipped her drink. "Yeah, I heard that about you. Not a guy who stops. Kind of a hardass."

"Depends who you talk to." Vic thought of Anne's sister and her accusations he wasn't a real cop.

Hanna lifted her cup and swirled the ice cubes around. "I only talk to the right people, so you'd better give me some background."

Vic found himself relaxing. He liked her, it didn't matter how old she was. She was prettier than spring, knew it, and he liked how she just charged forward, without any side trips.

"Background it is," he heard himself say, knowing he'd made the decision to ask her to help. "So Gretchen had some side deals. Let's just say she was a little different."

"Like?"

"At least one lover and an extra house. But that isn't the main problem." He waited for Hanna to absorb his words, but she didn't seem fazed.

"Okay." Her tone said get on with it.

"I suspect she was taking money to blow up cases, get some clients off."

Hanna sat back. "Jesus. No wonder the DA took you off the case. Election year."

"About right."

"Proof?"

"A guy who got off came in and spilled the beans. Apparently his mother paid Gretchen. DUI, long story, it boils down to either he wants his father to like him or he's trying to do the right thing. I'll give him the benefit of the doubt that it's a bit of both. We taped the interview, he refused a lawyer, we played it by the book. I'm sure a good lawyer would argue coercion, but I don't think my partner and I said more than ten words on the tape. The kid wasn't lying."

"How many cases?"

"Tough to say, but I would guess at least seven in the last two years. But it gets more interesting."

Hanna grinned. "I'll bet it does."

Vic realized she was enjoying herself, that she was hooked.

"Gretchen lost almost every case she passed to trial and her defendants got hit with massive jail sentences. Just a theory, but I think that if she offered the payout to someone and they couldn't come up with the money, then she took the case to trial and made sure they lost in a big way."

"Why wouldn't the defendant countersue, charge that she asked money?"

"I don't know, but I did talk to a bunch of families who lost a relative to one of those trials, and every one asked if Gretchen's death might mean earlier parole for their jailbird family member. That's the only thing I have."

"Oh yeah, I get that." She grinned again, showing perfect white teeth. "They teach us that early. To get people to plea deal, we tell them we'll get them an early parole opportunity. Minimize their sentence kind of thing. She could have turned that around and said if they came after her, she would make sure the jailbird never saw a parole board."

"Could she do that?"

"Not easily, but most people don't know that. They're talking to her, at that point she represents the entire judicial system, as far as they're concerned. People have no clue how the law works. But the whole thing is risky as hell. And who has the money to pay her off? I mean these are people who need to use a public defender."

"Right, I thought the same thing. But the DUI kid came from a wealthy family. I bet she picked her spots, that's why there's so few of them. But if a defendant comes from a large family they could tap relatives and raise the money. If the parents own a house they get a second mortgage. There's ways. The DUI kid said the payment was fifteen thousand dollars, but I bet that was higher than usual because she knew he came from a wealthy family. But that's not out of reach for some people if it gets their child out of jail."

"God. That makes me sick." Hanna pushed her drink away and sat back, her gaze on the pastries in the glass case next to the cash register. Vic could tell from her blank look that she was thinking and not seeing them.

"So that's where you come in," Vic said quietly.

Her eyes snapped back into focus. Again she waited.

"My partner and I interviewed both the people whose cases fell apart and the ones that went to trial in the last eighteen months. But we did it fast and to begin with we didn't know the right questions to ask. We can't do that any more because the DA shook us off the case. He's worried about the story of the payments coming out and he's asked his investigators to slow walk it. But I still want to get whoever killed Gretchen Stoll. To me, the families on those lists are the best bet, although we need to work the husband some more."

"Wow." Vic saw a conspiratorial gleam in her eyes. "But you still haven't told me what you want me to do."

Vic leaned forward. "Depose those same people. Get them under oath to say if Gretchen approached them for a bribe, or not, and if they paid her."

Hanna shook her head. "Doesn't make sense. Deposing those people would take weeks, just for the set up and arguing with their lawyers. They could refuse. But this is what I don't get. You could interview them from the point of view of Gretchen's murder, not the corruption. Why don't you do that?"

Vic sat back, impressed and annoyed.

"Oh I get it." Hanna sat back with a laugh. "Your commander went along with the DA. Told you guys not to investigate the murder, either."

"Yep. Baby went out with the bath water."

"But Vic Lenoski has no plans to stop."

"Seems like a waste not to keep going."

"You are a piece of work." Hanna crossed her arms over her chest, watching him. Her eyes were merry.

Vic matched her posture. "So tell me, are you happy just doing plea deals. Or do you want to get it right? Actually defend someone who needs it?"

Hanna didn't move and the gleam vanished from her eyes. "You play hard ball, Vic Lenoski. I heard you lost your daughter a little over a year ago."

Something thick and aching shifted inside him and anger rose into his throat. "Yeah. What's that got to do with this?"

"I can play hard ball too."

"I never doubted it. So what are you saying?"

"I'm the youngest woman in the public defender's office. This isn't some weird thing about you thinking I'm your lost daughter and I'll do what you ask?"

"Screw you. It's about what you said in our interview. I took the chance that you'd want to do something good for the public defenders office."

"By helping out a rogue cop working a case he's been told not to, a case the DA himself took you off?"

Anger jumped into Vic's throat. "There's a difference between bitching about what's wrong with the public defender's office and actually doing something about it. Which person are you? Maybe it's time you picked a side."

Hanna watched him, her entire body still. Vic realized he had hunched down as he talked, almost moved his shoulders into a boxing position. He forced himself to open them up, to sit upright again. The anger was still in his throat. Hanna blinked and the corners of her mouth twitched. She picked up her cup and sipped her coffee. "You know," she said, watching him steadily, "this might be the best cup of coffee I've had in two years."

Vic waited.

"Okay, here's what I can do. Forget depositions. They take

too long and I need to get other lawyers involved, stenographers, you name it, the DA will know what's up before I get out of bed tomorrow. What I can do, on my own time, is visit some of these people and have a conversation with them. Tell them I'm from the public defenders office. Get them on tape. If there's something there I'll know within a day or two. We can use the tapes as evidence to get the depositions."

Vic's throat loosened. "That's a start."

Hanna leaned forward suddenly. "And you need to understand something. Me bitching about the public defenders office when I talked to you last time, that's not a Pittsburgh thing. That's a national thing. I've got friends from law school in public defender's offices in the Bronx and St. Louis. Same thing everywhere. I saw your partner get angry in that meeting. She gets it. The people least able to afford a defense are the worst served. Me doing this isn't going to solve any of that, no matter how noble you make it sound. This is my point. The public defender's offices," she held up her thumb and forefinger an eighth of an inch apart, "are this far from being useless. We cannot have Gretchens in any of those offices doing what she did. We can't afford to be worse, because it's the difference between being functional and actually damaging people. So I'll do it for that reason. Not because you asked, but because we can't let it get worse. That and the DA and his elections piss me off."

"I'll take that." To his assessment of her, Vic added tougher than cat gut.

She half smiled. "And I bet you just happen to have a list of the people to interview in your coat pocket."

Vic slid an envelope from inside his jacket and placed it on the table. "I wouldn't want to let you down."

Hanna gave him a small smile and slid it into her large leather shoulder bag.

Vic leaned over the table. "None of this is personal, Hanna. It's exactly what you just said. But there was no reason to bring my daughter into it. Somebody burned Gretchen to death, even if she was taking money. I want my hand on that person's shoulder."

"That's exactly why I brought up your daughter. To see if you could handle it." She blinked. "I'm sorry about that, Vic. But I had to be sure you weren't some loose canon, that you were buttoned down and on target. I'm taking a risk as much as you are."

Vic smiled at her. "Yeah. But you kind of want to take that risk, don't you?"

Hanna stood up. "And that, Detective Lenoski, is none of your damn business."

"My card's in the envelope. Call me when you have something."

She smiled at him. "You can count on it."

"Boom."

She cocked her head, staring at him.

"Not a loose canon. Starting gun."

She turned on her heel, but Vic caught a grin on her face as she did.

CHAPTER 39

I t was just before seven when Vic parked on the street outside Cora's house. He tightened as he cut the car's ignition.
The street was doing it to him again, Dannie's street, he
thought, for all the days she had walked its length on her way
to school. He let himself out of the car, checked that he still had
the envelope with the photos of Chrissie, Carole and Susan Kim,
and walked to the front porch. Cora's car was in her driveway,
the downstairs lights on.

Cora answered almost immediately and led him around
a couple of boxes by the front door and into the dining room.
Today there was no tumbler of wine.

"Can we make this fast?" she asked.

"Let's hope," Vic answered. "You know, I bumped into Lily
Bauer today. Saw a photo of you guys together."

Cora sat at the table, her eyes narrow, as if she was looking into a sandstorm. "She called. Said you were talking to her
about her son and his public defender?"

"Yeah. Funny coincidence."

"Sounds like the public defender was crooked."

"We don't have enough to say. You know we have to chase
down every lead, right? Good or bad, stupid or smart." He slid
the envelope out of his pocket. "Anyway, now that you've had
time to think about it." He said the last sentence lightly, but he
could tell from the way she tightened that she didn't like his re-
minder about her behavior the night before.

230

Vic placed each of the photographs on the table in front of her and waited. Cora stared at each one individually. Finally she tapped her finger just below Carole Vinney's photo. "Tiffany," she said. "She just didn't show up one day for work. Called her number — I guess she lived at home — and got her mother. She said she'd left for work, just never got there. The other two were kind of like that. Although for Chrissie," she tapped her finger under her photo, "I heard that she disappeared the night after she was working. One of the other girls said she was supposed to give her a ride home but she wasn't around. Her," she tapped the photo of Susan Kim, "I don't remember well. She only worked for a few weeks before she stopped showing up. I remember her being impressed with herself, like she thought she was above all of us."

"Anything else? Any guys asking after any of them?"

"Not that I remember."

"Anybody visit regularly on the nights they were dancing?"

"Same thing. Nothing stands out." She separated Susan Kim's photo. "Although after she'd danced a couple of weeks two old guys came in to watch her."

"Old guys?"

"Guys in their sixties. Vietnam vets, I think, one of 'em had a baseball cap said that. But they only came in like three times."

Vic sat silently, scouring his mind. He was starting to feel run out. "How about Lily? Did she overlap with any of these women?"

"You should ask her, but yeah, I would think so."

"Did she work Bare Essentials long?"

"Not sure what this has to do with anything, but I don't know. She was like thirteen or fourteen years older than the other girls so we're closer in age. Before I managed the place I think she worked for like a year, then quit. But she stayed in touch and came back every once in a while when she needed money or we were short a girl. I had her number. She kept herself in shape and played up the whole MILF thing. Some guys are into that. We got along. I don't remember how often I had her come in."

Vic sat back and glanced about the room. The African art, he noticed for the first time, was missing from the walls. "Were the girls difficult to manage? Any problems?"

"Sure, most of them were lazy. I don't think any of them liked what they were doing, they just wanted the money. And after awhile they got benefits, medical and stuff, which is unusual, so they stuck it out longer. The guys who came in were either college boys trying to prove shit to each other or the kind who think women are toys. And a few guys were just weird or plain disgusting."

"Thuds come in often?" Vic saw her face harden.

"Look, I told you what I known about these girls. Thuds is something else."

Vic remembered what Anne had said, about how the missing women all had different colored hair. "Did you hire dancers as well? I guess you want some variety."

"No. Hiring was done by one of Thud's guys. They hire them and then move them around their clubs so the patrons have variety."

"And they must hire for variety." Vic tapped his finger on the table to call attention to the photographs. "These women all have different colored hair." A thought came to him, building off Anne's comment when they talked on the front porch of her mother's house. "Kinda weird they each have different colored hair. If they went missing separately you'd think a couple of them would have the same hair, but they all played young or under-age, and all four had different colored hair." He was thinking out loud and he cut himself off, not wanting Cora to follow his line of thought.

"Four? I thought it was these three?"

Vic forced himself to concentrate and saw Cora sitting very still, as if it mattered what he said next.

"There's a blond woman went missing about the same

time as these three."

"Stripper?"

"No. High school student."

"No way she connects to these three. You're talking about the blond you showed me last night?"

Vic stayed silent as a second thought trailed in after the first. If they all looked young, but had different colored hair, it was possible they were picked. Targeted. He hadn't thought of that before. Something cold moved along his spine. That meant kidnapping. Trafficking. He forced his gaze on Cora. She was staring at him, her eyes bright behind her squint. "Mind plays tricks on you," he said quietly. He glanced down at Cora's hands, folded on the table. Vaguely he registered that she wore no wedding ring.

Cora separated her hands as if she understood he was staring at them. "Anything else? I have to go soon."

Vic felt himself blink as he strained to bring his mind to bear. "Is there anything else you remember? Anything at all?"

"No."

Vic knew he was finished with her, but he couldn't move. She was his last lead, but nothing came to mind. Slowly, he collected the photographs and rose from the table. To cover his distraction he waved his hand toward the living room. "Your artwork is gone."

As Cora led him toward the front door she called over her shoulder, "You said that. It was cheap tourist shit. Just redecorating."

Vic followed her, and a few moments later was across Cora's front porch and onto the sidewalk. Inside his car his heart wouldn't slow down. A tremor ran through his hands. Trafficking. But he had no proof. Not even a thread of a lead, only a suspicion.

He put the car into drive and started home, trying to push the thought from his head. But he couldn't. It was the first theory about the women that made sense.

Dannie's face floated through his mind and before he

could stop himself a sound came out of him, guttural, something between a sob and a gasp. He clung to the steering wheel, his lungs aching. Trafficking was the worst answer, the one he couldn't accept.

But the idea of it was inside him now, alive and hot.

CHAPTER 40

When Vic woke the next morning he lay in bed and tried to reconstruct what he had done the night before. He couldn't. He remembered arriving home and working out, raging at the heavy bag, hanging onto it later with both arms, his breath as ragged as oak bark. What happened afterwards was a blur. He told himself for the hundredth time that he had no proof Dannie and the other women were trafficked. It was a flimsy theory; he had no facts to back it up, and yet it fit with the truth of a wedding ring. He rose and drank water from the bathroom tap with his hand. Downstairs he made toast and left for work, eating as he drove. Somehow, his mind started to work. Trafficking meant organization. Someone had to call the shots, make the plans, handle the logistics of abduction and transfer. It meant people to guard the women, ways to launder the cash. The implications curled in his head. It also meant the FBI.

Liz was already at her desk when he arrived at work, still mentally making a list of everything he needed to investigate. She looked up from her computer screen. "We got you-know-who at eight. You ready?"

Vic dragged his thinking back to Gretchen's case. He noticed that Liz was smiling.

"What?" he asked. Vic glanced down the aisle and saw Kevin's foot sticking out from his cube. He pointed at it.

Liz rolled her eyes. "The interview," she whispered. "Mark

Stoll. "I can lead."

"Sounds good." Vic sat down and took his computer through the start-up. When he finished checking his e-mails he did a records search on Cora Stills. No criminal convictions. On a whim he did the same for Lily Bauer and again drew a blank. 'I'm seeing ghosts,' he said softly to himself. Sitting back he called out to Kevin and waited for him to appear beside his desk.

"Kevin." Vic spoke loudly enough for Liz to hear. "Just so you know, DA took the investigation on Gretchen Stoll in-house. Crush agreed. We're done. Thanks for your help, though. We just need you to do a final write-up we can send to the DA."

Kevin didn't seem surprised. "Sure thing, I'm on it."

"Thanks. It was really a consult anyway."

"Yeah, but I thought you said earlier you were going to interview Mark Stoll? I nailed him with his card swipe data." He gave Vic a smug smile.

"I guess that goes to the DAs office." Vic warmed to the lie. "Give it play in the final report you put together."

From the corner of his eye he saw Liz shake her head in disbelief.

"Yeah, fine. I'll write up the final."

Vic heard the irritation in Kevin's voice, ignored it, and watched him step into his cube. His head disappeared behind the wall as he sat down. He guessed that Crush had already warned Kevin, and that now Kevin was e-mailing Crush to tell him Vic and Liz were dropping Gretchen's case, as required. He turned back to his computer.

A few minutes before eight o'clock Eva e-mailed that Mark Stoll was waiting in one of the interview rooms. Vic rose, and with a nod to Liz, they took the elevator downstairs and ducked into the closet-sized space where the electronic feeds from the interview rooms were monitored and recorded. One of the monitors showed Mark Stoll sitting in a chair, looking faded in a brown suit. With his sandy hair and pale complexion Vic thought he just about melted into the pale green wall. The lawyer beside him was broad shouldered and solid, his salt and pepper hair matching his grey suit.

"Dirt and stone," Liz said.

"Seems that way. You got the receipt?"

Liz held up a file folder. Inside was a copy of Mark's credit card statement with his water bottle and hot dog purchases from a South Side convenience store. "Wish we had the cell data."

Vic reset his pants on his waist. "That'll be enough to rattle him. And we have a warrant out for the card swipe and cell phone data, we can tell him that. Do you know that lawyer?"

"I saw him one time before. He was with a suspect for sentencing and I was waiting to give testimony for one of my cases."

"So he'd lost the case."

"Hardly. His guy got three months for beating up someone during a robbery. Second offense. Judge was pissed, but I guess he swayed the jury enough for them to drop the worst charges. If I was him I would have called it a win."

"Great." Vic nodded to the tech sitting nearby. "You're recording this, right?"

"Will be. Just give me the when to."

They entered the interview room, Liz first and Vic following, and seated themselves on the two remaining chairs. They'd picked the room without a table, which Liz preferred. Liz hitched her chair close to Mark. Mark's lawyer watched her, amusement in his eyes. Liz caught the look and shot out her hand.

"Detective Liz Timmons."

"Harold Jones. I'm Mark's legal counsel."

They finished the introductions and Liz stated that they planned to record the interview. She called out to the tech to start recording. A red light high on the wall lit up. Liz walked through the names of everyone in the room, the date and time, the case file number and then explained Mark Stoll's choice to have counsel present. She paused when she finished, holding the slim file folder on her lap. "Any questions?" she asked,

"I have one," Harold Jones said. "I'd like to know why we're here."

"Your client made some inconsistent statements during the course of a murder investigation. We'd like to sort them out."

"Oh, I'm sure there are perfectly reasonable explanations for what you may have misheard."

Vic watched Liz absorb Jones' statement without blinking and fought down a smile. *You're gonna have to do better than that if you want to rattler her*, he thought.

Liz took a few minutes to run through the date and time of their visit to Mark at the motel, the statements he made at that time, and how Vic and Liz found Mark Stoll in the South Side house. Vic watched Mark as she did this, familiarizing himself with Mark's tone of voice and comportment as he answered the questions. As she finished Liz started to open the file on her lap but closed it again. Both Mark and Jones shot glances at the file.

"So," Liz said slowly. "The inconsistencies." She started to open the file and, once again, stopped herself. "Let's start with your alibi. Would you like to revisit that?"

"What do you mean?" Jones cut in.

"It's a simple question." Liz smiled at Mark. "You told us that you were in your office the entire day when Gretchen Stoll was killed. Are you sticking by that?"

"Of course he is."

Liz started to open the file folder again but stopped and kept it closed. Mark couldn't keep his eyes off the folder.

"Yes," he croaked.

"Then let me ask you a question. We're getting a warrant for your company's ID card swipe data and cell phone location records. Will they both support that you were in your office the entire time?"

"Of course they will," Jones said quickly.

If it was possible, Mark paled a bit more. "Well," he said softly.

Jones snapped his head around and gazed at him. Liz waited. Vic noticed that Mark's fingers were suddenly active in his lap.

"I might have gone out to get a sandwich."

"Lunch," Jones said quickly. "Easy thing to overlook. My apologies."

"Right." Liz stretched out the word. "Perhaps, Mark, you could let us know where you went and how long?"

"Sure. I went to a place downtown. I was out maybe two hours."

"Long lunch." Liz smiled at him and Vic was reminded of the lifeless eyes of a shark. "So where exactly did you go?"

"I, uh, got a takeout sandwich from a food truck and sat in Mellon Green. On one of the benches there. By the fountain."

"For two hours?"

"I was trying to work out the right approach on a case I was working on."

Vic saw that Mark's fingers were now still and felt something slip away. Mark's voice sounded too practiced to his ear.

"And your phone would confirm that?"

"Oh." Mark smiled an apology. "I guess not. I didn't have my phone with me, I left it in my office."

Vic understood how clever Mark's story was. It would be impossible to prove he wasn't in the park. The burden of proving he wasn't there was on them. To confirm it, they would have to interview every single person who walked through the park that day, or drove by it, and every single person would have to say they didn't see him. But finding everyone would be impossible. Vic guessed that Mark really had left his phone in his office, and his location data would show that. He glanced at Liz and saw her making the same calculation.

Jones shifted back on his chair, struggling to keep a grin off his face. "Gonna be tough for you folks to find every single person who walked through Mellon Green that day," Jones said. "I mean no matter how many you interview, you might miss a person who saw him there. And people's memories are so damn

239

unreliable."

Liz ignored him. "But explain something to me." She stared at Mark and, without breaking eye contact, opened the file folder and removed the sheet of paper. "If you bought your lunch at a food truck, what possessed you to buy two hot dogs and a bottle of water on the South Side at 1:30 pm?" She held up the piece of paper in front of him.

Mark said, "I," and stopped. A flush crept along his cheekbones.

"Oh my goodness, Mark," Jones said quickly. "We'd better put a stop on that credit card. I believe someone stole the number."

"Right," Mark said quickly, without enthusiasm.

"We need to thank you for uncovering that, Detective," Jones said, ladling it on. "Who knows what else might have been stolen. Perhaps the store has video of whoever made that purchase so we can identify the thief."

Liz didn't answer. Jones sat back again, this time smiling broadly. Vic knew it was a chintzy excuse, but without video, the claim of the stolen card number might work in court. That was all they needed. Again Vic had the feeling of something slipping away, and for some reason he remembered sitting in the parking lot of the hotel where Mark Stoll now lived, watching the rain come down, the passing traffic shushing along the wet roads, the water beading on the deep blue of Mark's BMW in the parking lot.

He sat up.

"Mark," Vic said quietly. "Do you drive to work?"

"Sure, I..." he stopped talking as if someone had snatched away his voice box.

"Right. I'm guessing you pay for parking. You wouldn't have a receipt for that day's parking, would you?"

Jones was quick to cut in. "I don't think we have to provide you with anything without a warrant, but who in the hell keeps their parking receipts?"

But Vic was watching Mark stare at the floor as if he was

looking through a trap door into the deepest level of hell.

"But maybe we don't need a receipt," Vic said. "Because you have a lease arrangement and use your very own lease card to go in and out of the car park. Wealthy guy like you. So all we would have to do is check the data related to the lease card. I wonder if it shows arrival and departure times for your car. I bet it does."

"We're done here," Jones barked at him.

"I think we're just getting started," Liz said, shooting Vic a *thank-you* glance. "Mark, you need to think very carefully about what you say next. You can see we're closing in on the truth. You need to decide if you want to meet us halfway. Because we are going to find out the truth, it's just a matter of time. We do this every day, we have a hundred ways to figure out your movements. You might think you're clever, but you made mistakes. Saying you sat in Mellon Green for lunch, that's clever. But a credit card at a convenience store for lunch? Wow. Paying for your parking with the lease card is tough to avoid, that's so routine it probably never crossed your mind that it was important. But it's time to come clean."

"Mark." Jones leaned in close to him, trying to get his attention. "Mark. Look at me. We need to go. This is over."

Mark slowly raised his head, his eyes rheumy. "I don't know."

"Mark," Liz said. "Help me out. You know you want to. This has been bothering you for days. The first time we met you, you went on an on about Gretchen being a saint. But I think you were doing that for a reason. You were trying to convince yourself that Gretchen was a good wife. That she loved you. But you know better, don't you?"

"I said we're done." Jones jerked upright in his chair and placed his hand on Mark's shoulder. He glanced from Vic to Liz. "None of this stands up. The DA took you guys off the investigation. This interview gets thrown out. We're going."

Vic stretched out his legs so they almost touched Jones' bright black tasseled loafers. He turned to Liz. "Liz, remind me, who do we report to? Is it the DA or is it the mayor and city council?"

Liz nodded. "Oh, it's the mayor and city council. They appoint the head of Public Safety. Not the DA."

"Nice try, counsel." Vic smiled at him. "So you knew about what the DA did to us, but you came in here anyway. I bet you figured you could find out what we had on your client and then get it thrown out of court later. Well played." Vic pulled his legs back in and leaned toward Mark, pulling his chair with him so they were barely a foot apart. "So here's the deal, Mark. I think we have enough to charge you with the murder of your wife, Gretchen Stoll. Proving it will be tough, we don't have a lot yet, but we will take your life apart finding it. For starters we'll publically name you as a person of interest."

Jones interrupted him. "That's coercion."

"Not if we charge him," Vic said out of the side of his mouth, his eyes never leaving Mark's face. "Or, Mark, you tell us what you really did that day. We check that out, and if it fits you avoid all that trouble. All the press. All those people ripping apart your life."

Mark nodded hard.

Vic sat back. "So let's hear it."

Jones bounced onto his feet, hesitated and sat down. "I don't recommend this, Mark."

"I didn't kill her." Mark squinted at the floor. "But I wanted to know what was going on."

"So tell us." Liz rearranged herself in her chair, as gently as if she was worried about waking a baby. "We'd like to know what was going on as well."

Mark stared at the ceiling. "I was starting to think she was having an affair." He wiped his lips with the back of his hand. "Then she took the day off without saying why."

"The day of the fire?" Liz asked.

"Yeah. She said she was going to see our contractor, but I wasn't sure. So I left work and drove out to the house we're redoing. She was there, but only for like ten minutes. When she left, I followed her."

"And where did she go?"

"To the South Side. I didn't know about that house. She went inside for like fifteen minutes and then came back out with some woman."

Liz leaned forward, a slight frown on her face. Vic guessed she was expecting Gretchen to come back out with Dave Norbert. "Did you recognize the woman?"

"No. I'd never seen her before." Mark sucked down a large breath. His hand started to shake. "And they kissed."

Liz frowned. "Kissed how? On the cheeks like they were saying goodbye?"

Mark pressed his hand to his lips and tears welled in his eyes. He moved his hand. "Like lovers. Lip to lip."

Vic was aware of the ventilation system humming somewhere in the building. He couldn't remember the building being so quiet.

"And then what?" Liz asked huskily.

"They got in Gretchen's car and drove away."

"And where did they go?"

Mark shook his head. "I don't know. I, I was stunned. I was sitting in my car but I didn't feel like I was. I didn't want to know any of it. I guess I thought if I went back to my office it would all go away. I'd go home that night and everything would be fine. I didn't want to know what was going on."

Vic watched him. He knew the feeling. It was the same feeling he'd had when Dannie disappeared. He'd spent almost a year scared to know what happened. Not wanting to know. Being stuck between both impulses.

"So you went back to your office?" Liz asked.

Mark nodded again. "That's when I stopped at the convenience store. I knew I needed to eat, but I wasn't thinking straight. It was like I was dizzy. And I used my credit card. I ended up throwing all the food away."

"Okay." Liz sat back and glanced at Vic.

"Can you describe this woman in any way?" Vic asked.

Mark slowly shook his head. "I was halfway down the block."

Vic leaned forward. "Start with the easy stuff. What race?"

"White."

"Was she as tall as Gretchen, or shorter?"

"About the same height."

"And her figure?"

Mark blinked. "Curvy. I could see it from there. And she was wearing a tight dress."

Vic sat back. "And was she waiting inside the house when Gretchen got there?"

Mark nodded. Vic caught the glance from Liz. If she was inside the house it meant premeditation, and she had a key. Liz pointed at the microphone on the wall. Mark followed her finger and said, "Yes, the woman was waiting inside."

Liz studied Mark. "Who locked the house when they came out?"

He frowned and his eyes widened. "No one. They were kind of hanging onto each other and laughing."

The room fell silent. Vic looked at Liz and she gave just the slightest of shrugs. He knew what she was thinking. That the parking lease card would show that Mark did return to his office after he followed Gretchen to the South Side. He doubted there was enough time for him to get to his North Hills home and set the fire.

"You went back to work after that?" Vic asked. "Or did you follow them to your home in the North Hills?"

"I told you I didn't kill her."

"I think my client has been more than cooperative," Jones stood up, his deep voice filling the room. "We're leaving, unless you plan to charge him." He almost dragged Mark to his feet.

Vic stood, never taking his eyes from Mark. "Mark, why didn't you tell us this right away? During that first visit? You're a lawyer, you know the risk you take withholding evidence in a capital crime."

His voice was reduced to a whisper. "I just found out about it earlier in the day and then she's dead. I thought maybe it would all go away, that no one would find out. That I could just bury her and move on."

Liz rose and nodded to Jones. "You guys are free to go."

"Will charges be forthcoming?" Jones glanced from Vic to Liz.

"Of course," Vic said. "Mark lied to us. But we have more investigating to do and I'm sure that will lead to more questions for him. You should counsel him to be fully honest. And you would do yourself a favor by surrendering the lease card to us." Vic looked Jones up and down. "Today."

Jones glanced at Mark, who nodded slowly.

Liz signaled the interview was over and the red light on the microphone flickered off. Vic and Liz waited as Mark and his lawyer left the room, Mark's shoulders sagging. When the door clumped shut neither of them said anything for a few seconds.

"Could he have followed them to the North Hills and set the fire?" Liz said it to no one in particular. "We should have pushed him. He didn't answer the question and his lawyer didn't want to go there."

"Well, let's check the lease card. Put Craig on it as soon as we have it. Seems unlikely, though. He'd have to get into the house unseen, tie down Gretchen, chase off the other woman, set the fire and get back to the offices. I actually believe he was so stunned seeing Gretchen kiss a woman he didn't know what he was doing."

"Except buying hot dogs. A woman. Damn. I did not see that coming."

"Me neither."

They stood in silence for a few moments. Finally Liz looked at him. "We forgot to ask about the box of cash in the house. We need to hit that next time. But I'll do a three ring binder. Your way of doing things and that'll keep everything off-line."

"And don't let Kevin know what's up."

"Yeah," They left the room and walked to the elevators. As the doors shushed shut Liz turned to him. "You know what I can't get my head around?"

"What?"

"He got in his car and followed her. Instead of trusting her, or asking her straight up, he followed her. Secretly. That's what chickenshits do. Who does that? No wonder she cheated."

Vic carefully kept his eyes on the lighted floor number display, thinking about following Liz to Jayvon's high school. "Yeah, total asshole."

"Damn right."

Vic's phone vibrated and he slid it from his pocket, glad for the distraction. The screen showed Pokorny's name.

"Officer Pokorny," Vic said into his phone as the elevator doors opened and they stepped into the hall.

"Yeah, so, things got real interesting."

Vic squinted down the hallway, wondering what Pokorny meant. "What did?"

"Three a.m. last night, a domestic call, shots fired. I was nearby so I gave the North Hills guys support."

"Yeah?"

"Lily Bauer shot Denny Halpin. One to the shoulder."

"What?"

Pokorny chuckled. "I guess she has a temper. Anyway, Halpin made it out of the house, he was hiding outside when we got there. She was shooting out the front door. We got Lily in a cell and Halpin is over at Passavant Hospital. His shoulder's a mess but he'll live."

"No shit."

"Yes shit, and here's the kicker."

"Yeah?"

"Halpin's asking for you. Says he wants a deal."

CHAPTER 41

Vic told Pokorny he would go to Passavant Hospital and ended the call. He'd stopped walking as he talked and Liz was waiting for him. She arched an eyebrow at him. "Lily Bauer shot Halpin."

Liz was quicker to the question. "Why?"

Vic blinked as something aligned in his mind. He didn't know what, yet, but he was certain of a connection. "I don't know, but Halpin wants to talk to me."

"He knew you were investigating Gretchen, right?"

"Right. And Lily's son went to jail after Gretchen represented him. But Lily said Gretchen never asked her for money."

"So go see Halpin. Find out what he wants. That works out."

Vic forced himself to focus. "How do you mean?"

"I have to leave. I need like four hours. Everything goes right I'll be back by end of day."

Anger rose up in him but he tamped it down. "Again?"

"Yeah, Vic, again." She turned on her heel. As she headed back toward their cubes she called over her shoulder, "If this works right I won't need to keep taking off. *If* it works right."

Vic started after her. "Well, I guess that's something." But he knew she couldn't hear him.

◆ ◆ ◆

It was two o'clock when Vic reached Passavant Hospital. He entered through the emergency room entrance and showed his identification to the security officers at the door. They waved him around the metal detector without requiring him to remove his weapon.

Vic walked through several doors to the ICU stepdown unit. He spotted a North Hill Police Officer standing outside a door. When Vic approached the officer stopped talking to a young nurse and placed his hand over his weapon. Vic had the feeling he did it mostly to impress the nurse. He held up his badge wallet.

"Detective Lenoski. Denny Halpin in there?"

The officer stared at his identification and told him he had the right room as the nurse sidled away down the hall. "He's been asking for you." He waved a hand toward the closed door and peered after the nurse.

Inside, Denny snored on the bed closest to the window, his face turned to the parking lot. The bandage on his shoulder was almost the size of a laundry basket.

"Denny."

At the sound of his name his eyelids fluttered. Vic walked around the bed.

"Jesus," Halpin said. His eyes opened all the way and he searched the rolling tray next to his bed. Vic saw his eyes settle on a plastic pitcher.

"You need water?"

His legs moved under the sheets. "Yeah." It sounded like Velcro was splitting apart in his mouth.

Vic unscrewed the top of the pitcher and poured water into a plastic cup. Denny struggled upright in the bed, took the cup and drained it. Vic poured him another and he sipped at it. He dropped his head back onto the pillow and stared at the ceiling. "I don't know what they gave me, but man, it scrambled me."

"What did the Doctor say?"

"Bullet went right through. Nicked the clavicle and broke it. Doc said a year of rehab and I'll be able to predict rain the rest of my life."

"Gotta love doctors who think they're comedians. But it sounds better than a couple of inches the other way."

Denny lifted his head and met his eyes. "That's where she was aiming."

Vic topped off his cup with water. "Okay, Denny, I got word you wanted to talk to me. What's up?"

Denny gazed at the parking lot two floors below for a few moments. "I'm not taking the hit," he said finally.

"For what?"

"That Gretchen Stoll."

Vic's heart shifted a beat. "Start at the beginning, Denny. Start at the beginning."

"No, I need a deal. You want to hear what I have to say, I need a deal. I don't go down for anything."

"Not how it works. You tell us what you have and then we decide. But you need to know something. My next stop is Lily. Maybe she talks first and tells me how deep you're in. She has more reason than you to make a deal. So think about how you want to play it."

Denny reached for the tray, snagged the cup of water and drank. The lines on his forehead looked machine tooled.

"Okay, okay." He put the cup back on the tray. "I was there."

"Where?"

"Stoll's house. Right before the fire. I was waiting for Lily and Gretchen to get back. I needed to be there in case Gretchen didn't play ball."

"You were inside Gretchen's house, waiting for her and Lily to get back? So they were together?"

"No, outside the back door. And then they got back, so far so good."

"What were you planning to do with her?"

"Take her damn money, what do you think?"

Vic cocked his head, not following. "Her money?"

Denny frowned. "We figured she had cash in the house. A lot of it. Lily had already searched her place on the South Side, it wasn't there. Had to be in her North Hills house. We figured forty or fifty thousand bucks."

"How did you know there was money in the house?"

"You know why. You asked Lily about it. With her, you want the charges against you to go away, you need to cough up some dough."

"How were you going to make her hand it over?"

"Threaten to burn the place."

"Okay, so let me get this straight. You guys knew she took money to get people off their charges and you figured the cash was hidden in her house, so you guys were gonna jump her when she got home. Threaten to burn down her house if she didn't give it to you."

"Yeah. Pretty much. But we wouldn't need to jump her. She was going to do that herself."

"I don't follow."

"She liked being tied down. She was kinky that way. Lily was going to offer to tie her down, they'd done it before. Then we'd have her."

"But how'd she die?"

"Beats me."

Vic stared into the parking lot and spoke to the window. "Denny, none of that gets you a deal. And so you know, I can't make deals. That's up to the DA. But I need to know how Gretchen died and who did it. But you're telling me you didn't do it? So what are you giving me?"

"That's what I got."

Vic looked at him. "Okay. Let's do it another way. What went wrong?"

Denny sank back into the pillows. "Gretchen's damn husband showed up. No way I was getting into that, so I took off."

"He came into the house?"

"Beats me. He pulled into the driveway and hit his horn. Gretchen was tied down by then and Lily had come downstairs to let me into the house. I found a can of gas in the garage. Lily wanted to splash it around the bedroom and threaten her. Scare her. But when I heard the car horn and saw him standing in the driveway, I bolted. I wasn't getting in the middle of that."

"You're sure it was Mark Stoll, Gretchen's husband?"

"That's what Lily said."

"You left Lily in the house with Gretchen?"

"Yeah. With a can of gas. I went out the back door and over the hill. I had my truck parked there. I got in and waited for her. She shows up like fifteen minutes later, no money, and we take off."

"Anything else?"

"She stunk of smoke."

Vic shook a second plastic cup off the stack on the roller tray and poured himself some water. He sipped it.

"Where do you think that gets you, Denny? All you're doing is placing Lily at the scene right before the fire."

"She tried to kill me last night. She was more pissed at Stoll than at me. You do the math. But you're gonna talk to her next, right? What if she says she wasn't there? Or if she says she waited in the truck and I went in. She tries to pin it on me."

"You guys married?"

"Shit no. She only moved in a couple of years ago."

"If she says any of that stuff it's her word against yours."

Denny slapped his good arm against the bed. "Now you're getting it. You're gonna need leverage to get her to talk. My deal is because I give you the leverage."

"You just told me you guys were there. You ran off when someone Lily claimed was Mark Stoll appeared in the driveway, leaving Gretchen and Lily in the house. That's all I know."

"No, man. I told you what I don't want to be charged with. I was there, I'm not going to hide it, makes me part of it. I want a deal to not get charged with anything. I'm giving you two things on Lily."

Vic sucked back his anger. "Denny, you haven't given me one thing yet, let alone two. I'm pretty sure I can put Lily with Gretchen right before the fire," he said, guessing that Lily was the woman Mark Stoll identified as meeting Gretchen at her South Side house.

Denny shook his head. "No. Listen up. Lily was moving girls a year ago. She and some friend of hers. Snatched 'em off the street and kept then in my barn until they had the four they wanted. Then the friend and some guy drove 'em out west. I'll give you all the details. Throw that in her face and you got the leverage to make her talk about Gretchen."

Vic struggled to breathe. For the second time that day something aligned in his mind. "Is that why you burned your barn? You didn't want us finding anything related to the girls?"

Denny settled back into the bed and closed his eyes. He kept them closed for thirty seconds. "Yeah," he said finally. "You watch them CSI shows, they find evidence like years after. I am not going down for that. I came home one day and she's got some girl chained up in the back of the barn. Then it's four."

"And that's why she shot you. She didn't want any of this getting out."

Denny closed his eyes again. "Smart boy."

Vic took a deep breath but it didn't feel like he was getting oxygen. "Who helped her with that?"

Denny opened his eyes. "I'm just giving you a taste. Now you know I got something. You want that name I get to walk free. That's the deal. And I'm done talking."

Vic stepped closer "Is that friend named Cora Stills?"

Denny pursed his lips and frowned.

Vic's mind reeled.

Pay dirt.

CHAPTER 42

When he stepped into the hallway the officer by the door looked at him. "You okay?"

Vic forced his mind to slow down. "Lily Bauer, the woman who shot Halpin. Do you guys still have her or was she transported to county?"

"She's at county. Transported her this morning."

"Thanks. Keep an eye on him. He just told me he might be a witness in a second crime."

"Got it." His eyes shifted down the hall and Vic guessed he was searching for the nurse.

He found the elevator and double timed it to his car. As soon as he was moving he tried calling Liz but the call went to voice mail. He flipped on his red and blues and shot through an intersection, sorting out the quickest route to the county jail.

Thirty minutes later he'd signed the paperwork to talk to Lily and waited in a small room on the ground floor of the jail. It was utterly quiet, except for the distant clanking of gates and an occasional shout. The air was stale, the light filtered. It took twenty minutes before the door clumped open and a guard led Lily into the room. She wore a baggy orange jumpsuit and the look of someone who'd just had her teeth stolen.

"What the hell?" she said, seeing Vic. She turned to the guard. "I thought I was meeting my lawyer."

The guard, a short woman as wide as a refrigerator, shrugged and hooked her thumbs on her belt.

Lily stared at Vic. "I'm not talking to you. I only talk to my lawyer."

"I thought you might say that. So here's your one chance to rethink that. Denny's rolled on you. He's looking for a deal. He puts you in Gretchen's house right before it burns, and his leverage is the women you and Cora Stills trafficked. FBI is gonna eat you alive for that."

"He's a liar and a dinkshit. I only talk to my lawyer."

Vic leaned closer to her. "Your call, Lily. But right now I'm going after Cora, and I'm guessing she's gonna roll on you as well. So what's my name?"

"What are you talking about?"

"What's my name?"

"Lenoski, you Polish prick."

"Just making sure you know who to call. That's your shot to make a deal. And too bad you didn't find Gretchen's money when you were in her house. Because if you need a court-appointed lawyer it's gonna be one of the lawyers who worked with Gretchen. One of her colleagues who loved her, had lunch and drinks with her. If it's one of the guys he might have swapped spit with her. Of course that works for the women in that office too. Gretchen liked to go both ways, didn't she? You know all about that. But I wonder how much they'll want to see your rights protected. You killed one of their colleagues. Oh yeah, they're gonna give you outstanding legal advice."

Lily's face reddened and she shook her handcuffed wrists so hard the guard loosened her arms, ready to grab her.

"Lawyer!" she shouted at Vic, spit following the word.

"Lawyer or public defender?"

"Fuck you."

"So I'm gonna be clear. My name's Vic Lenoski. You think about it. You got maybe three hours. Call me in that time and you got one chance." He nodded to the guard, who was now grinning as if she'd just heard the funniest joke of her life. She tugged the back of Lily's jumpsuit and guided her out of the room. Just before the door thunked shut he heard the guard say, 'you are so screwed.'

Vic waited a few seconds and followed them out of the room. Ten minutes later he was in the car, headed to the County Courthouse and the DA. As he negotiated the traffic light his cell rang.

"It's me," Hanna said, when he answered the call. "Thought I'd give you an update. I took the day off and chased your list of names. Much more interesting than what I do most days."

"What do you mean?"

"You were right. I talked to two of the people who had a family member go to trial with Gretchen as their lawyer. Turns out Gretchen asked both of them for money and they said no. The family member went to jail and Gretchen told the family he'd have no chance of parole if word got out about her asking for money. They believed her and stayed quiet. But now that she's gone they're talking like crazy. Apparently eight thousand bucks was the going price. I have it recorded."

"Good. Give the recordings to Dave Norbert. If you can e-mail them to me do that as well. And something else. I've got Gretchen's killer down to two people. Her husband or Lily Bauer. I've got both of them at the scene right before the house burned. Right now Lily is in county lockup for trying to shoot her live-in. If you want a good case you should try and snag that one...I think she'll need a public defender. I think I can connect her to human trafficking as well."

"You do get the juicy stuff, Vic."

"Not what I would call it." He ended the call, maneuvered his car into a parking garage space and hiked up the short hill to the County Courthouse. He took the elevator to the DA's floor and presented himself at his secretary's desk. "I need to talk to Marioni."

Marioni's secretary was in her late fifties and looked as solid as her wooden desk. She studied him with eyes the same brown toughness of chestnuts. "Well aren't you the important one."

Vic had to physically stop himself from rising onto his toes and leaning over her. "It's about Gretchen Stoll, the public defender who was murdered."

"Kinda weird to be in such a hurry about that. I mean she's still dead, isn't she?"

"You want to catch who killed her? Or is that not part of your job description?"

They stared at one another. She let out a long slow breath. "You're Lenoski, right?"

"Yeah."

"I heard about you. I'm a friend of Lorna's. She could have done better." Vic concentrated on keeping his face still. Of course his one night stand from a few months earlier would be her friend. He felt greasy somehow. She let him stew for a few moments, rose, and with a quiet knock, disappeared into the DA's office. A few seconds later she swung the door open and motioned Vic to enter. Marioni waited behind his desk, standing, a frown on his face. In the overhead fluorescent light his face seemed oddly pale, his eyes hidden by shadows. His tie was loose at his neck.

Vic heard the door shut behind him as he crossed the office. Marioni waited for him to speak.

"I need a prosecution deal structured for someone and an arrest warrant for someone else."

Marioni thumped his desktop with the flat of his knuckles. "You don't need me to do that. We have a process. You don't need to come to me. You know that."

"I need them right now or we're gonna lose the suspect. I can't wait for your damn process."

"This better not be for Gretchen's case, I told you to step away from it."

"Yeah. Turns out every lawyer in town knows that. But the warrant is for someone who trafficked young women. Including my daughter."

Marioni straightened, staring at him. "And no connection to Gretchen?"

"It looks like a Lily Bauer committed both crimes, although someone helped her with the trafficking. The deal is for an accessory to Lily. For the deal he'll place Lily at Gretchen's house right before the fire and tell us about the trafficking case." Vic sucked in his breath. What he had said wasn't strictly true, he'd left out Mark Stoll as a possible culprit.

"She killed Gretchen?"

Vic struggled to keep his voice calm. "I can give you the names of two people on site at Gretchen's house right before the fire started. It's one of those two. But I need an arrest warrant right now for the person who helped traffick my daughter and three other women."

"That's FBI jurisdiction."

"Doesn't stop you from giving me the warrant. Then we hand her to the FBI."

"On what evidence?"

"Witness statement from Denny Halpin, he's the one wants the deal. They held the girls in his barn before they transported them. He'll give us the details if we give him a deal."

"Do you have an actual statement from him?"

"He wants a deal first."

Marioni hunched down. "You know that's bullshit, right? I need the statement for the warrant. We need to follow procedures."

"I need to arrest the woman who helped with the trafficking. Then I go to Lily Bauer and tell her we've got two people in custody willing to roll on her. She'll open up like a tin can and you'll have Gretchen's murderer. Without her it's just Denny's word against Lily's."

"And then the whole thing gets thrown out for a bullshit warrant."

Vic leaned over his desk. "You can work around that. But this woman is a flight risk. I've been in her house twice asking about the missing women. Second time all the art was missing from her walls and there were packing boxes in her hall. I didn't put it together until just now."

"No. Get your witness statement lined up and take it to the FBI. That's the deal. You hear me?"

Vic arched back. The silence of the long office was inside him, somehow, like air. It tasted of gutlessness. Marioni's eyes glowed bright and hard from deep inside his skull. Vic gently punched the top of his desk. "Okay, so we're clear. I walk out of here with an arrest warrant, you understand? If I don't, I go from here to the Post Gazette offices. I give their reporters recordings from the people Gretchen Stoll hit up for money to make their cases go away. I got three people on tape. One person who admits paying to have the charges against him dropped, and two others who didn't have the money, so she had the judge throw the book at them and threatened them to keep quiet. It was silence or she'd throw away the parole key."

"Bullshit. She couldn't do that."

"The families didn't know that. Either way, she threatened them. So here's my deal. I walk out of here with an arrest warrant or the press gets the recordings. Good luck with your next election."

"I'll have your goddamned badge, Lenoski."

"And the press will have their story. Here's your problem, Marioni. I got nothing left to lose. You know that. Why would I care? I just want to find out what happened to my daughter. The only one thing you care about is getting reelected. You proved that when you kicked me off the Stoll case. So right now, you and me, let's get the things we want most."

Marioni leaned over his desk, his tie swinging like an executioner's axe. "Screw your deal. Here's my deal. Fine, you get your warrant. But those recordings come to me, all of them, and you walk away from the Stoll case, you walk away so far you're on another goddamned planet. You don't talk about it, you don't write about it, you don't even think about it. And when your trafficking case lands, I get the credit. I'm front and center as the guy who wouldn't give up on it, I'm the guy who solved what happened to your daughter. And Vic, if that case doesn't land? You hand in your badge and walk. Screw your pension.

Deal?"

Vic rocked on his feet. It was as if all the air was gone from the room. "Deal," he heard himself say.

"Name for the warrant?"

"Cora Stills." Vic pulled an envelope from his pocket and tossed it on his desk. "Details are there."

"Good. Now go make me famous. And when you get back I'm gonna have something for you to sign so we both remember our deal. And. So we're clear. I also have it on tape." He held up his cell phone and tapped the front, so Vic could see the voice recorder was on.

Vic spun from the desk and let himself back into the offices and the clatter of people typing on keyboards, shouting into telephones and shushing across carpeting. He felt as if something was torn inside him, but he didn't care. As he headed toward the elevator someone fell into step beside him.

"Vic."

Vic blinked, focusing on the voice. "Vic," Dave Norbert repeated.

"Yeah." It was an effort to get the word out. They reached the office doors and crossed into the hallway.

"What's going on? I saw you in Marioni's office."

Vic stopped at the elevator. "I'm off the case, Dave. I made a deal with the DA. I got two suspects, you can figure them out."

Dave's dark eyes flared. "You're gonna be right there with me, Vic."

"Not this time." The elevator doors opened and Vic stepped inside, glad that it was empty, glad when the doors closed, glad he was completely alone.

CHAPTER 43

As Vic pulled out of the parking garage his phone erupted, Liz's name on the screen.

"Vic. What are you up to?"

"On my way to Cora Still's house. Denny Halpin is selling her for a deal. He said Lily and Cora grabbed Dannie and the missing women, kept them in his barn until they could ship them someplace. Marioni's putting together a warrant to arrest her on trafficking."

"Dannie is definitely one of them?"

"It feels like it."

"But you don't know?"

"I will."

"I'll meet you there, I'm headed into Pittsburgh."

"You done with whatever you went to do?"

Liz was silent for a moment. "Yeah, you might as well know. I've been having trouble with Jayvon. But I did the paperwork today, I got him into a new school district. Quaker Valley."

Vic frowned, bringing his mind to bear. "Don't you have to live in the district to put him in school there? That's in Sewickley."

"Yeah, well. Since you and Levon gossip like a couple of junior high girls, Levon and I are looking for a place together. Someplace in the district, maybe Sewickley."

Vic grinned, his whole body suddenly light. "I'm glad for you guys. Seriously."

"Don't get all gooey, Vic. And it bugs the shit out of me that you were right. He *is* a good guy. I realized sitting around worrying about him wasn't solving anything."

"You made the right move."

"Yeah, well, we'll see. Text me Cora's address and I'll see you there."

At the next traffic light he texted the address. He couldn't get the smile off his face. He thought about calling Levon and harassing him about it, but decided to wait.

Twenty minutes later he slid through the stop sign at the end of Cora Stills' street, looking for Liz's car, but his eyes shot to Cora's house. Smoke poured from an open upstairs window. The front door hung off it's hinges, more smoke churning through the opening. Liz's car was parked at an angle in the driveway. As he pulled in behind it he glanced in the open door and saw flames lapping at the steps to the second floor. Cora's car was nowhere to be seen. Vic jammed his car into park, scrambled out and jogged toward the house. As he did Cora appeared in the driveway by the rear of the house, where it curved to the garages.

"Lenoski!" she shouted.

"Vic pulled his Glock but kept it at his side. "You're under arrest, Cora. Trafficking. I got people ready to roll on you. Where's my partner?"

She spread her arms from her sides and her lips slid back showing white and even teeth. "You want me or your partner?" The sun glinted off her hair.

Vic glanced at the gaping front door. "Where the hell is she?" An upstairs window exploded and glass rained onto the lawn. Vic stepped toward Cora, the Glock heavy in his hand.

She raised a finger at him and wagged a no, shouting at him to come no closer. "Where do you think?"

Something quickened inside him, the way it did when a boxing match started. He hurried along the edge of the driveway toward her, one foot on the asphalt and another on the grass. Cora automatically retreated several steps, maintaining the distance between them. He was about to run at her when Liz screamed, the sound so shrill Vic stopped dead.

"Oh man, that sounded bad," shouted Cora. "Me or her, Lenoski."

"Liz," Vic shouted at the doorway. It radiated orange light. He glanced back at Cora, feeling under his sport coat for his radio with his left hand. Cora grinned at him and spread her arms, the movement asking 'what now?'

Somewhere his mind registered that his radio was in his car. Vic raised his Glock and shouted at her to lie down, but a low and guttural wail from the house cut to his marrow and turned him toward the sound. In the distance a siren shrieked. He glanced at Cora but she was around the corner of the house, her body hidden, only her face visible, her eyes crushed into a squint. Vic couldn't breathe. Something tore inside him and he roared out loud, holstered his Glock and darted for the front door.

Just inside the door the heat hit him with a body blow. Staggering he shouted, "Liz!" He instinctively buried his face in the crook of his elbow and lurched into the living room. He skirted burning couches, the smoke acrid in his mouth and nose. His eyes burned and watered. Through their blur he spotted Liz. She was lying next to the dining room table, her wrist handcuffed to a radiator pipe. He ran toward her, buffeted by heat as he passed the entryway to the kitchen. He dropped to his knees beside her. Her eyes were closed, her mouth hanging open. Vic struggled for his keychain and the handcuff key. "Liz," he shouted, his voice hoarse. Heat seared the inside of his mouth and nostrils. He straightened the key in his fingers, grabbed the handcuffs and dropped them in pain. He saw blistered skin where the hot handcuffs circled her wrist. Using the edge of his sport coat he grabbed the handcuffs and worked the key. They fell open. He jammed his arms under her and forced himself upright. He was dizzy and his mouth and lungs ached. He staggered toward the front door, Liz in his arms, the room spinning. She was too heavy, he started to lose her, her weight shifting in his arms. He launched himself at the front door but jammed his shoulder against the doorframe, ricocheting onto the front porch. His right arm dropped, useless, and he crushed Liz against him with his left arm, careening off balance, her legs dropping, the shift in weight throwing him forward. He pushed off the steps and in mid-air twisted so he'd be underneath her when they hit the ground. The smack of them landing sent a shriek of pain through his shoulder and his breath exploded from his lungs. He scrabbled to breathe, his throat aching. He staggered up, his right arm limp, and tried to get his left arm under her to drag her away from the fire. Two arms in a blue shirt grabbed Liz under the armpits and yanked her toward the road. Vic stumbled after her, the flashing red and blue lights of a police cruiser scathing his eyes. He turned and looked down the driveway but Cora was gone. Sirens screamed nearby and a fire truck thundered to a stop and shed firemen, one of them shouting at the others something about a fire hydrant farther down the street.

Vic was somehow on his knees, he couldn't get up. His right shoulder, where he had hit the doorframe, raged in pain, his arm hanging useless. His eyes dribbled water as if his face was under a faucet. Through the blur he saw an officer giving Liz CPR. Everything swam around him. He put his head down to get control of himself and catapulted into darkness.

CHAPTER 44

Vic swam upwards. His lungs ached and something pulled on his feet, holding him down. Dannie's face drifted past, laughing. He kicked hard and suddenly was in daylight, coughing, his stomach heaving, but there was nothing for him to throw up.

"Vic!"

He knew the voice. He heaved again and tried to get at whatever was covering his mouth, but pain stabbed his shoulder and his body shuddered at the shock of it.

"Vic, it's an oxygen mask. Keep it on."

Anne's voice.

It was Anne.

He felt her hand on his chest, over his heart, like a salve. He trembled all over, his eyes focusing. Above him was a white tile ceiling.

"Leave it on, Vic. You need oxygen. You're in a hospital."

He tried to breathe but his lungs refused to expand, as if a metal band clamped them tight. He turned his head and found Anne, bent toward him, her blue eyes searching his face.

He concentrated on speaking. "I'm sorry." It came out as a gag.

She pushed lightly on his chest. "No. You got Liz out. Stop."

"She okay?"

She patted him on the chest. "She's got a chance. You gave

her a chance, Vic. It's up to her now. Rest. You had a separated shoulder but they popped it back in. You got burns and you breathed who knows what chemicals. You need to rest."

"She got away."

"Who?"

"The woman who took Dannie."

Anne's hand on his chest curled into a fist and for a moment her eyes were both fragile and hard, then she reached out with her other hand and settled it on his brow. "You know who it is, right?"

He nodded, it was too hard to speak.

"Then you'll get her." She gazed at him. "I told you a few months ago that you would need to run into a burning house to save yourself. You did that. Now get well, and then you get that woman."

Vic nodded again, trying to think, but his mind wouldn't work. Darkness stole toward him from every corner, wrapping him, and he slid away.

CHAPTER 45

The next time he woke he was in half darkness and a deep silence underlay the soft beeping of medical machines. It was inky black outside the windows. Anne was curled on a chair by the side of the bed, a hospital blanket over her hips and chest. He watched her for a time, the way her slow breaths raised the blanket. Despite being asleep, her right hand clasped the gold cross on the chain around her neck. In the dim light he saw something of Dannie's profile in her jawline and nose, but just the ghost of it. He suddenly wasn't sure which had come first, Dannie's jawline or the ghost of her in Anne's face. Anne's lips moved, as if she was talking to someone, or praying, but he couldn't hear the words. A tear streaked Vic's cheekbone and he let it, too tired to wipe it away, too unwilling to wake the pain of his injured arm by doing so. He tested his breathing. It seemed easier somehow. And then he was asleep again.

He woke the next morning to a doctor and nurse standing at the foot of his bed. The doctor, seeing he was awake, lifted Vic's oxygen mask and flashed a penlight in his eyes. He asked him his name and the date. Vic got one of them right, but when he said in disbelief that he couldn't have been sleeping for three days, the doctor nodded and issued a string of orders to the nurse. Vic drifted off again, and when he woke discovered that he was alone in the room. On the roller tray next to his bed was a sticky note from Anne, saying she had gone home to shower and change. He struggled upright in bed and fumbled with the TV remote. Not long afterward someone entered the room.

"Nothing kills ya, does it Lenoski?"

Vic shifted his head on the pillow to find Sergeant Wroblewski standing over him, his bent nose catching the overhead light, his white hair falling over his forehead.

"I don't know about that."

Wroblewski, the most decorated cop on the force, the real power in their union and a font of knowledge about every cop who ever pinned on a badge, crossed his arms over his chest. "Buncha people keep tryin'. You keep popping out the other side. Fucking Energizer Bunny."

"Luck." Vic shifted a bit more upright. "How's Liz?"

Wroblewski grinned. "She woke up this morning. First time. She's got spit. Always thought it. Doc is starting to use words like 'guardedly hopeful.' Long way to go and she's gonna be out awhile, no question. She got some bad burns."

Vic realized that the oxygen mask was gone from his face, replaced by a tube that fed oxygen into his nostrils. "You guys get Cora Stills? Track her down?"

Wroblewski stayed quiet for a moment. "No," he said finally.

Vic turned to the window, angry. He spoke to the window. "I didn't see her car when I got there. How is that?"

"Best we can figure is that she was in the driveway getting ready to leave when Liz got there. Liz blocked her in so Stills pulls a weapon on her, uses Liz's handcuffs to lock her to the radiator. There's an alley runs down the center of the block behind her house. She drove her car through her back yard to the alley and parked there. Went back to the house, set the fire, and she's heading down the driveway to her car when you show up."

Vic didn't know what to say. Someone entered the room

and when he looked back Dave Norbert was standing beside Wroblewski, who shifted sideways to give him space. Vic saw a tightness along Wroblewski's jaw.

"Sarge," Norbert said.

Wroblewski eyed him. "That's the problem with cats, they keep dragging dead shit home." Wroblewski leaned over and gave Vic's left forearm a squeeze that could have stopped blood. "You get better," he said, and left him with Norbert.

Norbert waited until he was gone and then turned his dark eyes to Vic. "That guy forgives nothing."

"He's not that kind."

"Heard you were doing better."

"So far." Vic gathered himself. "What's up with Lily and Denny Halpin?"

"Both under arrest."

"Yeah, but who killed Gretchen? Her husband was still in it."

"Nah. Mark did go back to his house and it looks like he scared Denny out of there, but he was in an Uber. Pulled into the driveway, made the driver hit the horn and he got out so Gretchen could see it was him, then got back in and went back to his offices. Never out of the driver's sight. We got the driver's statement. Basically, Mark wanted Gretchen to know he was onto her, but he didn't have the stones to confront her. That left Lily. Remember I said Gretchen was crazy? She does like to be tied down in bed. And I'm not surprised she wanted to do it in her wedding bed." His face tightened and his eyes turned distant, as if he was searching for something. "I know because she and I did that, at least the tying each other down shit. When she asked me to do it at her house, I called it. I couldn't do that."

Vic saw tiredness come over him, how his lips turned thin and tight. He thought about saying something about everyone needing standards, but knew it would be piling it on. Instead, he asked, "So Lily and Denny are charged. Either of them rolling over on Cora Stills?"

Dave met his eyes. "I know it ain't what you want to hear,

but, yeah, they offered. Marioni turned 'em down. Said we have to make an example of them for taking down a public defender. No deals."

Vic felt something lift right out of him. "And Cora Stills got away clean."

"Worse than that. We found her car torched down by the Allegheny River. We don't even know what she's driving, or who she's with."

Vic couldn't breathe, couldn't fill the new empty space inside him with air.

"And one last thing."

Vic waited.

"DA asked me to give you a message. Said you need to bring the Cora Stills thing home. He's willing to give you a few extra weeks. He said you know what to do. He said you need to remember the deal." Norbert fell silent for a short time. "Anything you want to share?"

"No," Vic said, "that's between him and me."

"Didn't think so, but thought I'd ask."

Vic nodded, staring out of the window. "Thanks, Dave."

"No problem. You did the work here, I just cleaned up."

Something flitted through Vic's mind dragging a grappling hook. "Wait, there is one thing I don't get." He turned to Norbert, who shrugged and waited.

"I asked Lily if Gretchen wanted money to get her son freed. She said no. I believed her. I don't get that part."

A slow grin spread over Norbert's face and his eyes lit up. "Yeah. Lily told you the truth. Gretchen didn't ask Lily for money. She asked Lily to go to bed with her. That was the price."

"Christ." The pieces dropped into place like stepping stones. "No wonder Denny was so pissed at her. And turned on her. He thought she cheated on him."

"Yeah, I guess to begin with Lily said no, mainly because of Denny. But once her son was in jail she figured what the heck, maybe if she slept with Gretchen a few times it would get her son out sooner. And man, it pissed Denny off. That's why Denny burned down the barn and it's what led to the fight when she shot him. I think she's gonna use it as part of her defense, that Denny was jealous and went after her, so she had to defend herself."

Vic met Norbert's eyes. "Good work. That was the string I couldn't figure out how to pull."

"You pulled it hard enough Vic. That's why they went after one another. I was just picking up the pieces."

Vic held out his left hand and they shook, awkwardly, which Vic thought was about right given Norbert's history.

"Get well," Norbert said.

"Yeah, well, I have a ways to go on that."

CHAPTER 46

Vic napped, but was jarred awake by a memory of Cora Stills standing at the bottom of her driveway, squinting at him, the way she was laughing at him. He lay on his back, staring at the ceiling for a few minutes, his brow sweaty.

"There he is." Levon Grace entered the room, trailed by a gangly boy in his teens. Jayvon, Vic realized.

Levon stopped at his bedside, Jayvon a step back. Vic saw Liz in the boy's shoulders and forehead.

Levon stayed quiet, his gaze roaming Vic's face.

"Grace." Vic said finally. He nodded at Jayvon. "It's Jayvon, right?"

"Yeah." He stepped forward. "I wanted to thank you Mr. Lenoski. They said you saved my Mom."

"I got her out of the house, yeah. But it's up to her, now."

Jayvon stared at the bed. Vic had the feeling he'd been practicing the thank-you and wasn't sure what to say next. "How's your Mom doing?"

He pulled himself upright. "The Doctor says she's got a real good chance. But she needs a few months."

Vic saw how Levon was watching Jayvon, evaluating him as a father might when his son was talking to an adult about something important.

"Your Mom's tough, Jayvon. I've been her partner for years. She's gonna be back giving you a hard time soon enough."

He seemed unsure how to answer and settled on, "Yes,

sir."

Levon patted Jayvon on the shoulder. "Jayvon, can you check on your Mom? I want to talk to Mr. Lenoski."

Jayvon glanced at Levon and Vic caught a look of affection between them. "Yes, sir." He nodded at Vic. "Thanks again, Mr. Lenoski."

When he was gone Levon turned to Vic. "What happened shook him. He's using sir and ma'am all the time now. Like he hopes if he behaves Liz will get better."

"Can't hurt."

Levon looked around, then dragged a chair from the wall over to the bed. He sat down so they were at eye level. "I want to thank you as well, Vic."

"Liz told me you guys worked it out right before she got caught in the fire. You need to know she was real happy about it."

"Me too. She's starting to talk again. First thing she asked was if I'd signed the rental contract on the place we decided to live. She seemed a little pissed I hadn't done that already."

"So what are you doing here?"

Levon was silent for a few moments. "That's easy. I overheard that white-haired sergeant with the bent nose. He said you want to get that Cora Stills person, that she trafficked Dannie?"

"He's right. And yeah, as soon as I get out of here."

Levon shuffled the chair closer. His voice dropped. "I want to get her too."

Vic shook his head. "It isn't that easy."

"I find people for a living. It won't be that hard, either."

"No," Vic said. In his mind the pathway was suddenly clear, he knew exactly what he planned to do. "You need to understand. She took Dannie and three other women. Trafficked them someplace."

"And we'll get her."

"Not just her." Vic shifted toward him, so their faces were only a couple of feet apart. "You traffick, there's people working with you. Those women were chosen. Someone gave Stills and Bauer a shopping list, helped them move the women who the hell knows where, kept them all locked up, ran them, might still be doing it. I want them all."

A look came into Levon's eyes. Vic had seen it a few months earlier, the moment when Levon shot the man trying to stab Mary Monahan. "So we get them."

"Not just that," breathed Vic. His entire body tightened. "I want to burn it down. All of it. The guy who started it, the people running it, Cora Stills. I want to burn their entire god-damned house down."

Levon placed his hand on Vic's forearm. "Then we're thinking the same way, Vic." He searched Vic's face. "And I'm saying we start right now."

THE END

ACKNOWLEDGMENTS

Much like my first novel, *The Things That Aren't There*, this second book of the Pittsburgh Trilogy simply wouldn't have come into existence without the support, help, and patience of my family, Pittsburgh's community of writers and my publisher, Level Best Books.

First among these groups were my July 2018 Boot Camp members, who over the course of five weeks (at a fifty page-a-week clip) read the first draft. Led by the inimitable and always-prepared Annette Dashofy (an outstanding and multiple Agatha-nominated writer on her own account), Carol Silvis, Anne Slates, Audrey Snyder and Sharon Wenger identified weaknesses and strengths, corrected mistakes and managed not to laugh out loud (too frequently) at my annoying penchant for repeating words and phrases. I do hope to improve on that. I can't thank them enough. Their tenacity, support and guidance were critical to the completion of my submission draft.

Both of my Pennwriters' critique groups (Wexford, led by MaryAlice Meli, and Bridgeville, led by Barb D'Souza) read various sections of the manuscript, and over the years all of the members have proven to be trustworthy and insightful commentators. I'm lucky to belong to both groups, and especially for the support, laughter and community they provide.

Many thanks to Cyla Alcantara Marx, a long-time and valued family friend who just happens to be a professional proofreading demon, who knocked the manuscript into shape late in the editing process.

Thanks especially to Verena Rose of Level Best Books for her unwavering commitment to my work and her editing insights, and Shawn Reilly Simmons, who as final manuscript editor and cover designer quite literally brought this book to life.

Lastly, I do need to remind readers that my books are works of fiction. The characters are not based on anyone I know or have heard or read about. They, like my descriptions of the Pittsburgh Bureau of Police and the Allegheny County District Attorney's office, are rendered purely in service to my stories, not the actual people, events, departmental organization, working practices, and professional standards within those respected, honorable and long-standing Pittsburgh institutions.

ABOUT THE AUTHOR

Peter W. J. Hayes was born in Newcastle upon Tyne, England, and lived in Paris and Taipei before settling in Sewickley, a village just north of Pittsburgh. He spent many years as a journalist, business writer and advertising copywriter, but it was a six year stint on Wall Street as Chief Marketing Officer for a global investment company that really prepared him for crime writing.

His short stories have appeared in a variety of mystery magazines and anthologies and he has won or been shortlisted for several awards by the Crime Writers' Association (CWA) and Pennwriters. He is currently working on the novels of his Vic Lenoski Mysteries.

Made in the USA
Middletown, DE
25 October 2022

13519840R00168